# THE DANGEROUS MEN COLLECTION

## ALEX ABBOTT

PATHFORGERS PUBLISHING

Get an EXCLUSIVE book, **FREE** just as a thank you for signing up for my newsletter! Plus you'll never miss a new release, cover reveal, or promotion!

http://alexisabbott.com/newsletter

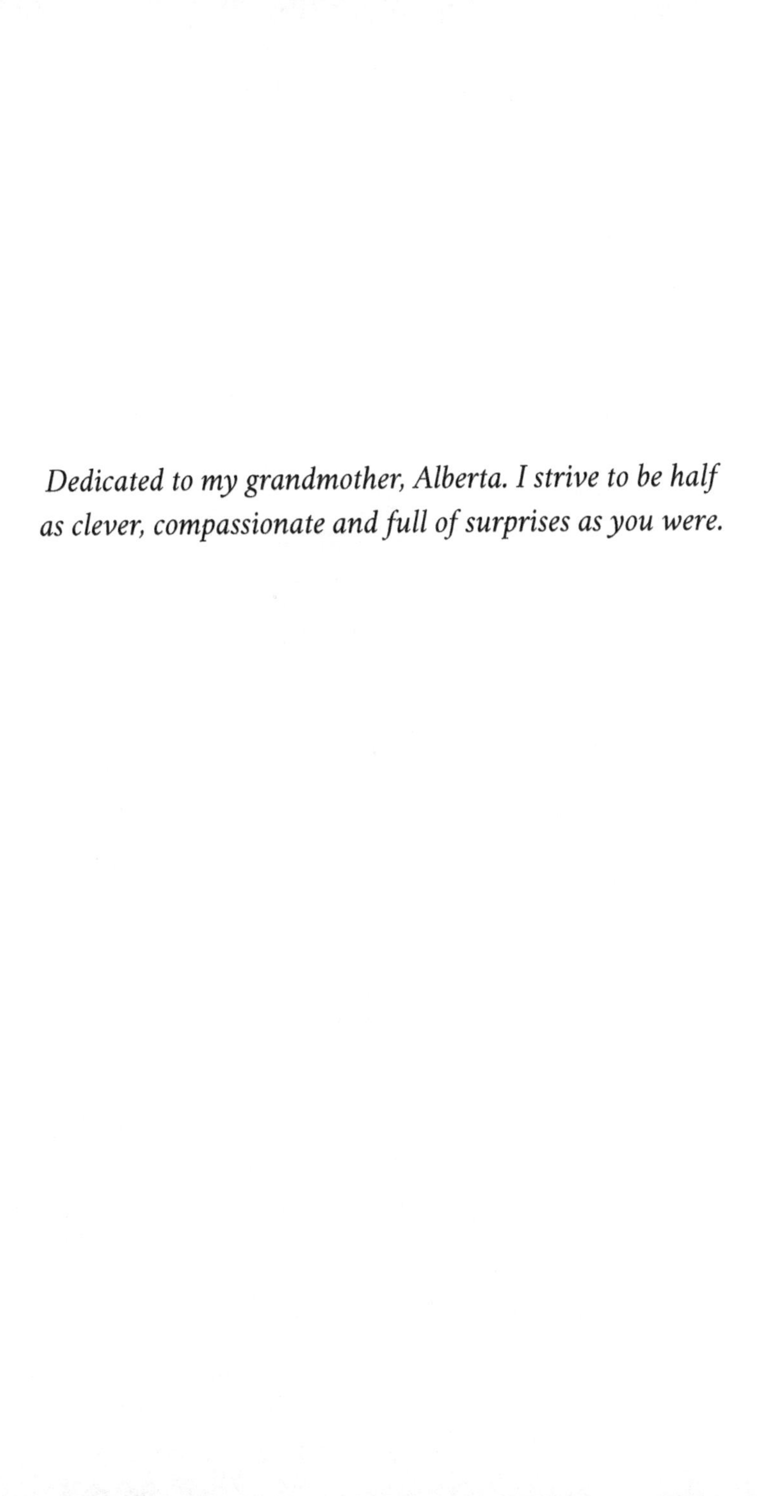

*Dedicated to my grandmother, Alberta. I strive to be half as clever, compassionate and full of surprises as you were.*

# PART I
# STRAYED FROM THE PATH

$\mathcal{A}$ngela couldn't decide which was worse: the white, fluorescent-lit walls that made her eyes hurt, or the dreary business-casual attire of everyone in the office? No wait, she knew exactly what was worse: the fact she was dressed just like them.

Her skirt went down to her knees, which was something she could say of no other skirt she'd ever owned past the age of twelve. And beneath that she wore a pair of hose that was binding and irritating and cut into her waist but still felt too loose around the crotch.

Her thick, black hair was done up in a simple, prissy manner that made her look like she belonged. And that hurt her, deep down. She didn't want to belong in a dismal office. Of course, the fact her thirtieth had come and gone and there she was applying for an entry-level job at a call center only made it worse.

"So tell me miss, why do you want to work at Omitrex?" asked the dreary man behind the desk, flanked by another balding fellow and a short, bitter looking woman that was probably not much older than Angela herself but looked at least in her fifties.

She looked between the three of them, wondering how they saw her. Some fresh faced, enthusiastic girl just ready to break into the exciting world of call-centering? She knew that couldn't be true. Had that ever been true of anyone else that had ever come into the room?

No, she knew it was more likely they saw her for what she was. A scrubbed up failure, desperately searching for the last end of the last rope that might save her. To allow her to *provide* for herself, and nothing more. The job ad had said twelve hour days, and no benefits until six months, though they'd tried to spin that as a positive thing. Angela knew, though, that most people never made it past the six months and the terrible starter pay to see benefits.

And those that did? Those that stared across at her in the uncomfortable interview room?

She'd seen people who'd gone through a war looking more cheerful.

Still, her pink, lip-sticked lips turned into a smile and she leaned in, touching her hands gingerly to the edge of the desk. And then, lies tumbled from her mouth.

"I just really love talking to people, and helping them to improve their lives." They knew it was bullshit. She knew it was bullshit. In the end, it didn't really matter, did it? They just wanted to know she could fit in and say the right lines to their bosses so that she made them look good.

"I've always been told, ever since I was little, I had a great phone voice." Her blouse felt too tight across her large chest. It was impossible to find one of those buttoned up pieces that fit right, and she'd had to pretty much clip it shut so that her breasts weren't showing from beneath the white material. Which she was pretty sure was see through in this glaring light.

That made the center man smile, the bald man leer a little, and the unpleasant woman glower even more. Angela assumed she must've hit it right then. There was clearly nothing she'd say to that'd make that woman stop loathing her. After all, Angela was staring at her own future there: Drying up and becoming embittered in some dead-end job, feeling her every asset waste away as she oversaw some tedious facets of a call center.

She'd be just as bitter about a lovely image of the woman she used to be waltzing in all smiles and beauty at that point too.

"Alright, thank you," said the man in the center,

jotting down some note and shutting the folder before him. "We'll have to finish with interviews and then you'll receive a call if accepted." Rising up from his chair he reached out a hand, "Thank you for coming in."

Angela stretched out her hand, keeping a light and gentle touch that was almost a tickle as she smiled at him.

"I'm very excited to hear back from you," she purred, tilting her head to the side for a brief moment as her green eyes wandered over his before she straightened up. She smoothed down the back of her skirt, over her toned ass, and picked up her little black purse.

The man that had been leering took the time to gather her black coat, holding it out for her, and she knew she'd gotten the job as she slid her arms in. She smiled over her shoulder at him and gave a little curtsey.

"It's nice to know there's still gentlemen in this world," she teased.

She couldn't wait to get the fuck out of that place. And then come back, every day for the rest of her miserable, little life.

# CHAPTER 2

The call had come almost instantly. She was still walking to the bus when her phone rang. The voice of that man so full of himself as he dispensed the piddling job offer as if he were offering up trips to Tahiti.

Arriving back at her dingy apartment, she felt like something was in order. She wouldn't so much as think celebration, because it felt more like preparing for a funeral. All her years of youthful indiscretion behind her as she prepared to settle in and try to play the role of the good lady.

Still, the urge to get out of that place was over-powering. She kicked off her bland heels and had her pantyhose off almost instantly, throwing them in a pathetic pile in the corner as she went to her closet. She didn't have much, but she was lady enough to know that she needed a little black dress and a pair of fuck-me-pumps if she was going to feel alive for an evening.

She needed to get drunk - on someone else's dime.

She looked into her mirror, sneering at the pink lipstick that made her look like a teeny-bopper and took it all off before starting fresh. By the time she was finished, she looked every part the vamp with her dark rimmed eyes and red lipstick. A simple black necklace and she felt much more herself.

She grabbed a black leather jacket, long ago stolen from a former roommate, and shrugged it on, leaving it open in the front.

Her apartment was low rent, in one of the seediest parts of Toronto. Flanked by a strip club with a broken neon-sign, and a series of barred up stores, including a pawn shop, it wasn't exactly the sort of glamorous lifestyle she'd dreamt herself living as a younger woman.

Though even as dark and dreary as the place got, it provided her a glimpse of an easier life. That busted up neon sign on the corner of the street advertising for nude girls bore the promise of money. Not easy money, she wouldn't call it easy, but it was less soul crushing than the office, and in much bigger amounts.

All the same, doubts nagged at her. How long could she keep doing something like that anyhow? And her competition would be girls a decade younger than her. Though she knew that wasn't a deal breaker, not for most men. Girls attracted a certain type, but a woman like her? She could manipulate any guy into loving her. Or so she hoped.

Still, she went the other way, to the dingy bar just down from her place.

Going to the liquor store would've let her get something to drink in peace and quiet back at her place, but she couldn't handle the misery of loneliness on top of it all. Besides, alcohol was expensive and her funds were drying up. That business suit she hated and all the others like it for a full time job didn't come cheap, after all.

She pushed in through the door to the sounds of dreary music to fit its look. Some awful foreign sounds, droning out of too-tiny speakers.

The place was hardly what one would call full, with its clientele a mixture of old, dried up gang-bangers of old and those quick on their way there. It began to give Angela second thoughts immediately.

Coaxing a drink out of a man was one thing, getting free drinks from repulsive old has-been crooks was another.

Though before she could turn herself away, out he came. A gorgeous young man, clearly ten years her junior if he was a day. Sleek black hair that was brushed back, smooth lightly browned skin and a cigarette that'd inevitably eat through his good looks someday, but not then. Not any time soon.

He froze the moment he saw her, letting her eyes scan over the simple white tee that was partially transparent and clinging to his muscles, and down to the black jeans that hugged his ass.

Captivated, he was slow to pluck the cigarette from between his lips with two fingers, exhaling a puff of smoke as he leaned on the bar, eyes never quite leaving her.

"Cuba libre," he ordered in a delightfully accented voice. To which the bartender replied in a rough, foreign voice of his own.

"Speak in English in here."

"Rum and coke," the young man repeated loudly, irritated with the old guy already as he continued to stare her way. Waiting. Waiting to see if she'd come claim a perch in the bar.

She hovered there like a little sparrow, uncertain and flighty. She knew the reason she hadn't instinctively gone to a better bar, and it was to avoid guys that look like him. Guys that reeked of trouble for her. She could see how the night would play out: her getting wasted on his dollar, then stumbling drunk back to her place at three in the morning, fucking until they didn't hate their lives so much.

And then there would be the regret.

But her legs apparently didn't get the memo because they started moving her forward, entranced by his masculine allure. A one night stand might not be such a bad idea, after all.

The floor was sticky and the music was poor quality, but suddenly that all drifted away as she smiled at him.

"Getting something for me?" she asked, that voice so filled with honey.

The young man's face lit up with a bright smile and he took a deep drag on his cigarette, clearly unconcerned for the smoking laws. But then, so was everyone in that dive.

His drink was put before him and he said:

"A glass of wine for this lovely lady," before sliding down the bar towards her, an aroma of fragrant spices about him, pleasant and enticing. "You look like a classy woman at heart," he remarked, a strange thing to say with how she'd trashed herself up. "But if wine is not your thing, maybe I will get it right on the next attempt."

Her lips quirked into a smile as she slid onto the stool beside him. Her dress barely hid her ass, and she crossed her toned legs, letting her shoe slowly pull away from her heel.

"I'm surprised they even have wine here."

He was sexy as fuck. There was no hiding that, with that mischievous glint in his eyes and his casual, slow mannerisms. As if he knew he were the shit, but was too modest to come right out and say it.

With a smooth complexion, and toned biceps, he was every bit the eye candy, and easily six feet tall.

"It's not great wine," he confessed, tapping some

ash from his cigarette into the provided tray that the bar shouldn't have even had. "But fuck it," he said in his rich accent, "if it's not to your taste, we will just have to go track down a place that has something which is."

He extended a hand to her, palm up, showing the smooth pads of his fingers and palm.

"The name is Romy, and regardless of what yours is, you are the most ravishing woman to have ever set foot inside this place, I can guarantee you."

She let her hand dip into his, her smirk not disappearing as she glanced around.

"There's not an awful lot of competition." But despite her words, her heart raced.

Yes, this was the distraction she needed to feel alive and vibrant again after feeling as though her soul had been sucked from her. She only had a couple days left of freedom before she started her new job, and thoughts of him?

Oh, she hoped they'd get her through the torture.

He took her hand and bent forward, laying a kiss upon the backs of her knuckles ever so softly. Marking himself as quite the gentleman with that move, though the attempt to be suave would've seemed so awkward on most any other man.

"Ah, do not take it for as empty a remark as it seems," he said, rising back up as her wine was placed before her, a bubbly sort of girlish drink that was most frequently served at bachelorette parties.

"When the strip club down the road closes up, this place is often graced with some very angelic forms. But yours?" he looks her over again pointedly.

"You suck all the light from the room," he said in a soft, approving murmur.

She had to admit, that was pretty slick, and she had to grab her glass to keep from making a fool out of herself. For a moment, a brief moment, she knew she was in over her head. That a guy like this could easily send her off the rails, all her progress towards being normal, staying on the good side of the law, slipping away into nothingness.

But there was that rush of excitement that she was drawn to, and she took a long sip of the overly sweet wine. She knew she should leave, before this went further. Accept the drink, finish it, then say she had somewhere to be.

That'd be the smart thing to do.

But then she finished off half her glass of wine in one sip, and her shoulders relaxed a bit.

"You're a charmer," she said softly, trying to play coy. As if she were the one with all the control and power. And she did, she reminded herself. He was nothing more than a young admirer, a man who appreciated her beauty.

His soft, smooth hand lingered upon hers as he let his thumb trace over her knuckles. A warm smile upon his handsome face for her before knocking back some of his own drink.

"A special lady like you must be bringing it out of me," he remarked in that Caribbean accent. "How come I have never seen you here before? If you had set foot through those doors," he said pointing towards the doors with two fingers off his glass, "I would have heard about it. And I would have remembered it."

His smile was downright infectious as he gazed upon her, his brown eyes such a lovely shade that they stood out even in that dimly lit hole of a tavern.

She could sense the danger within herself. The fact that she was so clearly enamoured, so readily entrapped within his charms. He was making her feel like a little high school girl, nervous and needy for more compliments.

From self-assured adult to teen lust in the span of time it took for him to order her a drink. Definitely wasn't a good sign, but still she licked cautiously over her made up lips and squirmed under his penetrating stare.

"I don't get out much," she admitted, and it was true. She'd been avoiding these seedy dives, and drinking, and dangerous men. So why had she come to *that* bar?

It had to be because she subconsciously craved it. Some part of her knew she was drawn to it. It made her feel alive, and after a day of feeling like she was a husk of a person, she needed that feeling.

"What a shame, and a loss for all of us men who

would fight for the opportunity to merely bask in your presence," he remarks with a white, toothy smile.

With her drink nearly empty, he waved the bartender over to refill her glass. The large, silver-haired man gave an impatient look to Romy however, and didn't recede until the young man reached into his tight black jeans and fished out some money.

With a roll of his eyes and a gesture back at the old Russian bartender, Romy spoke to her in an exasperated tone.

"Old man thinks everyone under forty is out to rob him," he stated, placing his cigarette back between his lovely lips.

"Little does he know, the true thief is you. And you steal hearts, not drinks," he tacked on with that smooth air. He was young, but he was practiced at being suave, Angela had to give him that.

"I don't mean to steal hearts," she said, teasingly. Most other guys couldn't have said something like that without her rolling her eyes at his corniness, but there was something about him and she squirmed a little. She remembered these feelings. The deep down, crazy, wild needs. The rush and thrill of the fast life, of hard men and their gentle words.

She had to get out before she fell too deep into this. To go back to her dank little apartment, lonely and horny and spending the rest of her life wondering what could have been if only she took one more drink.

She was torn between her genuine desire to get her life back on track, and to just put her toe just a little bit over that line she'd drawn in the sand.

Taking a long drag upon his cigarette, he rolled the fragrant smoke about his tongue as he tapped more ash from its tip into the tray. Exhaling a lovely grey cloud to the side, away from her, he remarked:

"A woman such as yourself does not need to try to steal hearts. As special and ravishing as you appear to be, I imagine it is like an aura you merely emit. A thieving aura that plucks the hearts of men from their chest. Only to leave them mercilessly left in your wake, trodden and stomped. And who could blame you?" he said, grinning then. "What woman would have the time to tend to so many enthralled hearts? You have a life of your own to tend to. Perhaps that is why you have caged yourself up for so very long."

Her head dipped down, black tendrils spilling over her cheeks.

"Is it that obvious?" she asked, a soft little purr to her voice as her green eyes rose to him from beneath her dark lashes. Her heart was racing, and part of her knew she had to run before she was ensnared. She worried, though, that it was too late for that.

"You are a woman that could not help but be obvious." Cigarette between two fingers, he pointed to her with them. "With that face, those hips, your… lovely curves," he remarked, letting his eyes and fingers trace out her figure before him.

"No, you were brought to us here on earth to be noticed. To be appreciated. Anything less is a crime against nature itself," he stated with a confident smile, so full of himself and his appraisal of her.

It had already infected her and as she finished off another glass of wine, she feared it was too late for her to stop herself, tumbling head first into trouble. But perhaps it wouldn't be so bad as that. Just a fun night to think back on, to get her through the drab days ahead.

What's so horrific about that?

"So. Romy," she purred with a smile. "Where are you from, mmm? Clearly not here."

He cracked a handsome smile that made him look even more insufferably dashing. The corners tugged up across his smooth cheeks.

"Cuba," he said simply. "I grew up there, but made my way to your lovely land not long ago. And so far… it has been worth it, if only for the opportunity to meet you. Because I have a feeling about you, and I do not just mean the sort of feeling all men get when you saunter on by."

He crooked a brow at her, looking saucy and daring before he finished off his own drink.

Part of her wanted to just grab him by his neck, pull him into her and mash her mouth against his.

But instead, she tried to remain cool. Calm. She knew guys like this, and they didn't want some eager little minx, unable to control themselves. Those girls were drama, and these guys... they tempted it out of even the most laid back of women.

So instead she grinned, as if expecting and deserving of the complement, all confidence and ego, just like him.

"Mmm, a feeling, is that it? And what feeling do you have about me?"

He never turned his attention from her, but he smacked his hand to the bar top and offered his empty glass out for a refill. The bartender dutifully made due on that, as the handsome young man continued to smile and attempt to seduce her.

"That you are a woman I could hitch myself to. An elegant lady that would make men out of foolish boys like me. With a Midas touch that let you take handsome young punks and inspire them to be great men."

He took his time studying her and slowly nodded at his own appraisal of her.

"Yes, you're a woman worth not just fighting for. No. Men will fight over any ol' pretty face. Men fight over everything after all," he remarked with amuse-ment. "You are a woman worth building something for."

Every time he spoke, he impressed her a little bit more. It wasn't even just the wine, or the complete lack of other interesting prospects. She was intrigued how this man, so little more than a boy, could be so cool in her presence. Angela was used to fumbling pick-up lines, or nervous deliveries, or shaking hands. But he seemed just as cool as his words and that unnerved her.

"You're going to make my head swell," she teased, resting her forearm on her knees and leaning forward, her breasts pressed together beneath her push up bra, the V-neck of her dress delving so tantalizingly low. That had to unnerve him, right?

No man was unshakable, she learned that again and again. Romy, for all his charm and suaveness, was no different on that front.

His eyes dipped down to the ripe valley and were caught in the trap she'd set. He stared a little too long for politeness, but shorter than many men she'd ensnared.

Muttering something in Spanish he let his eyes widen as he forced his gaze away.

"Apologies chica," he said to her, running a hand back over his glossy black hair to the back of his neck. "You make a man swell in other ways," he retorted, some of that suaveness lost as he chuckled. But he managed to make a stumble look endearing.

The accent certainly helped.

She gave a soft smile as she lifted her shoulders, righting her posture as she uncrossed her legs and slipped from the stool.

"I have to powder my nose," she said calmly.

Romy nodded his head and took another drag upon his nearly finished cigarette.

"Yeah, I'll be right here, beautiful," he stated, leaning against the bar, his shoulders back as his elbows perched upon the edge. The pose showed off his lean muscled physique, highlighting his beautifully male body in that tight top and jeans.

It was impressive that he made the most casual outfit look so good, and her eyes slid over him with such hunger. She managed to pull herself away, though, finding her way to the little bathroom that was cramped and could barely fit the two stalls and a sink. Still, she had it to herself at the moment, the florescent light blinking and stuttering above her.

She placed her purse on the counter and stared at herself in the mirror.

"You don't have to do this," she said to her reflection. "Just walk out. Don't even say bye. Easy as that."

But it wasn't as easy as that, and her reflection frowned at her pitifully.

Angela let out a sigh and shook her head, fingers running through her hair and fixing any perceived slights. She wasn't drunk. Barely even tipsy.

So why was she on the brink of making such a huge mistake?

She let out a sigh as she pulled out her phone. Maybe she should just text a friend. Have her come in and rescue her. But, pushing on the button, her phone flashed its warning at her. She'd forgot to charge it after the interview and it was at 4%.

"Piece of shit phone," she scoffed as she couldn't even make it stay on long enough to pound out a text and she threw it back in her purse, angrily. She was fighting with herself not to make the stupid choice, even as she knew that she'd already made it.

When she pushed open the door and made her way through the bar, she hesitated before she got to him. Just walk out. *Just walk ou*T. She pleaded with herself, but it was no use. She stopped next to him, her fingertips tracing along his bicep.

"Miss me?" she cooed, and inwardly, all of her common sense screamed at her to run, but she ignored it.

That light touch of hers was like a jolt of electricity. He had been arguing with the bartender, leaning onto the bar as she came up and took his attention back, claimed it all for herself with that one act, and those two words.

He smiled at her brightly, as if seeing her for the first time all over again.

"Ahh, you are back," he remarked, his cigarette gone and his new drink half-drained. "You were greatly missed," he added on, lowering one arm and smoothly sliding it up along her own, resting at her elbow. "If we were at a decent place with some respectable music, I would ask to sweep you off your feet for a dance."

Angela laughed, shaking her head.

"So take me somewhere that there's music." Maybe that'd help. Distract her mind from what might happen next. An excuse to blow off some sexual steam without disobeying her 'no bad-boys' rule.

His eyes widened at her words, obviously exciting him with the prospect. What he said was given in casual jest perhaps, but her acceptance of it had him practically jubilant. It took him a moment just to calm himself down as he grasped her arm.

"Ahh, go dancing with a lady I do not even know the name of?" He swayed his index finger at her, back and forth, "So very naughty." He grins toothily at her. "Some of my friends have a club, good music there. But how could I take you on my arm and dance with you before them all when I would not even have a name to tell that would pass from lips to ear and lips to ear until they are all gushing about my miraculous fortune?"

She barely heard a word he said, so enchanted by his accent that she just followed the dips and the ways the words tumbled together. It was a beautiful way of speaking, and she was smiling before she realized what he was even saying.

Then, she bent towards him, leaning up on the toes of her black heels and said, very softly, in his ear, "Angela."

"Angela," he repeated, as if it were some

sorcerous word that granted power with it. His lips spread wide across his face, nearly from ear to ear.

He reached back, plucking up his drink and downing the last of it in one quick go before turning back to her.

"If you'll accompany me, Angela, I'll take you to the Tropicala," he took her free hand in his, squeezing it affectionately. He reached into his pocket and pulled out a phone, dialing up a cab company and calling them to their location.

She pushed herself into him, so eagerly, as her mind cried out for her not to go with him. But she wanted this rush. This one last thrill before she buckled down and became the person she never wanted to be.

What could happen in one night, anyway?

When he brought her outside, and the cool air hit her, she was surprised by how dark it had gotten. She was glad she'd worn her jacket, and hugged it around her body a bit more.

"Your friend owns a club and you come here instead?" she asked, her ears finally free from the horrible music from the pub.

His arm was around her, behind her back so he could grasp her opposing hip. The young man loved the closeness, the contact with her. As the cab pulled up, he opened the door for her to let her in.

"I had things to do over this way," he remarked simply.

When she tucked her legs into the car, he shut the door for her then went around to the other side, climbing in next to her with a smile.

"Tropicala," he told the Indian driver before looking back to her. "I think you'll like it. It's new."

"Sounds exotic," she teased as she leaned her shoulders into the seat. The cool air should have sobered her up enough to know this was a horrible idea, but she was drunk on him. On the rush, the thrill of misbehaving. Of going back and taking back the promise she'd made to herself after breaking things off with Jake. No more bad boys. No more guys that'd get her into trouble.

But oh, Romy, he'd get her in so much trouble. But just for one night, get it out of her system. A little taste of rebellion.

Romy's hand found its way to her knee, resting upon her smooth skin as he leaned over to point out at something through her window. It was clearly an excuse, though he made it all so convincing nonetheless.

"That building," he said, pointing to some structure she didn't recognize, "was where I had my first job after arriving here. A lot nicer than you'd think from the outside."

It was done so smoothly, but his hand slid down from her knee, across her thigh, rubbing against her warmly.

She played along, acting oblivious to the creeping

hand even as her breath caught in her throat.

"What did you do?" she asked, the terrible music from the cab having replaced the terrible music of the pub, the staticky sound making her voice sound so much softer than she'd intended it.

He was a young man, couldn't possibly have been far into his twenties if that, so she had to wonder if he was making the whole thing up. How many jobs could he have even had already?

"Nothing special," he said with a shrug of his shoulders, still casually stroking her supple thigh. "I moved some cargo, that sort of thing," he said. "Ah, we're nearly here now," he said, pointing out her window again before the cab made a turn and brought her down a dark but festive road.

His caress was a little too gentle for her to buy him lugging cargo, but she pushed the thought aside. This is just one fun night. An escape.

She licked over her lips as she glanced around her. She'd not been paying that close of attention to where they were headed, and a little bead of fear developed in her chest before she promptly ignored it.

"What type of music do they play?" she asked, not caring for the answer. She figured Cuban, by the name, and what friends he'd likely have. Immigrants tended to hang out with other immigrants, after all.

"Good stuff," he said with a playful wink. "Cuban, but also other things, more popular music around here," he explained as the cab pulled to a halt. He tugged another bill from his pocket and handed it over to the driver as he stopped the meter.

"Let me get that door for you," he insisted to her, climbing out and quickly rounding about the vehicle to pull open her door and give a gentlemanly offer of his hand. "A lady like you should not have to do such things on her own, no?"

She thought back to the man who had helped her with her coat, with the coy way she'd teased him about being a gentleman. But Romy took it up several notches, and she didn't feel that glibness towards him.

Angela, instead, enjoyed it as she slipped one high-heeled foot out of the cab, then the other, struggling to right her skirt as she stood up and slung her purse over her shoulder.

She looked up over the club, drinking in the exterior in the dark, the flashing lights illuminating bits and pieces of the building. It looked to have once been brick or some other old fashioned home, retrofitted to blend into the bars that now surrounded it. Toronto was a fast changing city, and condos were all the rage, so more and more stores were popping up in former houses.

Lively music filtered out onto the streets, that Latin beat in the air which was such a change from the usual. The city was an immigrant nexus, but most of them were Asian from her past experience.

Romy offered her his arm and took her into the club. True to his word, the bouncer at the door gave the man a nod of recognition and let them pass on in. The place inside looking a mix of a fresh, new club with fancy lighting and expensive sound system, paired with a lively musical sound and atmosphere that was so very foreign to Angela, but still reminiscent.

"Welcome to the Tropicala, my beautiful Angela," he said, moving towards the steps down onto the dance floor, where so many young, hot bodies moved and gyrated. The enthusiasm there was all the more pronounced after coming from that dreary little bar back where she'd met Romy.

There was life there. What she'd been looking for.

It was infectious and she shrugged off her jacket, quickly abandoning it at the coat check and leaving her shoulders bare. After so long of pretending to be someone else, someone stuck up and prissy and perfect, she was excited for the chance to simply... dance.

"Get me a drink?" she asked, having to lean in and speak to his ear over the loud beat.

For that brief moment as she whispered to him, he had his arm about her waist, holding her close, their two bodies intertwined.

"Anything you wish," he said in a smooth, breathy voice, sounding so taken with her. And he was. For all his suave charm, he was utterly and completely smitten with Angela.

He disentangled from her reluctantly, leaving her to stand there at the edge of the dance floor. So many bodies moving and gyrating all around, more than a few sets of eyes going her way as she managed to draw some attention.

The average age there had to be more than a couple below her own, but her resilient beauty kept her a focus of attention, and not in a bad way.

One man was making his way to her, big and broad, a confident grin on his face as he hooked his thumb towards the dance floor and offered her his hand.

Romy returned at that point, two drinks in hand as he moved up between the two of them.

"Hey, beat it man," he said in a heavily accented voice, sounding more aggressive than she'd yet heard him. As he'd said, men would fight for anything. Especially her.

Angela accepted the drink graciously, giving a gentle but apologetic smile to the other man. "I'm here with someone," she shouted enough to be heard. Still, he wasn't a bad looking guy and she drank him in before turning back to Romy.

"Ready?" she whispered in his ear, her nose brushing along the outer lobe as she spoke.

Romy softened at that, and the big man backed off, hands held up as he gave them their space.

"You are too precious to be left alone for long," Romy remarked, handing her a mixed cocktail. Something looking very fruity and sweet, and strong judging by the aroma of alcohol off it. "I figured I might have to come back here and fight a flock of men off."

"I can handle my own fights," she teased, taking a sip as the strong taste of rum hit her. Ohh, it was definitely a double.

Still, against her better judgement, she took another, longer drink.

"And I know who I'm here with," she finished.

Seeing that young, handsome face so alight with pleasure at her words made them worth it. He slipped back in against her, his tall, lean form swaying to the beat of the music a little as he sipped his own drink and put his arm about her.

"You understand men well," he remarked, his rum-tinged breath so close to her as he moved against her a little, before they had even made it to the dance floor. "I bet very little gets passed you."

That was a compliment she so desperately wanted to hear, and she rewarded him with a flirty smile as her hips circled into his hand. And then she'd grabbed it, guiding him more quickly to the dance floor before turning to face him.

It was so warm, the heat of the writhing bodies filling the air, their energy contagious as she took another sip of her drink and then held it in the air, safely, as she began to roll her hips back and forth.

Many of the other dancers were going at it much more vigorously, but together they made a sensual thing out of it. His body moved with such agile grace, exemplifying his youth and masculinity so well as he rocked his form with hers.

"My friends are going to be dying to know who you are all evening," he remarked pridefully, his ego already pumped so high just from pulling her into his world a little. "You'll be the talk of the gang for weeks."

That word didn't go missed by her, but she brushed it off. Language was more fluid than that, especially for someone learning it as a second language. Clearly he just meant his buddies, and Angela purred.

"But you know so little." Her free arm went around his neck as she downed the rest of her drink and set the glass on the railing. It was a strong drink, no doubt, and she took the excuse to hold onto him more eagerly. Her hips ground against his, her motions small and seductive against his.

His eyes rolled back into his head at that contact, the grind of her hips to his, and he shamelessly swelled within his jeans as he downed the rest of his drink in mimicry of her.

Once unencumbered, he brought both of his hands to her hips, and let his fingers move back towards her round ass cheeks. Their two bodies picking up their pace as he guided her into a more rigorous dance, moving his body with practiced grace. He was a dancer, there was no doubt about it.

"I need to know more," he agreed with her sentiment, looking into her emerald eyes with a spark in his own. "I want to know all there is to know about you," he said with a grin of excitement.

She pressed her chest against his, her gaze rising to him as she grinned her naughtiest grin.

"Oh, I can't tell you that," she purred. It was harder to hear, to talk, and for that she was grateful. There was no need to ruin her illusion as a delicious bombshell.

Each shift of her hips threatened to raise up her skirt a little more, his touch enough to raise it up a few centimeters, but she didn't care. She was feeling sexy as hell, and there was no need for her to be a prude that night.

He furrowed that smooth brow of his and put on a wounded look that only made him all the more endearing.

"No? Not even a little?" he asked in that delicious accent, his hands sliding down over her ass cheeks and now brazenly kneading their supple mounds as their bodies moved to the lively music faster.

"What do you do?" he asked over the music. "You move like a dancer," and those words were said as the utmost compliment. He was a man who more than just enjoying dancing, appreciated it as a craft it seemed.

"I'm nobody." It was truth and lie, mixed together in a flirtatious manner, pulling him into her. "Just a girl."

She could feel her body so eagerly reacting to his touch. She'd been single for the better part of three years, though the last time she fucked someone was just a couple months back. It hadn't been great.

"Just a girl," he repeatedly mockingly, and for a moment it created some worry of her age bothering him. Of being an impediment, or maybe just the reminder at all. "You are a woman who brings men to their knees. No mere girl could do that," he stated firmly, his voice growing huskier with lust as they moved together, their bodies gliding with liquid smoothness.

Her forehead rest against his shoulder, hiding the flush across her cheeks that both the alcohol and the complement had caused. She swallowed, her mouth tasting so sweet from the drink, and one of her hands moved along his bicep before she looked up at him once more.

"But nothing I can tell you about me will be better than the fantasy," she insisted.

Those fingers of his sank into her fleshy cheeks, tugging her skirt up just a bit more in his hunger to feel her. To experience her body as they writhed and danced beneath the glow of the colourful lights.

"And fantasy with you is worth a king's bounty," he said over the noise, savouring the feel of her body against his. "But maybe I want them to have the fantasy. And me to hold the flesh and blood woman."

Oh, he knew just what to say. Just what she needed to hear.

It sent a shiver down her spine and a gasp from between her lips as she looked up at him with such dangerous desire.

"I'm a nobody, in a shit job, in a shit life. And I need you to distract me from that."

It was the kind of reaction that earned disappointed stares, or sympathetic frowns.

Instead, Romy gave her a bright smile, as if she'd just presented him with the opportunity of his lifetime. A twinkle in his eyes as he leaned in close to her ear, their cheeks brushing together smoothly.

"I was born just to distract you from life, I think. And I will make one hell of an effort to do just that," he pledged, shutting his eyes and nuzzling against her for a brief moment amid their scandalous dance.

She was oblivious to the bodies around her, to everything except him. His touch enveloped her, making her swoon against him. She was drunk on his affection, and it felt so good to be wanted. To be craved, as he craved her.

Angela felt all those little fears, the cautions and barriers she had in check slipping away into the aether, and she smiled up at him so deviously.

"I'm surprised you don't have someone."

"If I had, I think one look at you would wipe my memory of her and all before her," he remarked smoothly amid the gyrations of their body. He never really grew winded at all, his flexible body moving with such grace, never pausing, though a faint sheen of perspiration grew on his smooth skin, reflecting the lights.

"But no," he continued, speaking close to her ear over the music, "I have never settled in with a relationship. But for you?" His eyes flashed wide, and that was no bullshit she detected on his lips, or in his expression. "The exception is already made."

But all she could do was giggle and laugh, half drunkenly. She couldn't believe him, even if he did sound sincere. But quickly she silenced herself on his mouth, pressing her sweetened tongue in against his, her hand on the back of his head as she eagerly made out with him on the dance floor.

That kiss came as a surprise to the young man, but a most welcome one.

He squeezed her about the waist and slid one hand up her spine to push through her hair to the back of her head. His tongue lashed against hers, ravenously hungry for her as he returned her kiss passionately, grinding their bodies together slower then, heeding the music less as they caved into desire.

It felt so good to have that passion boil over, to

feel so desired and wanted, and there was no turning back for her. She needed it. For so long she'd yearned to feel that affection and need, and she ground against him so crudely, oblivious to everyone else.

Those soft, smooth-talking lips of his mingled with hers and they made out shamelessly on the dance floor. Romy showed no hesitation about it, and if his friends watched, all the better by his reckoning. If his mind had been clear enough to reckon anything at that moment, that is.

His one hand knitted through her thick, lustrous hair, the other pawed at her ass, tugging her skirt up scandalously high as they made out.

She was grateful she'd decided to put on panties, for she was almost certain that they were peeking out. She parted from him for a moment, her green eyes scanning his, as if asking what he wanted to do.

He licked his lips as their gazes locked, savouring the lingering flavour of her mouth on his. He was breathing heavy at last, not from the dancing, but solely from his excitement for her.

"Your place or mine," he put forth the option, though it was not posed as a question. As if to say: pick A or B.

"Yours," she said, both curiosity and practicality working together. It'd be safer, and probably closer.

Besides, she was sick of her dingy little apartment.

She kissed him again, hungrily, before pulling back and practically dragging him to the coat check and grabbing her leather jacket.

It was impossible for either of them to say how long they'd been dancing, grinding and kissing. Time had ceased to have meaning during the course of their drawn out conversation amid the noise and press of bodies in the club.

Romy took control once they were outside, pulling her along with him as he led her to a nearby building. The front was a store, a pawn shop in fact, but unlocking it he took a side passage up the stairs to the apartments above.

The going was slow, because he kept stopping to kiss at her in turn, to paw at her flesh in his over-anxious hunger.

Every second was agony, her self-control and hedonistic desires warring with each other even though one had clearly already won. Her hands were all over him, down in his back jeans pocket, grabbing at him anxiously as her breath quickened. Twice she nearly stumbled over in her high stilettos, only to catch herself on his arm.

When they came to his door on the fourth floor, he pressed her to the wall and kissed her deeply, thrusting his tongue into her mouth as he fumbled with his keys to unlock it before finally, after several failed attempts, throwing open the door to his clean, sparsely decorated apartment.

A couch, dinner table and chairs were the only furniture in sight through the living room and eating area. A not too small place for the city, but far from lavish. It looked like he'd only recently moved in.

But it was worlds better than her place, at that moment, if only because of the proximity.

She pushed him inwards, closing the door behind him as she let out a little moan, her fingers in his hair. She felt him out so eagerly, down over his strong back and arms, and then her fingers were on the button of his jeans, pushing it through the hole.

Romy was backing into his hallway, watching with excited eyes as she pawed at him, then expertly began to disrobe him. His jeans drooping down as that button was loosed, showing where his hard, six-pack abs formed lines down towards his groin.

"You are too damn amazing," he remarked, bringing his own nimble fingers to her dress' skirt, tugging them up in his effort to get it off her, or at least bind it around her waist. He managed it up to the bottom of her ribcage before he could get it no higher, revealing the lacy black panties beneath.

His room was nicer than the rest of his place, with a queen sized bed, a small book shelf and dressers. Clothes were strewn about, but not terribly badly, and the window overlooking the bed was open, showing them off to the narrow street below.

Her fingers went to the zipper on her dress, finishing what he'd started and revealing the matching lace push up bra, her simple black necklace delving towards her cleavage as she shook her hair out and stared at him.

She was so aroused, it was hard to contain herself, but she wanted to drink him in. To remember his form, his smile, his everything.

He looked at her body, utterly entranced by her large bust wrapped only in her bra, and the taut outline of her quim below. But he was eager to give as well as receive, and he pulled his tight top up over his head from the bottom, showing off his well-defined abs and pecs, letting his bone-necklace tinkle as it smacked back to his collarbone.

His shoes were next and he was freeing himself of his jeans, showing the bulge of his manhood beneath his briefs below. Before they too were dragged away to let his cock spring forth from their confines, excitedly hard.

God, it had been so long since she'd seen a cock, and just the sight of it was enough to make her mouth water as she closed the distance. Her fingers went behind her shoulder blades and quickly unclasped her bra, shrugging it off and revealing her large chest.

It'd been a curse when she hit puberty, but a blessing ever since. The nipples perky and hard as she kicked off her heels, lowering her almost half a foot and making her have to look up at him a bit more.

Her hand went to his abs then down, grazing across his member and then clasping it as she pushed herself up to kiss him once more.

Romy's hands went to her breasts immediately. The boy was hardly to be blamed for it, those large breasts so weighty in his palms, the flesh so supple and yielding. He toyed with them as they kissed, let his thumbs tease her elastic nipples as his cock throbbed so thickly in her grasp with his excitement building.

He was rock solid, in a way a man could only be a few times in his life. That thick member pulsed with life and he pushed her back towards his bed as their lips smacked.

She allowed herself to topple back, to feel her head and shoulders and ass press into the large bed as she stroked him with such need. It wasn't a soft stroke, but it was skilled and hard and filled with her own hunger as she kissed him with more ferocity.

Romy was atop her immediately, his fingers only reluctantly leaving her breasts to curl into the waistband of her panties and tug them down. Sliding them across her thighs and tugging them from her feet before tossing them to his floor.

Her panties were slick and her scent quickly permeated the air, her legs spreading around him as she pulled him towards her. She was desperate for it, for him, and caution was slipping from her mind.

Months with nothing, and then there was him, so vibrant and sexy.

The excited look in his eyes said it all, he was ravenous for her, looked like he was just presented with the best day of his life as he lunged atop her once more.

Her naked, nearly hairless slit grazed against the underside of his cock and she whimpered, her clit throbbing with desperate need.

His mouth clamped to hers, his tongue delving deep as he clasped a breast in one hand and her thigh in the other. He pushed that full leg back up as he ground his bare cock flesh against her cunny, the gorgeous young man absolutely wild as his spine arched and he moved with the same grace he had on the dance floor.

There was very little thinking done then between either of them, and he angled his hips to pierce her cunt with his steel cock, jab down into her depths.

She screamed. It'd been so long, and she felt so tight, and he felt so huge.

It was one of the most intense things in the world, the first time after a draught, and her back arched and her body ground against him, desperately taking him in as far as he'd fit. Her calves wrapped around his ass, dragging him into her and moaning so loudly.

It was reckless, dangerous and everything she wanted to avoid that night. Everything she knew her life depended on steering clear of, yet there he was, that gorgeous young Romy, balls deep in her, with nothing separating their loins.

He let loose such a low and sultry moan that rose up out of his chest as he pulled back his hips that very first time. The sweet relief of her cunt no less intense to him, than his cock was to her.

Clutching her large breast in one hand, her ample thigh in the other, he began to pump into her atop his bed. The sight of the two of them there visible through his bedroom window as they began to rut like thoughtless animals.

She could feel his heat, his hard form as it rubbed and rut against her. She brought her hands to his neck, forcing his mouth to hers as she kissed him with such delight. Nothing else mattered then, nothing but the sensations of their bodies as they writhed together and she let out another loud cry as he picked up the tempo, stabbing into her hard.

Just two days from then she could be condemned to a life of meaningless office work, but for that brief moment she wanted to savour living with her beautiful young lover.

His pace grew fast, the sound of his balls slapping against her ass resounding through the sparse room. Romy bent her back into the plush, thick comforter as his own dark shaft plunged down and pulled out again and again, filling her loins with his manhood.

A muffled 'yes' escaped him from betwixt their

kissing mouths, his hard body slamming down into her voluptuous frame.

Her lips then moved downwards, over his jaw and to his throat, tasting that light, salty taste with such relish, a moan travelling from her mouth onto his skin. It was a pleasant little vibration, and her nails dug into his back, holding his chest tightly to hers so that each rock of his hip sent them both rolling back.

"Fuck," she hissed, gasping in a breath before her mouth was back on his skin, indiscriminately kissing.

She'd been with many lovers over the years, many men, and though he wasn't the most skilled of them, he knew his way with her body better than most, and his enthusiasm and energy — his sheer gorgeousness — made up for all the rest and then some.

Romy angled his hips and thrust deeply into her with such an expert angle, his throbbing cock glistening with her honey in the room's white light. Each pound of his body between her thighs making her thick tits jiggle and sway.

He was panting near her ear, his mouth then seeking out her lobe in turn as he keeps the passionate thrusting going, even in the face of his cock's intense pulsations.

God, how did she get so lucky and so unlucky as to find him? Of all the people she could have ran into, he was the one who had the power to make her break all the vows she'd made to herself.

He was the one who was able to make her act like a stupid kid again, hell bent on self-destruction and fucking up her normal, boring, stupid life. She wanted this feeling of loss of control, of passion and carelessness, and he was so good about doing just that.

She screamed his name, her calves pressed against his ass so hard, begging him in further.

His body was racked by a trembling shudder, and he quaked atop her through a noisy moan. Romy was doing his best to make the moment last, to savour his time with her, to pound the last remaining traces of their senses out of each other's brains. But she felt those tell-tale signs, the little hints that a man was at their limits with her pleasure inducing body.

He slid his hand up her thigh, and used his thumb to try and prod at her clit. To circle that little bundle of nerves and coax a climax from her as he gasped and moaned.

"Angela," he groaned out, and that simple use of her name was said in such a way it meant so much more. It was a plea for her to join him in his climax to come, it was a tipsy declaration of his fondness and adoration for her.

It was a young man's cry of lust and love.

And that itself was nearly enough to throw her

over the edge. She was so slick and wet against his thumb, throbbing so heatedly as she whimpered. Her breath caught in her throat and she was so close. She just needed a little bit more, and she ground her body against his with such desperation.

Then there were stars as her body exploded for him, her nerves spasming and muscles tightening as she clasped herself to him so desperately. Her pussy pulsed, begged him to cum, milking him of that seed.

It was a foregone conclusion, that young man had teetered at the edge and the clenching pull of her cunt was more than he could've possibly fought against.

Romy's eyes shut even tighter and his mouth went wide as he let loose with a loud, noisy moan that filled his whole apartment. That throbbing shaft twitched and spurted, spewing his thick, creamy seed into her depths. Nothing between them as they both spiralled into carnal bliss so heedlessly.

His thrusts went on long, carrying through their intense body quaking climax as he blew his load within her. It was as if the momentum of his thrusts carried him on after that, when he slumped atop her paler body, thrusting and bucking in the dying throes of his orgasm. Until he was panting and heaving atop her. His soft lips kissing at her neck tenderly.

She didn't want to stop, and she kept rocking

with him, each thrust bringing another little spark of energy through her form.

It was bliss, and it was only when he slowed that she realized what she'd done, but it was too late for her to care. To do anything about it. So heedless. So stupid.

But that was what living was. Making dumb choices because a hot, young guy with a sexy accent and a ripped body wanted you.

She shifted to kiss him again, deep and passionate, as he slowed atop her, within her.

Her insistent rocking coaxed him on, brought forth that youthful energy. It was as if it sparked more than a moment's pleasure, but that proud manhood in him.

Romy rocked his hips and kissed at her hard, rebuilding pace as he lifted some of his weight from her.

The slick, wet noises of their loins smacking together filled the air after he'd made her cunt so messy with his seed. And he worked his lips back to hers, kissing at them fondly as he huffed and panted.

Her fingers ran through his hair, her eyes burning with affection as she looked at him with such adoration. Her final stand before being a normal person. She couldn't have asked for better, and that smile graced her lips once more before pressing them against him.

# CHAPTER 3

The day began late, but it began with a bang. There was no denying that.

Angela's new boy was as ravenous when he awoke as he had been the night before. Well, more so really. He treated her to another long session with his morning wood, then together they retreated to the shower together where they slipped and nearly fell on multiple occasions, but never let it impede them from fucking again.

"I've got some work thing to handle today," he explained as they climbed out of the shower, his sun-kissed flesh glistening with moisture. Though as he handed her the towel he seemed to hesitate, looking her over. "You can chill out here though," he offered, shrugging his shoulders, "if you like."

She was surprised by the offer, and her brief

smile said as much. Though she still hesitated. She'd sobered up, of course. She hadn't drank that much, after all. Certainly not enough to hide behind the mistakes she'd made in the last twelve hours.

This was just a one night fling, right? She'd convinced herself of that much. So why was she so unwilling to leave and go back to her dull, dreary existence?

Oh. Right.

She looked him over, all beautiful flesh and youthful vigor, and she craved more. She wanted him. She wanted the way he made her feel.

She wasn't ready for it to end.

But still, she took in a deep breath.

"I have a few things I gotta do too."

He nodded to her, giving a smile.

"Of course, whatever you need," he remarked before leaning in, placing another warm, succulent kiss upon her pouty lips before beginning to towel off. "I'm headed your way if you could use an escort back," he offered with a cheeky smile.

Whatever the night before was for her, she saw she had a new admirer.

"Sure," she smiled back at him.

Perhaps this life of mediocrity wouldn't be so bad, if she had him to look forward to after a long week. She wrapped the towel around her breasts, her hair wet around her shoulders, her makeup washed off. She was just her, and he didn't seem to mind at all.

It was refreshing.

# CHAPTER 4

"So you live up this way then?" Romy asked her, walking her down the street in the midday sun. They'd slept in late and were forever getting out of his place thanks to their twin libidos.

He looked good, a slick short black jacket on, left open, and sunglasses on his head as he took her towards her depressing little apartment. On her last day of freedom.

"Yea, for now," she said with a shrug, as if it were only a matter of time before she was moving up in the world. That couldn't be further from the truth. Even with the new job she'd not be able to move out for a while. If ever.

She still wore her dress and heels, the walk of shame the next day. She'd even missed that.

"I mean, it's a place, right. Good enough." She forced a smile.

Romy looked up over her sad little apartment building and smiled to her. For a moment she thought he might cringingly patronize her about it. Instead he shook his head at her and screwed up his lips.

"Nah," he stated as they came to a halt at her front door. "Not good enough for you by a mile," he asserted firmly, smiling at her so handsomely. "Once I earn my way up to a big, ritzy condo, I'll have to take you along with me. Show you the good life."

She laughed, a soft, polite laugh of being offered an impossible dream. Her eyes sparkled as she looked at him, and none of it was diminished.

"Well... I'd get your number, but my phone's dead." She brushed some of her long, dark hair from her face.

With a broad smile he pulled out his own phone, though she noted it was decidedly better than the one he'd pulled out the night before to call the cab. Unlocking it and entering in a few things he handed it over to her in offering.

She noted instantly her name was listed as: Beautiful Angel.

"Slick," she teased as she quickly typed in her digits, saving it and handing it back to him. Makeupless and slightly hung-over, and he was still quite the charmer.

"So... I guess I'll be hearing from you soon,

mmm?" she purred gently, stepping towards him and giving another little kiss.

Romy grasped her by the waist and turned that little kiss into something a bit more, unabashed with his affection on the midday street as their lips smacked noisily.

"I'll be in touch before you know it, chica," he promised with a delighted grin.

Her nose brushed against his and her heart fluttered in her chest. She had to push herself away, fumbling with her keys as she disappeared into her bland little building, a brilliant flush on her face. She could feel her heart thumping in her chest, her stomach turning with such excitement and new sensations.

She took the steps slowly, her heels clicking on them as she made her way up to her floor, down past the ugly stucco walls with the terrible brown paint. When she arrived at her own door, and made her way in, she immediately threw herself down on the couch.

Angela knew she'd done so many stupid things in the past half day, but she couldn't stop smiling at the thought of some sweet little twenty year old lusting for her so hard. In her mind she replayed it, over and over, every stolen touch, every passionate embrace. He made her feel so very deeply, in a way she hadn't in such a long time.

Just a little taste of freedom before she was locked away in the grey, dreary walls and fluorescent lighting.

# CHAPTER 5

Thoughts of her last night of rebellion got her through to the next morning. Though nothing could prepare her for the reality of a day job.

Angela found herself playing the walking dead as she trudged into the office, operating on the cheap, lousy coffee she had at home before the blinding white of the office greeted her. Reporting in at the front desk, it was the balding, leering man who came to welcome her to her job.

"Hey welcome to your first day at Omitrex," he said. What he lacked in enthusiasm, he made up for in his slurring sleaziness. "Lemme show you to your station," he instructed, waving her to follow him through the long, bland corridor.

"I'm just *so* excited to be here," she practically purred, trying not to roll her eyes. She was terrified of acting normal, of letting it show how repugnant she found not only him and that place, but the fact that she had to be there.

Pink lipstick stained her mouth, her sleek, dark hair pulled back in a bun. She felt like a nun in that blouse and skirt and itchy pantyhose and boxy shoes. It was quite the contrast from the bombshell who had landed herself such a sexy guy not long ago.

A sexy guy who hadn't called her back, or even sent a text.

She was trying not to dwell over it, but at eight in the morning, long before anyone in the world should be awake let alone at work, she couldn't help but think on it with a pout. At least if he'd texted, she could read it fifty times like a crazy loon.

She looked over the faces of her so-called co-workers, with their curious and yet still bored expressions as they yapped on their phones, grumbled about how slow their computers were. It was vapid and dull and Angela just kept giving a glowing smile to everyone as if to say they couldn't beat her down.

But she already felt dead inside.

"Here you go," he said, taking her to a long table situated up against a blank, white wall. No window. Not even a cubicle. "I'll just run you through the basics real quick and then you're set to go…"

All throughout the brief explanation of her tedious new job, he leaned in over her awkwardly, tried to peer down her top and was generally obnoxious. It wouldn't have been so bad except he stank of so much cologne it made Angela's eyes water.

"You all good?" he asked after that, placing an unwanted hand on her shoulder, though in truth her head was already aching from the incessant chatter of the other workers on either side and all around her.

"Perfect," she lied, just desperately wanting him to be gone. She didn't cringe away from the touch, though. She didn't need anyone to tell her how quickly her ass would be fired if she insulted her supervisor on day one. He wouldn't even need an excuse.

"Great! Just remember no bathroom breaks until lunch and always keep your eye on the quota. Though you get it a bit easier since you're just starting out," he said, squeezing her shoulder before walking off. "Just come get me if you need anything!" he called out, abandoning her to her mind numbing new task.

Where did going to get him fit into her tight new schedule?

# CHAPTER 6

By the time the day was over, her mascara was flaked and her eyes were strained and her head thumped like a jackhammer had pounded away at it. There were points she wasn't even sure she could make it, but she needed the money. She need the stability.

Her pantyhose had run up her thigh as she'd run to the washroom on her lunch break - thirty minutes! - and by the time she was headed outside she didn't even remember most of the previous nine and a half hours of her life. It was a blur of boredom and frustration.

She just couldn't wait to get home and slip into a bath. At least she could still afford that small pleasure.

No sooner than she had begun to sink into the tub than her phone rang. Another perfect event in her day. She couldn't even take a moment's peace to settle in.

She ignored it. She couldn't deal with anything but the hot water over her naked skin. She had to remember to change her ringer from that obnoxious default one. She let her head drift beneath the surface of the water to drown out the sound, soothing her head.

How could she go back and do that every day? To get used to that mundane torture?

She had lit a couple candles, cheap ones she'd gotten from the dollar store just in case there was a power outage, and they smelled sickeningly sweet but she just needed to feel a bit decadent as she rubbed the bar soap up and down her toned leg.

Surely life had to hold something better for someone like her. She was bright, and sexy. She could do anything if she put her mind to it, her parents had told her. But that was before she'd dropped out of University and gotten herself mixed up in other people's troubles.

When she finally got out and wrapped herself in a towel, her skin pruned from the water, she found her phone waiting, the message light flashing. Turning it on showed a missed call. And a text.

The number was foreign to her, but the text immediately made it all clear.

*"In your neighbourhood tonight. Won't you come out and play, my lovely chica?"*

She felt her heart race, her stomach flip. Oh, she wanted to. She did.

But she had work in the morning.

*"Gotta get up at 6:30 tomorrow,"* she wrote before reluctantly adding a frowning emote and hitting send.

And then she clutched the phone in her hand, swiping it awake whenever the screen went dark, waiting for his response like a teen.

The response came back before long:

*"You're breaking my heart!"* it read, but was then followed quickly by another.

*"Could meet at the bar near you. Just for a bit! I NEED to see you again, chica."*

Her fingers touched along the screen, over the words, as if they had body and spirit all their own. She took in a deep breath and glanced around her dingy room. A drink wouldn't be bad. A single drink. And if anything went further, well... she'd bring him back to her place and kick him out before the clock struck twelve, as if she were Cinderella.

*"One drink,"* she texted back before tossing the phone down on her couch and drying her hair. Everything was done so quickly as she pulled on a jean mini-skirt and a red top that showed off her cleavage. Her makeup done light — this was just a drink at a dingy pub — and she stepped into her sexy heels.

Going over to her phone, she turned it on once more.

*"Like telling me I get just one heartbeat. It is at least more than the none I would have without you!"*

She'd never been under any illusion he wasn't dramatic. She probably should have used caution, but instead it just made her grin like a maniac. At least boy drama was more exciting than the bullshit life she had to lead during the day.

*"Leaving now,"* she quickly texted back, checking to make sure her battery still had juice before throwing it in her black purse. She pulled on the same leather jacket she'd worn last time and then waltzed down the stairs as if she had the world at her fingertips.

At least for a little while she could fantasize that was true.

# CHAPTER 7

The dingy bar was not much changed from the last time she'd seen it, still she got looks from everyone around. But the only one that mattered was Romy. The handsome young man was quick to turn and see her, his face lighting up.

"You didn't give me much time," he remarked to her as he advanced with arms out to embrace her. "Lucky for you I was almost here already," he teased before leaning in to giving her a passionate kiss. None of that fire lost between their first night and then.

She softened against him, her green gaze penetrating as she stared up at him. He was just as gorgeous as she remembered, and even more into her.

"Well, I don't have a lot of time," she teased right

back, poking his ribcage playfully. "So we should make the most of it."

He'd retained the tight white top that showed off his abs beneath, but instead of the jeans he wore a crisp pair of black pants to match his blazer, it was the right mix of casual and cool on him. He made it look damn sexy.

"Already ordered you your drink," he retorted, pointing to the bar, where another glass of that bubbly wine awaited. "Would've got you something else, but… the options are limited here, as you've no doubt guessed by now," he remarked with a wry smile at her.

"I'm not too picky when other people are paying." Her bland, boring day slipped away from her as she stood so near to her lover, inhaling his scent and just enjoying his company.

His presence was intoxicating, and as they walked over to the bar and picked up the glass. She slipped into the seat, crossing her legs as she looked at Romy.

"What brings you here tonight?"

He was all charming smiles, so dashing and handsome as he sat next to her, his hand reaching out to rest upon her thigh comfortably.

"Got someone I need to meet for my brother," he shrugged his shoulders and added, "nothing big. Just a quick drop off. And hey! A perfect excuse to meet with you again. I've not been able to get you out of my mind since we met," he confessed in a low tone of voice.

She could have truthfully said the same, but instead she played it cool and gave him a flirtatious smile as she took another small sip of her wine.

"When's he coming?" she instead asked, her foot slowly teasing against his pant leg.

He took up his own drink, a simple rum and coke as before, helping himself to a generous mouthful.

"I dunno," he confessed with a shrug as he places his drink back down. "Kinda stuck waiting for a bit." He pulled his lower lip into his mouth and looked her over. "You look bangin'," he stated, though with the way he looked at her it didn't need saying.

It certainly didn't hurt to hear, though, and she smiled down at her outfit as if she couldn't even remember what she'd thrown on.

"Well thanks," Angela said, leaning in towards him. "I was glad to get your text today. I needed an excuse to get out of the apartment." It was a nice way to give him both a complement and act as if it were no big thing.

"I would have texted you sooner, buuut—" he paused and shrugged his shoulders, "didn't want to seem desperate." He laughed softly with his confession, bashfully scratching the back of his neck.

"I know you're busy with your job," he said to her, seeming to want to broach a topic carefully, "but… I was thinking you and I could go on a real date. Full deal. Show you off to my friends and family at the Tropicala. Or any ol' place you like!"

He was adorable when he was trying hard to win her over. It wasn't often he betrayed anxiousness, but it endeared her when he did. Made him seem more human.

More harmless.

She smiled at his confession and reached out, touching her fingers to his knee.

"I think that'd be really nice," she purred. "I get weekends off."

"Friday night?!" His eyes flashed wide and hopeful, the excitement palpable as he scooted to the edge of his stool nearer to her. And though it was clearly the soonest time, realization sank into Angela that it was still four whole work days away.

Four more days of that stifling hell that was called 'work'.

She tried not to let that thought bring her down, and she gave a demure nod. It'd give her something to look forward to, right?

"Sure, that should be fine." She clasped his knee before sitting back up and finishing off her wine. It was beautiful and cheap and bubbly and she loved it.

Angela looked across at her newest admirer, and all those old, familiar feelings began to worm their way into her. The heedless desire. It was almost cruel to meet him when she was trying her best to behave, because oh, he had the ability to make her do very, very bad things.

Romy's hand went to hers, and he squeezed her slender digits as he sipped his own drink, then lifted her hand up to kiss upon the backs of her knuckles.

It was nice just to sit, to be near to him. To enjoy his company and the way the alcohol warmed her veins and made the aches of the day slowly disappear. She took time to touch him, gentle, exploratory little grazes of her fingers against his jaw, his knee. Nothing overly lewd, but done with such appreciation, trying to commit every detail to memory.

To take something back with her to the office in the morning.

"What does your brother's friend look like, anyway? Should we be watching for him?"

"They're not friends," he clarified quickly, but then softened further, continuing to pay her all those little signs of affection. "It's not a big place, I'm sure we'll notice when he comes along, probably won't even be until after you have to go back," he said with a delightful pout, played up just enough to be fun and cute without over doing it.

He was such a charmer.

"Such an evil job you have, keeping us apart like this," he stated, moving his stool in so close to her, so he could get his arm in around her and stroke her thigh.

"You don't even want to know the half of it," she

said with a soft sigh. And she didn't even want to talk about it, but at the same time she wanted to scream about how horrific of torture it was.

Her hand rested atop his, caressing his flesh with slow, gentle motions atop her thigh.

"But at least you made my night a lot better." Angela's lips quirked into a smile. "Shame you have to wait."

Those beautiful eyes of his lit up, and it wasn't so much their colour that made them lovely. Though their hue of hazel was delightful, it was the curious patterns in them, an almost sort of emerald tinge that brought such life to his gaze.

"Ah fuck him," he said, casting off his responsibility that quickly. For her. "He's not goin' anywhere, and if he cared this damn much for his delivery he'd have shown up sooner, no?" he said with a toothy smile before leaning in and kissing her upon the lips soft and slow. "A lady like you does not come along more than once in a lifetime."

"I hate it when people are late," she purred, leaning towards him.

Deep down, Angela knew she was falling into a dangerous trap. Cute Cuban men, waiting in shady bars for relative's non-friends?

It was all too familiar to her, but she ignored every bit of her gut instincts, pleading with herself to not pay it any mind. Not read into it.

She couldn't give up the distraction he brought

her, the amazing sex, the thrill. She wouldn't sacrifice that so soon. Just the week. Get her through one week, with this cute young guy, and she'd be settled. Find something else to do with her time. Make friends with her co-workers, learn to not hate the itch of pantyhose and the constant watching of her shirt buttons.

But for now she was isolated and bored, and he brought colour into the world.

He lifted his hand up from her leg to stroke the tips of his fingers along her cheek, brushing back her glossy hair as he admired her beauty. It so easily could've been an act, all those little things, but with him she was convinced it was genuine.

He was suave and charming, but he wasn't *that* good of an actor.

"I don't even give a fuck anymore," he confessed softly, letting his fingers knit through her hair, around her ear, as he leaned in, kissing her deeply. It was such a sweet, passionate time, amid such a bizarre backdrop. None of the other haggard old fucks in the bar showed any kind life compared to the flame they lit together.

Angela relaxed into it, feeling herself get lost in all those things that had been missing in her life, and his warmth spread to her.

It was just what people did. Slaved their days for these little chances of life, and as she parted from him, smiling as her forehead rest against his, she was okay with that. If only just for the moment.

"I meant what I said about one drink," she purred.

He stroked his hand back through her hair, giving her plush lips a few warm kisses as they sat practically atop one another. The both of them looking more like teenagers than the adults they were supposed to be.

"Maybe I could come back to your place," he offered softly, "just for a bit."

His eyes fluttered, those long dark lashes of his so beautifully accenting his face. Yet those words… as dangerous as they were tempting.

But that sense of being wanted, it was overpowering, and she was nodding before she could stop herself. She was running on his high, and she had to force herself to take a deep breath and calm herself.

"Maybe for a bit. If you won't get in trouble."

"I'll worry about me," he said to her with a masculine, reassuring husk, letting his hand slowly descend from her face to rest at her hip, where he squeezed and tugged her towards him a little closer. "Besides, there are certain things in a man's life that are worth getting in trouble over. And a ravishing woman is at the top of that list," he declared so smoothly, kissing her lips again with such warmth and affection.

As much as she was smitten with the way he

made her feel, he was absolutely taken with her. There were no doubts about that.

He gave her such a head rush. His every touch was like electricity running through her, and she was at his mercy.

"C'mon then," she murmured before she brushed her lips against his, and she knew the wine was no excuse for this mistake. No, she had to own it, and she was willing to do just that.

They both stood up from their bar stools, and Romy nodded his head towards the bartender.

"Hey, Dmitri, I'll be back, okay? You tell the man I just had to step out," he said before putting his arm around Angela, grasping her hip and walking her to the door and out onto the cool evening streets of Toronto.

He didn't need to be directed to her place this time, and guided them both there, their path a slow, meandering thing as he kept kissing at her lips, her cheek, her neck. Insatiable for her the whole way there.

"You drive a man wild, my Angel," he said to her with such reverence and passion.

She clung to him as they walked, silly giggles fluttering from her lips every so often as she looked at him with such lust. Every time he spoke, every time he touched her, her insides fluttered and her sex throbbed.

He was like a drug to her, and she wanted more. And escape from the mundane.

It took longer than it should have before they were stood outside her building, drunk off each other's presence.

She didn't know what time it was, but with him, it went so quickly. Her long, dreary day dragged, and her exciting night would be little more than a blip.

She stuck her key in the door, letting them in to the relative warmth of her crummy building, and she practically ran up the stairs with him in toe. Each step resounded up the stairwell, and she glanced back at him with such excitement.

Grinning up at her, his hand was placed rather firmly upon the round curve of her ass over her jean skirt. He was shameless with her — they were shameless together — as they ascended her stairs to her apartment. That dingy little place, smaller than his, but more cluttered with the trivial effects of a foolish, wasted life.

None of that mattered though, he was just excited to be with her, and she could've lived in a dumpster and it wouldn't have mattered judging by the look on his face as he touched and kissed her. His two hands upon her hips as she backed into her apartment.

She locked the door behind them, and then led him into her room. She'd done a bit to try to tidy it up, but clothes were still thrown over the dresser and there were some books strewn on the bedside table. It was a sparse little room and as she sat down on the bed it squeaked, but she didn't even feel shame.

No, instead she kicked off her shoes, beckoning him towards her with a wide grin.

"We don't have a lot of time," she teased breathlessly.

He stripped off his jacket, the act pushing his shoulders forward, making his lean but prominent pecs and abs stand out through his tank. He was hungry for her, and looked so good; a tall, well groomed beauty of a man.

His shoes came off next, and then he undid the belt of his pants before he found himself unable to resist, and leaned one hand on the edge of her bed to kiss at her lips.

"Your scent drives me wild," he said in a ravenous husk, kissing his way down from her ear, across her sensitive neck.

She watched him with such fascination and need, stripping out of her own shirt and tossing it towards the collection of discarded clothes. Then she quickly undid her bra, eyes dropping to his belt.

"Hurry," she moaned as she pulled her arms through the straps, revealing her large, round breasts and the perky nipples set atop them.

God, it was just what she needed. Sweet, blissful distraction.

He dropped his pants and then soon after his underwear with it, and he pressed in over her, his throbbing cock prodding against her as he climbed over both her and the bed, making her shimmy back across it.

"I want you so bad right now, babe," he murmured to her between smacks of his lips, one of his hands rising to fondle and squeeze at her gloriously large tits, the young man entranced by those beautiful mounds and their resilient perkiness.

She bit down on her lip as her skirt shimmied up over her hips, staring at him with such appreciation.

"Is that so?" she teased, holding it in just how much she wanted him in return. It wouldn't do to give him the upper hand, to let him think he'd tamed her. Even if she did so willingly spread her legs for him, she wanted him to know it was her doing him the favour.

He was a gorgeous young man, with a ton of charm to spare, but she still had at least ten years' experience on him, and a body that made any man tremble.

"I haven't been able to calm myself down since our night together," he confessed breathily, pushing back and spreading her legs so wide, causing her skirt to become nearly a belt as he teased that pulsating member along her slit just a bit. Just a brief moment was all he could handle of that moist, velvety quim, before he began to push it into her raw again. A deep, throaty moan escaping his lips.

"Tell me about it," she hissed as she wrapped her legs around him, shoulders pressing into the bed as her body arched. Fuck, she knew she should make him grab a condom. Hell, she'd even bought a little box and it was within her reach.

But she couldn't bring herself to wait. It was careless, and reckless, but she instead tugged him in deeper, needing that full, human contact.

Romy wasted no time pumping his girth into her, filling her with his meaty shaft as he again and again sank down to the utmost depths of her cunny. The lewd slap of his balls to her ass filling the room as they began their newest tryst. Their latest abandonment of all reason and decency to rut like animals on base instinct alone.

"I've not been so tortured—" he gasped and trembled atop her, within the hold of her legs, his dick swelling inside her, "—since I was a little boy. Thoughts of how fucking good you feel, how good you look… smell," he was shuddering with excitement, squeezing her one plump breast as he built up speed.

He knew just what to say to drive her crazy, just what to do. Her mind was dimmed as she pressed her breast into his hand, the hard nipple rubbing against his palm as she squirmed so wantonly.

Her emerald gaze met his for a moment, a dark

smile gracing her lips as she wriggled beneath him, tilting her hips just so to let him go deeper.

Which was exactly what he did, that young buck atop her pounding faster, harder. He took her warning about time seriously, pumping into her so hard, so fast, so damn good. His fingers clenched into her breast and thigh as his face contorted in strain; from the pleasure more than the exertion.

"You feel so fucking good," he strained out, neck tense as he tried to hold back. She could see it, the way his beautiful young face contorted so. He wanted to savour their moment before it was all torn away. And for what?

She fluttered her eyes closed, and forced herself into the moment, to experience it fully. The way he smelled, the hardness of his body, his groans filling her ears as her cunny squeezed him so tightly.

He was delicious, a dangerous treat that she wanted more and more of. Even when he was fucking her she was looking forward to another taste.

Her breasts rocked against her ribs as he fucked into her, and her calves tightened against his ass, keeping him from pulling back.

Romy let loose a throaty, deep exhale as he fought the tight clench of her cunt, resisted the over-whelming pleasure of her depths to put as much of himself into pleasing her as he could. He was so full of desire and excitement, wanting to please her even as his body was being overwrought with sensations of his own.

"Gonna cum," he gasped out, squeezing her breast tighter as he trembled and his dick swelled, throbbing inside her lewdly.

That was her cue. Just loosen her legs, and it'd all be okay.

It took everything she had just to loosen them a little bit, feeling that failure grip her. She shouldn't have fucked him raw, and she knew it, but she was a fuck up. She knew that even better. She had such a hard time resisting temptation, and even though she'd gotten herself back on the pill, the doctor had reminded her that it's not effective immediately.

Her calves tightened against him again anyways, and she threw caution and good sense into the wind.

Romy came within her, not for the first time. Not even the second. No, she'd been far more reckless than that even. No claims to innocence could be made as he spurted his seed into her fertile depths, no claim that it was just a slip up. She'd welcomed him in and encouraged him. Because life was so void of meaning elsewise, that doing that one, animal thing — rutting, breeding, whatever you called it — just made it all bearable.

If only for a moment.

That brief second he bucked atop her and came so damn hard. His groin mashed to hers, his neat, trimmed bush against her mons as he shuddered and loosed all he had. That handsome face contorted into a strained expression of intense, overriding pleasure until he stilled atop her and broke into a gasp.

That was real. That visceral feeling that swam in her stomach, that made her mind turn to mush. How could anyone say anything else?

She looked up at him, breathing so hard as her heart pounded in her chest. Her mouth parted as she watched him come down from his pinnacle, that slow bit of disappointment eeking in. Disappointment that it was over and that he'd soon be leaving her.

She wrapped her arms around his shoulders, clinging onto him so needily.

An older or more jaded man might've been quick to leave, to disentangle himself from her. Her Romy however put his lean-muscled arms around her and squeezed her tight right back. He pushed his tongue into her mouth and made out with her passionately. Even as his dick laid within her, spent for the moment, he was passionate for her. He pushed his fingers through her hair to the back of her head and kissed her as if none of the preceding sex had occurred.

She loved the buzz of lust, that first spark of romance and need. They were such real emotions, heightening every moment to the limits. It made the duller parts of the day even more so, and the best parts amazing.

It was like being manic, addicted to the one source of joy as her tongue lanced against his with such a frenzy.

Yet even as disappointment began to sink its venomous fangs into Angela, her young lover only began to pump his hips again. Not with some slow, final tease, but the stirring vigor of youth and virility.

He wanted her bad.

No paranoid doubt from the petty gods of society could undo that truth. Her lover boy was ravenous for her, and he wanted to show it. Every inch of that sizable manhood of his.

It shouldn't have taken her by surprise, how quickly he was able to bounce back. She'd experienced it that first night, but had simply assumed it was that first lust, that little tease of one night.

But she bit down on her lips and pulled him into her, pussy muscles massaging his cock back to life as she ground her hips into him.

He was a dangerous man to fall in love with. There were no doubts about that. He was addictive. Like cocaine, he gave her an instant high and she wondered how she'd live without him after it all. After... what?

Thinking about the future was painful, and not just because it seemed so bleak. But because any future she thought up couldn't include being pounded by that hot young stud forever. It was the sort of passion that burned hot for a while like a fuse, before it triggered dynamite.

"I don't wanna leave you," he groaned out.

She giggled it off, those dark, creeping thoughts as she brought her mind back to him and his needful grinding.

"It's only a few days," she purred. "How long can that possibly be?"

"Forever, when I am not inside of you," he professed, kissing her plush lips back as he pumped into her at a less rough pace, savouring the sweet feel of their loins together. All sense evaporated in him, he just greedily wanted more of her, and if she let him he'd not leave the entire night.

But some small sense of responsibility had already started gnawing at her mind.

"I can't fuck up and be late tomorrow," she said in a whisper, sounding so regretful and feeling it even stronger.

His motions slowed, but only a little. He kissed at her face, stroked her side with his hand as they were entangled in one another, slowly rocking atop her creaking mattress.

"I don't want to make you late," he professed to her softly, his voice so sincere. But so needy.

She kissed him, gentle and soft, before she pulled

back and gave him a wicked grin, as if she didn't feel the same longing.

"Besides, you have to meet your brother's not-friend."

Romy cursed in his native tongue, then kissed her deep and hard, biting her lower lip before tugging back, pulling that plush morsel with him before letting it snap back into place.

"To hell with him, I'm fucking the hottest woman in the whole city and beyond," he declared in that rich accent, enough conviction behind his words to convince the judging angels.

She could lay there all night, rolling around in her squeaky bed, kissing his vibrant self 'til dawn, but instead she shook her head.

"I really gotta be ready for morning," she said, and almost felt proud of herself for that little moment that she felt adult. Until she realized just what being an adult apparently meant.

The athletic young man came to a slow halt, and paused over her. Their eyes met and then he gave her a soft kiss upon the lips before he pulled back away with a shiver, rolling over onto his elbows.

"You make a man never want to stop," he remarked in a breathy voice. "How is it you do not already have a rich man in your life?" he asked, looking over at her, genuine curiosity on his face.

But she had to look away, a little frown marring her face. She had a rich man in her life, and that ended just as well as she could have expected. She had been in *love*, though.

"Well, if I were, I wouldn't be free to have met you," she teased after the moment of darkness passed.

He supported himself upon one arm, then hooked the other around to cup her jaw in his palm and stroke her cheek with his thumb soothingly. He guided her face back towards him, smiling at her softly.

"I will be a rich man one day, a very rich man," he said with such confidence, such gusto. "If I was not sure of that, I would never have left home. So if you stick by me… be my girl, I will take you to the top. Where kings of men decide the fates of us all."

Angela smiled at him, feeling that carnal pull, the desire to be lifted out of the hell that was her life.

But she knew young men, like him, with dreams of grandeur, and there were very few ways to the life that he was describing. All of them were the ones she was trying to get away from.

She still kissed his lips, though, as she pulled away from him and fixed her skirt.

She couldn't do it. Those words, those sweet, alluring words, were like poison.

If he had wanted a response then and there, he never showed it. Without breaking stride he simply got up, picked his underwear and pants off the floor, then started dressing.

"You'll call me before Friday?" she still asked, since she knew then was not the time and place for a conversation about their far off and non-existent future.

"Sure chica," he said with a smile to her. "Hearing your pretty voice will soothe me through the week, no?" He tugged his jeans into place, sealed up the belt and bent over, placing a warm kiss on her lips. "You'll keep me in mind, won't you?" he asked so sweetly.

"Of course," she said on a whisper. She knew that to be true. It'd be impossible to get him out of her head right then, even if it was so wrong.

She was a sinner, and she was never good at paying her penance.

# CHAPTER 8

$\mathcal{A}$ngela felt the shower pour its soothing warmth over her, yet it was hard for her to enjoy it. Despite the youthful obsession that now tinged her existence, it was as if she could feel the presence of that woman. Like her, but younger, prettier. Immortal that way. Wiser, older. Like her mother.

*You really couldn't even make it a full day of work without fucking up,* came the woman's dissatisfied tone, so full of snark and a bitter edge.

Angela didn't need to turn to see the crossed arms, the stern expression. Of course, the woman didn't exist outside her mind. Her conscience, whatever the fuck it was.

*A box of condoms right there next to your bed even, and you just let it slide. Fuck some young punk without a care for anything. Not your health, your future. You're already playin' catch-up on twenty years of fuckin' up. And miserably at that.*

Angela cringed. She'd spent so long drinking and worse, trying to silence that nasty, chiding voice at the back of her mind, that strange manifestation of everything she hated about herself.

*It's just a bit of fun,* Angela lied, knowing it was futile. That subconscious woman saw right through her, into the heart of the matter. She couldn't cut it, living a lame little existence, going to work every day for shit wages. She wanted the thrill of danger, of something more.

She craved her fucked up life, but the price she had been forced to pay was too much. That was why she got the job, trying to run from the fact that she barely got out of jail alive, her soul shattered and her spunk disappeared.

And she tried, earnestly, to get her life back together, to do the thing that she was supposed to do. But she'd seen the easy money, the high living, the things it did to people - both good and bad.

*Fun,* came the bitter, angry retort. *Yeah, it'll be a lot of fun headin' to the pharmacists again. Trying to hide that look of embarrassment. You had it in you to do so much better. Now look at where you live. A rat hole you would've been too good to set foot in just a few years ago. But I guess this is where you belong. At least until you're out on the streets, dried up and beaten down.*

Angela's body tensed, the insult jabbing at her

most tender areas. But then, her subconsciousness knew all the spots to hit her that hurt the most. She could already feel her shoulders trembling and knew that what she - it - said, was right.

It was only a matter of time.

*I was only better when it came to dealing,* Angela hissed back with as much venom as she could, trying to hide that internal pain. *And we both know how well that turned out.*

*So what you're telling me is that you're just a total fuckup, so why bother at all? Oh please. Such a child, even as you wither away. Many have had it rougher than you and done much better. You just won't stop living for the cheap, immediate thrill.*

There was no more, nothing else to say as she shut off the shower and made her way out to towel off. Though no sooner than she opened the door she heard a terrible roar from outside.

It was an alarming sound, and she was drawn to her living room window. Out there in the dark streets she could see a motorcycle pull up at the bar just down the road where she'd met Romy. Upon it was a towering man, clad in leathers but even still, looking gaunt and lanky. Even from her distance he looked sickly pale in the streetlights luminescence, his hair cropped short.

It was a strange, momentary thing.

Her nose crinkled up as she towelled off her hair,

shameless in the window as she looked down upon the man.

"Fucking bikers," she hissed against the cheap window pane, rolling her eyes. If there was one thing she knew? Bikers were either obnoxious, or they were trouble.

The clicking of cheap keyboards, the sound of endless repetitions of the corporate script. The call center was a droning, draining job for Angela. She couldn't even get through the early hours without a headache.

So when she saw the balding man come up to her with his awkward grin, it hardly made her day seem any better.

It was her third day, the second having been the most excruciatingly mind-numbing, demoralizing experience of her life. More so than prison in some ways. Yet she pushed through it without another fuckup. Without even turning to her new beau.

"Hey, gotta talk for a minute," said her boss, sitting his large back end upon her desk, pushing some of her things awkwardly away as he made himself comfortable at her expense. "Got a few things to cover— oh but hey, first, how's it going?" he asked, using the papers in his hand to give her a light, condescending pat on the shoulder.

"Oh, perfect," she smiled, seething beneath. The energy it took to simply say that was excruciating, but she managed. Her head throbbed and she kept wishing he'd fall, get swallowed by the table. Anything but talk.

Talking at a job was always a bad thing, especially when she was working with such ridiculous restrictions. She'd been holding in the urge to pee for at least an hour and she squirmed, her itchy pantyhose only adding to her pain.

At least in jail she was able to dress comfortably.

"That's great," he said in a way that hinted he truly didn't care. He was, of course, already looking through the report in his hands before she so much as said it. "There's a little issue with your response times. You're new and it's only been a few days so I'm cuttin' you some slack here, but you've gotta move through the script quicker. Don't let the callers keep you on too long before bangin' out the next one, okay?" he asked, shooting a look to her over the rim of his ancient, out-of-style glasses.

Her smile tightened, her eyes darkening as she nodded up at him. It was getting harder and harder to keep up the prissy, excited personality she'd had at the interview. Three days in and already her life was being sucked from her.

"I'll do my best, Sir," she said in a strained voice.

"Of course you will," he said, reaching out and patting her shoulder directly this time with his hand. He moved to get up then but instead stopped.

"Oh! I almost forgot," he said, flipping through the papers again. "Oh yeah, here we go. To finalize the whole hiring process we need to get a criminal record from you. It got forgotten in the whole process somehow, but no big deal, right?" he said with a big smile. "So just get that into us A.S.A.P."

He pushed himself off the desk and walked off, giving another employee a light thwack with the rolled up documents. As if the office weren't a place for adults, but some other demeaning extension of school.

Her face fell.

Right. Of course. The record check. Of course it hadn't been a happy accident that they hadn't required one, simply something forgotten in the bureaucratic process.

She pushed her papers back onto that area her supervisor had sat and felt that pit of dread well up within her. Once more, her past haunted her future, ruining any chance of going clean she had.

She was going to have to find a new job. Again.

ngela spent her night fighting off depression, malaise, the crushing sense defeat. Though it wasn't easy; reading through the job listings online was horrible. Doing so on the tiny screen of her phone more troubling still. So many of them wanted online applications, but she didn't even have digital copy of her resume she could send through the damn thing.

It became so easy to forget them anyhow. A series of jobs that sounded all the more soul crushing for how hard they tried to make mundane, mind-numbing work sound glamorous. She was old enough to read through bullshit after all. Hell, you had to be able to do that from a young age, other-wise you were a sap taken in by everyone and every-thing in society.

Just as her resolve began to waiver, and her

thumb went down to the telephone icon — just itching to call Romy — the blaring sound of a motorcycle again resounded outside. Its deafening noise echoed between the buildings, and demanded the attention of all who lived and worked on her street.

She was drawn back to the window, to peer out onto the street.

Only to see the same man again. That towering, lanky man in his leathers. He looked no less haggard than before, some other dried up old fuck, she surmised. He'd fit right in at that bar, with his thin, pale-white hair and gaunt looks.

Then her eyes trailed to the bar and she was filled with a sense of emptiness, of longing, and she had to push herself away. She couldn't fuck it up again. She needed to avoid the things that had put her behind bars - including men like Romy.

Though that didn't stop her from being excited for Friday night, as much as she wanted to pretend it did.

She'd have to find a library that was open late and use one of their computers.

*My glamorous life*, she sighed bitterly.

# CHAPTER 11

It had been Angela's first day of putting off her boss about the record check. She didn't expect the office would give her many warnings; they fired people left and right for every ridiculous reason under the sun. There were always more desperate folk willing to snap up those jobs, after all.

So it was a night at a public library.

The old building was well kept on the outside, but inside she could practically smell the deteriorating effects of budget crunch. The library of books was clearly maintained with an attentive hand, but the place was being held together by the librarian's sheer will, it seemed.

The rows of computers available to the public were all in use when she got there, with others waiting to get at them. Despite the hubbub about the death of libraries, the poor and desperate lined up to get access to the internet where they could.

She signed her name on the ledger for a crack at the PCs and sat herself down. All around she could see the sights of the old library, the old tomes, the book club gathering on the level down below made up of a lot of grey and white haired individuals. The young people using the public venue for studying with tutors. The middle-aged folk walking into the public records section, undoubtedly in search of some connection to their past that would give them an idea of... what?

Angela doubted the answer was anything but: nothing.

Though as she sat there waiting, her phone began to buzz and ring. It sounded in the quiet area, drawing notice to her before she quickly got it out and saw the name flashing.

Romy.

She took the phone into a quiet nook.

"Hey," she said softly.

"Are you operating in secret, my Angel? You sound so... mysterious this evening," he remarked with smooth tone of voice, so delightfully charming.

There was no way she could bring herself to say, *"Oh, no, I'm just at the local library, waiting for a chance to use a computer that was old when you were born."*

Instead, she just giggled softly and purred, "Wouldn't you like to know?" It was almost second nature to deceive, to keep people uncertain as to just how bland her life truly was.

"That question shall leave me awake tonight wondering, my Angel," he remarked with a mischievous lilt to his voice. "You aren't being a bad girl, are you? I mean, it is a work night. If you were going to be bad you should've called me over and I'd have made your night as bad as they come. Even if I had to tie you to that bed of yours," he added on somewhat darkly.

His words twisted her stomach with both desire and that nagging sensation of fear, of letting herself fall too deeply into his alluring presence. She licked over her lips, eyes darting to one of the people giving her the stink eye, even as she whispered.

"Oh, don't tease me like that," she cooed, and already she could feel the heat between her legs throb with desire.

"Me tease you?" he retorted. "I thought you were the one teasing me, with that sexy little voice of yours. Trying to lure me over to your roost so that I have no choice but to pin you down and make you mine for the night, whether work agrees or no," he remarked with a sly, devilish tone that made his words all the more irresistible.

And she wished she were home so she could tempt him to do just that. But she wasn't, and part of her was relieved.

The boring part. The part that wanted to stay out of trouble.

"Naughty boy. Can't even wait another day?" she purred back, unable to resist.

Romy gave a deep, needful groan.

"Not when you talk like *thaT*," he stressed, and she could practically hear him squirming on the other end with need. "When you are my woman, I am going to have to tie you down to *my* bed so you cannot get away with being so naughty without consequences, beautiful."

She wanted so badly for him to keep going, for him to tell her all the nasty things he wanted to do to her, but she licked over her lips and swallowed. She had to get this stupid job hunting thing underway. She couldn't afford another week unpaid.

"And what do you have planned for tomorrow, huh?"

"Tomorrow? I am going to swing by and get you, then take you out to a lovely meal. Real fancy, something worthy of *my* date," he proclaimed, sounding so very proud. "After that, we will go to the Tropicala, where I shall introduce you to my friends and family, and make them absolutely die of jealousy as we rock the dance floor."

She couldn't wait, and was practically squirming right there in the library. Every time she thought she could just avoid him, ignore his lure, his voice and words tempted her otherwise. She was so weak, and weaker still to his charms, and she had to still her breathing to regain that edge of power to her voice.

"What time should I expect you, lover?"

"How about I come by and pick you up around seven? That give you enough time to get ready, my beautiful lady?" he asked, such a charmingly considerate tone to his voice.

Though right as he said it she noticed a spot opening up at the grungy old computers.

She smiled at his words and then cursed under her breath.

"I'll be ready. I have to go now, though, okay? See you tomorrow," she purred, unable to hide her excitement even as she stealthily moved towards the computer.

"Just make sure you wear somethin' to accentuate that gorgeous body of yours, beautiful. It should be a crime to not show that body off."

With that their conversation ended and she was stuck, sitting at the filthy keyboard before her preparing her resume to search out more miserable jobs she'd certainly not get.

ngela was already having a hard time finding decent clothes to wear out. She'd had a beautiful closet full of all the clothes she could ever have wanted before life cruelly snatched it from her, and she had to start practically from scratch.

Still, she had to admit, she looked smoking. Her hair was left down, all over her bare shoulders. The halter top dress paired with the push-up bra and the fuck-me-pumps made her legs look longer and more slender, her ass more rounded, and her tits huge.

Her makeup was all crappy drugstore stuff, but she knew how to accentuate her looks like a professional, and by the time seven rolled around, she was ready.

Sure, there was the unspoken rule about making her date wait, but she was too old for those types of games. She knew what she wanted, and she wasn't going to pretend that she needed to make him wait for him to want her.

Her phone lit up with Romy's call promptly on time.

"Hey chica, is it okay for me to come claim you now? Or should I pay you proper respects and wait down here a little longer? Don't worry, I understand if you need some more time," he said to her so smoothly.

She grabbed for her purse and was ready to run out before she stopped and looked in the mirror once more, fixing the stray hair that otherwise ruined her perfectly put together look. He tempted her to lie, but she couldn't stand staring at the dismal walls for any longer.

"I'm ready," she replied, the smile apparent on her voice.

It'd been a long day, and she dreaded what would likely come on Monday, so she simply opened her door and slipped out to meet him, all eagerness and excitement.

As she came down the stairs she could hear the then familiar roar of a motorcycle, it reverberated through the building and up the stairwell even. As she came down to the bottom of the stairs and exited into the lobby of the building, she could see Romy out in the streets. Even in his stylish outfit, however, it was the towering biker that loomed over him ominously that drew her eye.

He looked pissed.

"Shit," she hissed, and stopped in her tracks as she took in the scene, her heart instantly thudding hard in her chest. She was torn between what her gut told her to do - get out of there. Just turn around as if she'd never seen a thing.

But the other part of her, the part she was constantly fighting to keep in line? That told her to go over there. To help Romy calm the guy down.

Romy was dressed in a very nice, slick black suit, a pressed crisp shirt undone at the collar with a bundle of roses in hand. Though he looked too distracted with the towering man to do anything.

He jabbed his finger at Romy's chest, and Angela could hear his low, booming voice through the glass.

"Don't fuckin' miss your appointment next time. Or else there'll never be a next time, hrmmh?" he said in a strange manner, head tilted, eyes wild with repressed rage.

He looked scary up close, haggard and lanky, yes, but he was immense and had a look about him.

The look of the guys that she needed to avoid. He was dangerous, and not in the cute way.

She felt a tremor go through her as she stared, first at her gorgeous boy-toy and how jaw-droppingly cute he looked with his bouquet, and then back to the towering man. He had to be at least six-foot-five in order to make her lover look so small by comparison.

Angela couldn't move, her knees shook as she took in a deep breath and fumbled for her phone, stabbing in the police number but not yet dialing it.

Just in case.

She could see Romy try to calm the man, holding out a hand that got smacked away. His voice was softer, harder for her to make out. But when the towering man's eyes moved towards her, he stopped, frozen.

He couldn't have seen her holding the phone, it was tucked out of sight. But he looked to Romy again.

"Next time do business like a professional," he insisted, then stomped off towards the bar. Leaving Romy to deflate a little, the tension melting away.

A less auspicious start to her date than she could have hoped for, and she pushed through the door and went to Romy's side, touching his arm gently as she let her phone drop back into her purse.

"Are you okay?" she asked softly, her gaze chasing after the man as he left them.

Romy turned to her quickly, looking a bit surprised but hiding it well. His face immediately lit up and he looked her over, giving a sharp whistle.

"No," he said breathlessly. "Call an ambulance baby, I'm about to die of a heart attack. You're too damn beautiful for me to handle," he remarked, not even missing a beat.

And that cocky attitude of his softened her worries, and she relaxed a little.

"Those for me?" she asked, her green eyes dipping down to the bouquet with a wry grin, flicking some of her hair from her face.

Romy followed her gaze down to his hand, then feigned a little shock before holding them up to her.

"Oh yeah!" he said with a bright, handsome grin. "I was going to bring them up to your door so you could put them in something, but…" he trailed off, then shrugged his shoulders. "It's not a big deal. You're just lucky you didn't have to see me break out some fisticuffs, my beauty."

She let out a soft laugh as she accepted them gratefully and glanced back at the lobby door.

"No harm in running them up now," she said, licking over her lips and trying to plead with herself not to get so carried away. But she knew she would. She was itching for more, and that brief brush with danger did nothing to quell her desire for rebellion.

Romy put his hand upon her hip and then brazenly down to her ass, cupping the cheek as he led her back inside.

"Alright, c'mon. We've got that dinner reservation to make, after all," he remarked cheerfully before they climbed the stairs to her place.

She stepped with an additional wiggle in her hips for his pleasure, up those stairs with the practiced click-click-click of her heels on the tile. Fumbling for her keys she finally made it inside and gave him a kiss at the door.

"If you come in, we'll never make the reservation."

Romy's eyes widened in a daring sort of gesture before he blew her a kiss and waited.

"Just don't take too long or I'll have to come in there and maul you, my beauty," he called after her as he stood in her doorway.

She was impressed he didn't protest, and quickly moved inside. Really, she should have just locked the door, pulled across the chain, and left the night at that. Gone taken a nice long bath. Distance herself from Romy and the dangerous man that threatened him.

But every time she tried to push him away, that stronger voice within her told her that she had nothing else in life. No other light, no other hope or prospects. A person could go mad without any break in the monotony, so she instead dunked the flowers in a glass along with some water before heading back out.

Her arm laced around him, holding herself tight to him.

"Ready?" she purred.

"Any more ready and we'd never get out of here," he remarked with a husk, placing a kiss on her neck just beneath her jawline. With his hand upon her ass, he guided her out of the building.

# CHAPTER 13

The restaurant they arrived at was nicer than she would've thought; the menu had no prices on it, and that alone spoke volumes.

"I've never eaten here before," Romy confessed after seating her and hearing the waiter out for the specials. "But my brother assures me it's the finest. And you deserve no less," he remarked across the table to her, reaching his hand out to touch hers.

"I haven't either," she purred back. Her fingers interwove with this as she glanced around at all the high end finery. She couldn't believe she was there. It was a jarring contrast to the fast food places she frequented, late at night.

And it reminded her once more why she'd avoided dating and friends and anyone else for so long. She knew that once she had another taste of that life, she'd want it back. That was exactly what was happening, too. She could feel herself become more and more drawn, not just to his virility and charm, but to that air of mystery he had about him.

The fact that she knew that he and his brother were into something shady as hell.

"It smells really good," she said as she leaned back in her chair a little, crossing her legs so that her skirt pulled up. She felt like a low-class hooker in a high-class bar, but even that didn't bother her so much as the gnawing feeling that she was so close to the brink. So close to toppling over that edge and doing something bad.

Romy squeezed her hand in return then shut the menu.

"How about you have the butternut squash and smoked ricotta ravioli and I will try the braised veal," he stated more than questions her, looking so handsome and full of himself across the table. It was clearly an expensive suit he wore, very stylish and tailored to an excellent fit.

The waiter came by then all prim and proper.

"Some of your finer wine, my lady deserves only your best."

She had to face it. She was enamoured with him. That cockiness, that desire to please her... It made her feel more like a Queen than the pauper she truly was.

The sensation was addictive, and her ruby lips were tugged into a smile as she rubbed her thumb along his flesh. Just the little bit of a tease, to connect with him on that primal level as she looked over his handsome face and broad shoulders with such a sense of appreciation.

His thumb brushed over hers as the order was placed, their expensive wine was served and they gazed at one another. The wine itself wasn't particularly appealing, the sort of expensive yet not appetizing wine one expected when they paid top dollar.

"I hate your work," he said to her abruptly. "It keeps you away from me too much. And I am coming to realize I need a woman like you in my life. It is an awkward thing to have to dance around your schedule when all I want to do is have my hands all over you, night and day."

"I hate my work too," she grinned, though for different reasons. At the same. Her eyes wouldn't stop trailing over him, wondering how she could have gotten so lucky to find such a charming and sexy man in such a dingy little bar.

"But we all need a job, right?" she asked, but she knew the answer. It was just a gentle little probe for him to tell her more about what, exactly, he was into.

"Sure," he responded smoothly, "but some jobs are different from others, yes? I like my life with a little more freedom. A little more... opportunity. One can't grab up the big chances if they're locked away in a fixed schedule, no?" He said, smiling across at her.

Romy lifted her hand up and kissed her fingers tenderly.

"You should be my woman," he said affectionately, looking so very suave and charming in his crisp black suit, that edgy latin flair to his appearance even as he managed to look so dapper. His sleek, dark hair styled very nicely, not slicked back this time but up and to the side a little. He looked like he was straight out of a fashion magazine.

"Flexibility comes with a price," she said as her head canted to the side, her smile never faltering even as her heart began to race. She kept hoping he'd just come right out and say it, to quiet those doubts that told her she was wrong about him.

She knew he was into shady business, but still she tried to convince herself it probably wasn't all that bad.

"Everything has a price, beautiful," he said, kissing her hand again before drinking some of that expensive wine. "But if you were to be my woman, my price would be simply that you be mine. My lover, my regular date. The lady who follows me to the top, and I will get there," he boasted with a smile. "I know you have probably heard other young men say it, but if you tie yourself to me? I will take you in, look after you, ask nothing but you love me, physically, emotionally."

Things that would come so easy to her. He was tempting her, and she felt, not for the first time that night, that dangerous hand begin to grip around her ankle, tugging her towards ruin.

She lifted her own glass of wine and took a sip, ruby lipstick staining the glass as her green eyes worked over his face. He was gorgeous. Charming. What more could a woman ask for in a man? Especially one who was promising her the world?

Her thumb brushed along his and she forced a small smile.

"My lover, you're acting like I'm a stray dog," she teased.

That made him look bashful and apologetic. His face tucked down, not looking her in the eye any longer.

"Forgive me," he said smoothly. "Perhaps I am getting ahead of myself. I am not yet a great and powerful man. But I am a greedy man, greedy for your time, your affection. How I find myself longing for the freedom to come home to you whenever I wish it. To spend sweet moments with a ravishing beauty and make a life together."

With a shrug of his shoulders he amended, looking back at her.

"Perhaps it is still too soon, and I am being impetuous. You have not yet met my family and friends even!"

It was then their food was brought before them, meals that seemed to be more about how they appeared than anything else, arrayed upon the plate before them like some modern works of art.

She let go of his hand, instead bringing her napkin to her lap as she looked over the food and wondered how hungry she'd be after finishing it. Still, she smiled as if it were the best thing in the world, her eyes sparkling at him as the waiter departed once more.

"I don't mind impetuousness," she said as she reached for her fork, grasping it as she watched him intently. "But I still don't know much about you."

"After tonight, perhaps that won't be so," he remarked back to her, her lovely young beau smiling brightly as they ate.

The timing was impeccable, for before they could finish the next course of their meals there arrived a couple. One of whom she could immediately guess a relation to Romy. He was a towering man, another giant standing at at least 6'5. He wore a fine suit that looked like it came from the same place as Romy's, and the woman with him was a statuesque young lady, lovely as she was tall.

Romy stood up and rounded the table to grasp the man's hand.

"Javier," he said, giving the larger man's hand a firm shake and a show of respect before moving to the woman with him. "Evelyn," he said, kissing the back of her hand. "I would like you both to meet

Angela, my date," he said, holding out an arm towards her, quietly urging her up to his side.

It was a good thing that she was a practiced liar, always keeping that face of hers controlled. It was something she'd learned when she was younger, growing up on soap operas and finding the wealthy to be so fabulously manipulative and closed off. They lied with a straight face, and raised Angela to do the same.

She stood and smiled graciously at the couple as her slender shoulder rest against Romy's arm, her head just slightly canted in curiosity.

Romy put his arm about her in such a familiar manner, introducing Angela to them both.

"Angela, this is my brother and employer, Javier," he explained, gesturing to the man in the white suit with the dark, dreaded hair.

"A pleasure," he returned in his deep, booming voice, reaching out to take her hand and kiss it in such a refined, gentlemanly manner. He was clearly about her age, and the woman with him just a few years younger, her mid-twenties.

"This is Evelyn," Romy moved on, "his wife." Though looking at them, Angela swore the two were siblings rather than a couple. For Evelyn was Amazonian tall like the man, the same exact dark hue to their skin, the same hair and hints to their features. Even their clothes matched, her tight dress a white number that looked to be the exact same cloth as his suit.

"The pleasure's mine," Angela purred.

She looked over them both from beneath her heavily made up eyes and acted as if she weren't surprised or annoyed by their sudden presence. Which, she was. She wanted to know more at the same time she feared it, but she never let it show.

A couple like them? Even if they weren't into something illicit, they could make her do dangerous things, and for a brief moment it darkened her smile.

"If you wish to join us," Romy said, looking at her with a questioning gaze, "I don't think it would be a problem to have them pull another table over to ours."

"Not at all," Angela replied, that smile never faltered for a second even as he presented a question that was impossible to refuse in public.

"Certainly," came the deep, baritone response from Javier.

Romy saw to rounding up the wait staff to perform that task immediately, the tables rearranged and food was brought for the new pair almost as soon as they sat down.

"Romy has mentioned you often," stated Evelyn, looking between her and Romy.

"I can see why now," added Javier, none of the charm to that statement that she'd expect from the younger brother. He just remarked on Angela's beauty as a matter of fact and little more.

Her eyes flit to Romy, her smile a bit softer as she took another sip of her wine, her legs crossed beneath her too-short dress.

"Well, I'm flattered," she replied as she felt her heart pound within her chest. That fear of being boring was haunting her, of having nothing interesting to say in conversation. What could she even talk about? *Hey, I was living a really awesome life before going to prison, and now I work at a job that's even worse'?*

"Do you two come here often? Romy said you recommended it," Angela said to Javier.

"We do," said Javier, nodding slowly before taking a sip of his fine wine. "It's important to treat yourself to the finer things."

"To really remind yourself of how far you've come from scrounging for food just to survive," Evelyn added on, sitting like an empress with her shoulders back, such stiff but elegant posture.

"They were the first of my family to make it here," added Romy. "They built a whole lot out of nothing, it's amazing," he stated with such reverence for their feat. Not them; Angela could note that much. He revered the accomplishment, not so much the people who made it. A finer distinction.

"I absolutely agree," she said, only partially lying. She'd been the one scrounging for food, then living the high life. Then it all came crashing down and once again she was scrounging for food. The problem with fast money was that there was always someone else willing to step in and take it all away in the blink of an eye.

And yet she so relished being back in a fine restaurant, eating food she didn't care for with company she had to force small talk with. It was certainly more exciting than the lies she'd have to spin at work on Monday.

The new couple were not the chattiest, and Angela could sense a certain imperious air about them, how they both sat and spoke, the way they moved or didn't. They acted like royalty more than the sort of criminal element she suspected they were.

"So what do you do?" came the question from Evelyn, eating her curious dessert with but the tiniest of forkfuls. "Romy mentioned you were a busy woman with your employment," she said, her accent heaviest of them all.

Well that was a loaded question, and her eyes shifted to Romy as if looking for support that she knew he couldn't give.

"Nothing exciting," she said as she looked back at Evelyn, tilting her head just so with a smile. "It's just a casual job for now, doing..." there was a pause, "fashion design for a friend. She can't keep me full time, but it keeps me occupied lately."

It was a bold lie, but she didn't want to get to the heart of the matter in public.

"Only part time?" Evelyn said before taking another miniscule bite of her dessert. "I would have thought worse with how Romy seems to pine for you so."

Romy did his best to keep his cool, but a quick glance showed the slight crack in his veneer, how he tried to hide his embarrassment about Evelyn's reveal.

"They are still new love birds," remarked Javier casually in his low voice. "Give them time," he said, not even raising his gaze from his own plate as he broke off a more generous bite.

Angela was pretty sure she hated them both and gave a broader smile at Romy, as if trying to protect him.

"I'm certain my friend feels the same about me. She's the one stuck working with me twelve hours a day this week," she teased as she looked to Evelyn, her posture going a bit more rigid.

"She has a show coming up soon and needs as much help as she can get right now, but that's the nature of her business. Feast or famine."

Romy smiled at her affectionately from across the table.

"That is a something I can sympathize with, the ups and downs, the unpredictability," he said softly, looking every bit like a smitten young man, even in the presence of his superiors who she'd seen him noticeably tense up around.

"You are still getting situated in here," Javier said. "Give it time and work hard, you'll do well. But don't ever trick yourself into thinking that just because we're family you've got it easy ahead of you. Nobody gets it easy up here."

"It's boom or bust," Evelyn added, done with her half-finished yet meager dessert.

Angela gave Romy a subtle 'family is the worst' look before she quickly let it disappear.

She tucked some of her dark hair behind her ear, looking between the two guests and, for a moment, wondering how anyone went to a restaurant in white without leaving looking like a slob.

"That was delicious," she cooed softly before taking another sip of her dessert wine, the sweetness a relief from the bitter wine of earlier. But even the alcohol couldn't make the situation more comfortable.

*You don't belong here*, her subconscious reminded her, forcing Angela to think back on all the awkward dinners and parties she had to attend in her life before. How much she hated them.

Sitting alone in her apartment night after night, though, was the worse torture. Even worse than prison. In prison, she knew who she was. How to get through. Count down the days until she was free again.

But when life becomes a prison, there's no end date, and no future to look forward to. Just bleak, expansive failure. As far as the mind's eye could see.

As the meal approached its end the conversation changed.

"Angela and I are going to the Tropicala next, might we see the two of you there?" asked Romy, standing up and placing down the money for all four meals, a ridiculous sum all paid for in cash, of course. Only further solidifying what she knew to be true: his work wasn't legitimate.

"No," Evelyn said, moving over to stand beside her husband-sibling and drape off his arm.

"We have business elsewhere to attend to," said Javier. "Enjoy yourselves there though, cause no trouble," he intoned.

She was practically her age, and yet he was patronizing her and she had to resist rolling her eyes as she went to Romy's side. It was a mirror of Evelyn and Javier; though Angela thought they were the more attractive side.

And much more fun.

"I'll keep him out of trouble," she lied with a smile. She couldn't even keep herself out of trouble let alone someone else.

It wasn't until they were safely out of the building that Romy spoke up any further in confidence.

"Don't mind them," he said, squeezing her hip

and rubbing along her side reassuringly. "They are tough on the outside, because they have to be. They aren't as big of pricks as they seem to be," he added on with a wry grin and a kiss to her neck. "And they were much nicer than they are to most. They were really impressed by the beautiful woman I've managed to wrangle."

And the lies she so expertly weaved to make her life seem less bland, no doubt.

Her fingertips traced along Romy's jaw as he kissed at her so brazenly, a soft moan filling the air between them as he chased away her stress.

"The meal was lovely," she murmured, the wine having hit her after she'd stood up and made her more languid in response. "Thank you for treating me."

Romy kissed her back with no less passion, his tongue entering her mouth as they kissed upon the doorstep to the upper scale restaurant. He only broke away with a gasp to look her in the eye and breathe heavily.

"I want to treat you all the damn time," he remarked, before one of the attendants came up.

"Excuse me, sir," he said to them. "But a Mr. Hevia sent word down that you may take his car as you leave." He extended the keys on offer to Romy, who stood a little dumbfounded for a minute.

For a second she thought they were going to be told off for making out so eagerly, and she couldn't stop that soft smile or the relief that flooded her as she fought back a flush.

"No way…" he said, taking the keys and turning to see the stunning vehicle parked and waiting there for them.

Her gaze followed his, widening a little bit as her lips parted. Whoever Mr. Hevia was — she assumed his brother — he had taste beyond pale. And money to spare, on top of that. The sleek, black vehicle looked not gaudy, but stylish and clearly expensive.

"You're well liked," she purred into his ear, though his surprised said it was likely she that was liked.

Romy looked to her out of the corner of his eyes, then walked slowly towards the vehicle. He let loose a sharp whistle but then unlocked the doors and opened the passenger seat for her.

"You must have really made quite the impression if you got us this," he remarked with a toothy grin. "Hop in before Javier changes his mind," he added on enthusiastically.

She slipped within the black, matte vehicle, looking around with appreciation clear in her gaze.

The siren's call of the hard, fast life she'd left behind had become a wail, and she could no longer drown it out by sense and reason. She relaxed back in the leather seat, inhaling that clean smell of a fine vehicle, and fluttered her lashes closed.

What was the point of living a half-life? Miserable and lonely and desperately bored?

When she could have so much more, dropped at her feet, just for being herself.

Of course, she wasn't so naive as to believe that was truly all there would be to her life, but for those precious seconds as he rounded the car, she let herself dream.

When Romy climbed into the driver seat beside her, his own face betrayed the excitement he felt, mirroring her own. He grasped a hold of the wheel with one hand, and reached over to touch her leg with the other.

"I"ll have one of these myself before long," he pledged quietly. "Until then… let's enjoy this, huh?"

He started up the car, let its engine rev to life as if it were a feral cat.

It was beautiful and she spread her legs just slightly, letting him feel along the smooth flesh.

"So he's never done something like this before?"

"Never," he said, letting his hand slip away from her leg just long enough to switch gears before it returned, trailing along her inner thigh. "For no one. He doesn't even let the others clean it," he said, sounding so surprised and excited still as the car began to pull out.

"He's not my real brother," he explained out of nowhere. "It's just a thing we say."

That made the lending of the car even more

surprising, and her fingers roamed along the interior with no small sense of appreciation.

"So who is he?" she asked as her fingers found one of the speakers, brushing over the little bumps. She then leaned in, putting on some music, the sound quickly filling the air before she turned it down a little.

Romy didn't answer, not right away. He drove them through the streets of Toronto, letting his one hand stroke along her smooth inner thigh, up scandalously high beneath her skirt even.

"We're in an operation together. A business operation," he explained to her softly. "He's the boss, and in it we're all like family. All of us Cubans, by birth or through our family lines, you know?" he said, glancing to her only momentarily.

Her fingers rest upon his, staring out the window as the lights flit by in a hurry, giving him a nod.

She did know. She knew that his brother had him meeting tough looking bikers in a dingy bar, and that no one his age who didn't come from money owned that car without doing something illegal.

"Sure. People have to stick together," she said softly, just above the music.

She'd assumed drugs. After all, that was her entry into the underbelly of the world.

So it came down to whether she was okay with it or not, and as each second ticked by, his warm touch and tender smile tempted her further and further.

"That's right," he said, letting his fingers brush between the nexus of her thighs as he drove them through the streets, going a little too fast for safety's sake. But could she blame him? Would she have done a single thing differently?

He was a bad boy, but more than that, he was a bad boy with a slick sense of style, a gorgeous body, and the most charming mouths she could have hoped to find. Plus he had a libido out of the world, and she squirmed against his fingers, just thinking of fucking him again.

"Just wait until you meet the others though," he said with a smile, "you'll like them much more. Not as generous, but good people. They will fall in love with you the moment they lay eyes upon you, my beauty," he said it with such a sing-song, poetical voice.

"I can't wait," she breathed out, her gaze upon his handsome face. She could probably tempt him to pull over, to fuck her right there in the car. Her head spun with the thought, her grin turning dark as she licked over her lips.

She could see that even without the conscious effort, Romy was tempted to pull over and do just that. The glint in his eyes, the lascivious lilt to his grin.

He managed to hold himself off just by his sheer desire to show her off, however, getting them to the club.

They parked around back and Romy got out, letting her out of the car to walk her through the VIP entrance at the side. He offered her his arm and she took it, a bright grin on his face as he led her on in.

She wanted to say she felt nervous, uncertain of the whole thing.

But the truth was, that awkward dinner, and the luxurious ride had put her back in her old head-space, back in the game. She clung closer to Romy, her skirt hiked up around her thighs a little as she pushed up her cleavage a bit more.

"How do I look?" she asked, fixing her hair with a slender finger.

Romy looked her over, never missing an opportunity to appreciate her beauty slowly.

"Like you're ready to give every man in the club an insatiable lust for you," he declared almost breathlessly. "You're unreal, babe," he said, giving her a kiss on her neck and lingering a little over long, nibbling and suckling at her skin until he was risking derailing their even getting inside.

That might've happened even, except someone broke the moment.

"Romy?" called a voice, sounding crisp and local.

They looked and saw a tall lanky man, about Romy's size, with long hair brushed back to nearly his shoulders. He was much paler, with a larger nose.

"Abel!" Romy said loudly, excitedly, and the two

men broke into bright grins. Romy disentangled from her and gave the man an embrace, the two of them slapping each other's backs before they broke away.

"Angela, this is Abel, Abel… meet my beautiful lady," he said, a little presumptuously in his excitement and eagerness to impress his friend. Though she could tell the kind expression was genuine.

She smiled as she held out her hand, trying to look as beautiful and sultry as Romy made her feel she was.

"Nice to meet you, Abel," she cooed, her hip cocked to the side.

Abel wasn't a terribly handsome man, but he was a decent man if first appearances meant much. He reached out and took her hand not with a suave hold, but a cordial grasp, giving a respectful squeeze.

Though none of that was to say he didn't look dazzled by her.

"We all said Romy was bullshitting us about his new lady, but miss…" he looked her over but did so quickly enough to avoid leering. "The reality far outdoes the hype."

"I told you she was amazing," Romy said with a jab of his elbow at Abel's side.

She took the complement like a woman used to taking compliments, with a practiced air of flattery and acceptance.

"Romy," she tsk-tsked. "You're going to give me a

swollen head before the nights through if people keep saying that."

Her dashing young lover looked a little bashful for just a moment before reaching out to touch her arm and gently direct her towards the door.

"C'mon, there's more to see and do inside. You're not leaving are you Abel?" he asked his friend.

"No, no way," Abel replied, following them into the noisy club, with its bright, flashing lights.

The VIP entrance took them up through a set of stairs to a portion of the club that overlooked the rest. With plush, leather couches and a private bar and tender, it was the sort of reception reserved for movie stars.

"Romy!" came another voice, and a small, curvy white woman came rushing up to him. She threw her arms about the handsome man, having to practically toss herself up at him. "You handsome devil!" she said, before sliding back down, the whole leaving Romy looking at Angela with an awkward expression. Though any jealousy Angela might've felt was ameliorated by fact it all looked and felt very chaste and friendly, rather than familiar.

Angela could sense sexual tension better than anyone, and she got none from the two of them.

"I keep hearing you have yourself this amazink lady?" she remarked with an Eastern European accent Angela wasn't entirely sure on the origin of.

Romy cleared his throat and indicated towards Angela.

"Svetlana, I would like you to meet Angela. Angela, here is our resident cheerleader, Svetlana," he said, doing the whole introduction with such an air of dry amusement.

"Cheerleader, hey?" Angela asked in a friendly tone, smiling at the other woman. With another man, she might have felt jealous. But Romy? He'd have to be the stupidest man alive to fuck around on her.

He was clearly deep in lust.

Svetlana herself was more pretty and cute than sexy, with some softness to her figure she wore a skirt and tank top, but draped herself in a knitted-mesh top, and high socks. She looked adorably young, but it was hard to place her exactly. The dimples in her pale cheeks really sold the look though, and she rushed up to Angela, her bracelets jingling.

"That is correct!" she said pleasantly. "And I am so glad to be meetink you at last. Our dear Romy has become a Romeo this past week," she declared in such a curious mix of that Eastern accent and cutesy tone.

Angela felt a little taken in by it, feeling her own body soften with the pure enthusiasm of the other woman. It was refreshing to be around someone so excitable and open, compared to the closed and stiff dinner they'd had.

Her hand reached out for Romy's, a smile upon her mouth.

"I think he's been setting expectations too high," Angela confessed with a self-deprecating grin.

"Not at all!" Svetlana insisted with a bat of her hand against Angela's arm, the girl smelling like bubblegum up close. "You are every bit as ravishink as he insisted you were. Against much resistance I might be addink."

Romy pressed in against Angela, holding her hand as he looked just a wee bit embarrassed.

"Not every day a man feels his heart plucked out and sees the lovely criminal make off with it. It leaves an impression," he remarked.

It was then a large bull of a man came lumbering up the stairs behind the bar. Built like an ox he wore a vest over his mandarin collar shirt, with braided hair down his shoulders. He looked different from the rest, and Angela quickly guessed he was a native.

"Daryl!" Romy called out to the man, garnering the towering giant's gaze. "Come meet my beautiful lady, Angela. Angela, meet Daryl."

The man came over to her, his footsteps able to be felt through the vibrations of the floor, even over the beat of the music. He extended a hand to her that dwarfed her own ridiculously.

"Well I can see why you were the focus of Romy's

obsession lately," he remarked in a low voice, so calm and even-tempered.

For a moment, a brief second of time, Angela felt overwhelmed by the attention, by the reminder of Romy's affection. But flattery quickly took hold and she smiled brightly at Daryl.

"Thank you," she purred, a smile twisting her lips happily as she let her hand be clasped within his. "You all are too sweet."

Romy pulled her in tight against his side, rubbing over her waist and hip warmly as he gave her a kiss on the neck.

"Now you can't all accuse me of embellishing on her beauty," Romy declared smugly to them all, seemingly having won some triumph among friends and colleagues.

"Forgive our Romy," Svetlana said in her cheerful, accented voice. "He is still new among us, but fast risink in fortune," she said as if his victory was hers. Angela got the impression she took everyone's victory as her own, she seemed that kind of person.

"No newer than you, Svetlana," muttered Daryl before going back to the bar to tend to his business.

Angela let his lips and hands work against Romy, unabashedly, as she smiled at Svetlana.

"And when did you get here?"

"About the same time as Romy," she confessed. "Just a couple years ago," she stated with a nod.

"But she got here a month or so sooner so she

thinks that counts for a great deal," Romy remarked. "I'll get you something to drink," he stated, kissing her once more before heading over towards Daryl at the bar. It left her with Abel and Svetlana alone.

"So how did you two meet?" asked Abel casually, leaning against the railing overlooking the club. The music wasn't as overbearing up there in the VIP section, thankfully.

"At a bar near my place," Angela said, her gaze following after Romy for a moment before bringing it back to Abel. It was the simplest and most honest answer, and she followed with a smile. "And then he brought me here."

"We missed you that night," Svetlana chimed in.

Romy returned then, a mojito in hand for her as he smiled affectionately.

"Hope you enjoy this, I made it myself," he boasted with faux-ego, flashing a wink at her as she took the drink and he twined his arm about her waist. "You all were being good to my lady, I trust," he said with a playfully accusatory tone to the others.

"You were only gone a second," Angela teased. "We could hardly get in a scrap in that amount of time."

She kissed his cheek as she snuggled into him, taking a sip and feeling that little burn, the coolness, washing down her throat.

Romy savoured his own drink a moment before pointing to the rather mundane looking Abel.

"Abel here is my partner. We spend a lot of time working together, him and I. I know I can count on him in a clinch," he declared in praise of his friend, earning a shy smile and a bashfully appreciative look from the man.

"It's good to stick together, otherwise you get eaten alive," he replied, a bit quietly for the club.

Angela nodded as she looked between the two, the alcohol warming her up. She kept moving slightly to the beat of the music without even noticing, her hips swaying back and forth as she smiled.

"Always good to have friends," she agreed, leaving the *what do you do* part of her question unasked. It wasn't the time, and she'd just get more sly lies anyway.

"We don't get very far without them." Though in her experience, they were also the first to throw you under the bus in times of trouble. Perhaps she was just unlucky.

Abel came in close to talk with Romy confidently, but being so close Angela could pick up on every word.

"Hey man, we gotta go over that job we talked about, I think we can hit the sh—" Romy elbowed the guy.

"Shut up man, c'mon," he said, looking to Angela. "She doesn't wanna hear that shit," he said, protectively squeezing her side and giving her a kiss. "We'll talk about it later, okay? Come on by my place tomorrow."

Abel looked between her and Romy.

"Oh sorry," he said apologetically, looking rather upset at the prospect of having offended his friend and Angela.

"It's fine," she smiled placidly. "Though it is Friday night. Pretty sure it's criminal to talk about work on a Friday night."

Abel backed away and gave a friendly smile and nod. Though her sly word choice didn't seem to go over Romy's head at all.

"C'mon," he said to her, draining his drink and tugging her towards the stairs that led down to the dance floor. "Let's go have some fun, huh?"

"Just keep it in your pants, you two," Svetlana said with a big, cheeky grin at the two of them.

"I'm not wearing pants," Angela shouted over her shoulder with a grin, her skirt already hiked up threateningly high as she went down the stairs. She clung close to Remy as she finished off her Mojito, placing it down on one of the railings as she smiled at him, coming alive once more.

With the sound of Svetlana giggling disappearing over their shoulder, the two of them descended into the crowd of hot, writhing bodies, and Romy couldn't have looked happier or more proud about taking her with him.

"You are too ravishing," he remarked with such praise, sliding his hand from her hip around to her lower back. His other hand took hold of hers and lifted it up, beginning to move and sway upon the dance floor to the beat of the music. "Luckily there weren't too many of the gang about to overwhelm you. Some of them would be rabid with such a beauty like you before them."

She pressed her body to his with such heated desire. Having to be respectable and proper, first at the restaurant, then in the VIP section, was driving her crazy and she pressed her lips up to kiss him with such eagerness.

A purr pressed forth from her mouth against his, tongue flicking along the seam of his mouth.

"The real problem would have been that the more of them there was, the longer it'd take to get here," she teased.

Romy's eyes twinkled excitedly, and he squeezed her hips, let his hands slide down to cup her ass cheeks and knead them lewdly right there on the dance floor through her thin dress skirt.

"You devil woman," he taunted back at her as they moved, his legs carrying him about with such grace and agility. He was as nimble on the dance floor as he was with his words, if not more so. His legs moving on up to his waist with such fluidity, he had the makings of such a professional dancer.

"I hope you'll understand if I say: you need to

come home with me this evening," Romy said with such determination. Such sheer obsession lighting the fires in his eyes. "I won't take 'no' for an answer," he remarked, and though it was the sort of thing said in jest, he made it sound like anything but.

The sort of thing that made her head go light and her lips drop open as her heart raced. There hadn't been a doubt in her mind where she'd end up, what he'd do to her at the end of the night. She doubted everything else, about why she was tempting fate so, why she was risking throwing everything away, but never the fact that he was going to have her again.

She ground against him as her hips moved to the beat of the music, her body pressed to his with such excitement as her lips lingered on his throat.

"That so?" she purred.

That growing bulge of his manhood rose up between their bodies, and it only became worse as the music changed tempos and Romy pushed her away and twirled her around. Only to tug her back in and grind his cock against her plush ass, letting that length lodge between her ass cheeks as they moved.

"It absolutely is," he husked into her ear after pulling her back up against his chest, his lips finding her neck, then making their way up to her earlobe. "I am going to make you mine the whole night through, whether you agree to be my woman or not. And then come the morning, I'll have you again.

Maybe twice. Before I let you have the choice of going. It's beyond fate," he said with a tight grasp upon her hips.

She ground against him with his arms wrapped around her as she purred and shimmied. He felt so good, that fine fabric of his expensive suit so sensual against her as they moved.

She was addicted to him, she understood that. The rush he gave her, how he left her wanting more and more. Even though she knew it was dangerous to indulge, she kept telling herself, just once more.

One more time and she'd be able to stop.

Those long fingers of his trailed down her thighs, then back up her sides, spidering out across her form, sinking into the sides of her breasts as he felt her up.

"Can you feel that?" Romy husked into her ear as the music beat and the heat of all those gyrating bodies surrounded them. "All those eyes upon you? Every man's gaze just devouring you up whether he wants to give you that power or not?"

Their brazen display was occurring right at the heart of the club, and even with her eyes closed, she knew he was right. His friends were watching them. Soaking in their wildly sensual motions.

But it didn't make her shy. Instead, she danced more seductively, taking more time as she ground against him, her fingertips tracing along his body and neck as she let him grope her so lewdly.

"You're a devil," she teased with such longing to her voice. He was everything she'd been missing in her life.

Romy spun away from her for just a moment, but only long enough to pull his jacket from his body and give it a toss up into the VIP section where Abel caught it. Like a good lil' accomplice and underling.

He undid another button upon his shirt, showing more of his caramel chest as he took hold of her and danced face to face again. A look around told Angela that not only was she the center of attention for half the club, but her date drew a sizable portion of the other. So many women — and a few men — were looking on at her stylish, dancing partner.

"I don't know about that," Romy replied to her, "but he's certainly had a hand in just how hard you're gonna get fucked tonight."

It sent a lewd shiver down her spine and her breath caught, then was exhaled with a low moan as her smile darkened at him. She resisted the urge to silence him with her mouth, to press her flush lips against his and caress his tongue with her own.

Instead she just stared at him with lidded eyes, the rocking of her hips so sensual as she pressed her form to his.

"Dirty boy," she finally breathed. His words had twisted her stomach, made her pussy throb with wanton need. But she loved the tease.

Romy's eyes were lit up with impish mischief,

and their legs moved together as he held her hips and stroked along her figure.

"I am going to make you into my own little personal cum slut this evening, gorgeous," he pledged with a dark murmur, right before lifting her arm up over her head and giving her body a twirl before everyone. Taking hold of her afterwards he dipped her down low and kissed her plush, painted lips. "And you are going to love every minute of it, I promise."

She already knew she would, and her motions were so fluid as she longed for more. For the evening to be over so that she could go to his place and enjoy her boy toy. Fuck away all the concerns and fears and worries she had, and just have him pound her into the present.

"You should be careful," she purred. "Or else I'll take you right here."

Romy laughed at that, a devilish laugh of amusement as he pulled her up and the two began to rock each other's hips into one another in a lewd simulation of sex as a dance move. Some others had been doing moves no less raunchy, but with the agile, fluid motions of Romy and Angela's bodies, it looked downright scandalously authentic.

"How about you just beg me to take you back to my place instead, huh?" he husked at her through the intensity of their motions, the titillating sensations.

"I've never been a beggar," she breathed out, but

already she knew he'd make a liar of her. Mouth moving to his neck, leaving her lipsticked mark on him as she moaned into his skin and then nipped him, just enough to send a sharp little jolt through him.

Their hearts beat heavily, and he released a sudden gasp at her bite. He made her pay for it though with such a stunning maneuver, spinning her away from him, leaving her without his touch, his feel. Only to tug her on back in against his heaving chest.

"I can dance all night," he said to her breathily, and he looked to her like he could. Like he had countless times before. "Or do you want to find your way back into my bed with my cock balls-deep in you?" he taunted her, trying to coax that beg out of her lips.

She was so close to capitulation, and she kept trying to choke it back. But his words... Those, combined with the sensual way he moved, there was so little point in resisting but to torture herself a little bit longer in his embrace.

"C'mon," she said simply, but her eyes were lidded and her lips parted with such a lusty gaze.

He grasped her hip tightly with one hand, the other at the small of her back, controlling her motion, her distance from him. Taking such charge of her body and how it moved and swayed with his, keeping her in check.

"Cum on where?" he asked with a quirky smile, his voice low and taunting. "You have so many lovely places I would just love to cum upon."

She sucked in a breath.

How did he twist her into such a simpering, needful woman? It had to have been a long time since her last boyfriend. There was a time she would have simply laughed off his charms, his sweet words. Treated it like a joke.

But now it made her shudder with delight, and she bit down on her lower lip to try to hide her lust filled grin.

"Take me home and you'll find out," she tried to purr back, her voice so laced with desire.

He was grinning so widely, so confidently. He leaned in against her, letting her breasts mash against his lean, hard chest.

"Did I hear a please in there?" he remarked softly into her ear, before tilting his head and offering his own ear to her lips. Awaiting the plea to make it all happen.

For a moment she hated him, hated how much she wanted him. How that word slipped so easily from her lips.

"Please, Romy."

It was sweet torture to give up that little bit of power to him, losing the upper hand, all because her body was warped with pleasure and need.

That little surrender was all it took, he pulled her

with him immediately back towards the stairs up into the VIP section. He was in a rush.

"Hey bro!" he called out, and Abel turned to him, plucking up Romy's coat from the railing beside him and tossing it to the man.

"Have fun you two!" he called out and there in the background was Svetlana waving a hand energetically.

But it was all a blur to Angela, excitement and passion wild in her eyes as she stayed close to Romy, unable to stop herself from touching him. The entire week had been building up to a crescendo, and she could barely hold herself back any longer.

She was simply desperate for it, for him. For Romy to fuck her pain away, to let the feelings of being worthless slosh away into the aether.

She kissed along his neck, hurriedly, purring as he brought her out into the cool night air.

His place was right nearby, and with his jacket slung over one shoulder, Romy led her to it, revelling in those shower of kisses upon him.

They climbed the stairs into his building, and when they got to his place, the change was immediately noticeable. His once barren and white place, now had a large leather sofa, an impressive TV and surround sound speakers to go with it.

Though none of that was of particular interest to either of them then as he slammed the door shut behind them and pressed her into the wall to kiss her hard, thrusting his tongue into her mouth.

Her arms wrapped around him immediately, pulling herself up as her thighs parted and squeezed around his hips, her skirt rose up over her thighs as she ground so lewdly against him. She was all passion and fiery need, so desperate to feel him inside her once more.

Her lips parted and she let out a tiny whimper of delight as her green eyes flicked open and looked at him with such lust. He was such a gorgeous man, and she was no less enamoured with him than he was with her.

Angela smiled, dark and devious before she lunged in once more, kissing him hard and deep.

He rocked his hips, and Angela could feel that rock hard shaft of his press betwixt her thighs through his pants. If any of his actions had laid any doubt, the feel of that manhood against her dispelled them.

Romy lifted her from the wall, held her up and carried her into his bedroom, where he dropped her to the mattress and began to undo his belt. Those eyes of his glittering with excitement as he looked her over, peered up beneath her lifted dress skirts.

She was completely unashamed at the fact that she wore no panties, the barest glimpse of her slit visible as she let her legs part. Then she teased up her dress further, lifting her hips so that the skirt wrapped about her waist, her thighs pressed tightly closed, teasing him.

She watched him with just as much enjoyment, though, her eyes glued to the unveiling of his hard cock.

The thick, hard member sprang free, pulsating and veiny, so full of desire. He didn't waste his time with any of the rest, the fine shirt, his shoes, he went for her, unable to restrain himself any longer as he grasped a hold of one of her thighs, sinking his fingers into its underside, and gave a hard thrust, immediately impaling her upon his raw, throbbing cock.

The loud groan that escaped his lips filled the air as he imbedded himself to her depths, that handsome young man so enthralled with her.

Angela cried out loud, her mouth parted as she squirmed against him with such hunger. She was soaking wet and offered no resistance as he penetrated her, head tossed back with a triumphant, "Yes!"

Romy was wild with his lust for her, clutching her thigh so tightly as he suspended himself on one hand. His hips began to rock and he was thrusting into her enthusiastically, wasting no time to build up speed but taking her with an intense force.

His dark, lean muscles pumped and his balls slapped against her, punctuating the air as they began to rut mindlessly again.

Her hands went into his shirt, popping his buttons open as he peeled it back, showing off that smooth chest and rocky abs of his as he fucked her so enthusiastically. The filthy words coming out of his mouth peppered the air as he swelled and spurt his precum into her depths.

Her hands went up along him, gripping his arms, his hands, his anything. Just constantly moving, fluidly, over his body. She wanted to feel him, every inch of his flesh, even as her mind went blissfully quiet.

All that remained was him, was that sweet sensation of his body pounding into hers. Little yelps and moans escaped her lips as she ground against him, her hips lofted to let him fuck into her deep and hard.

Romy took the offering, and thrust as deep into her as their two bodies could manage. He filled her with his lust, slid his hand up from her thigh to clutch at her heavy breast flesh.

Her nipples tightened against his palm, growing with her own arousal as she moaned his name, her throat going raw with her screams and cries.

"You're such a hot fuck," he growled before burying his face into her neck and biting at her, nipping her smooth skin between his teeth as he pounded her and made the bed shake all around them with the motions of their screwing.

She moaned louder as he bit her, completely

unrestrained and unconcerned about what any of his neighbours might hear. It didn't matter that it was the middle of the night. She was too worked up to worry about such silly concerns, lost in herself and her lover.

"You're so sexy," she gasped back, her body arched and moved with his, the pain jolted her awake and kept her entrenched firmly in the present.

His white shirt slipped back from his shoulders and down his arms, and with a distasteful shirk he managed to free himself of it entirely, to let it fall to the floor as he continued his mercilessly hard and fast pounding.

The beautiful motion of his smooth, caramel form pounding into her was hypnotic by itself, even detached from all the sexual nature of the act. They were like a work of art, her soft, voluptuous form rocked beneath his hard, lean one. Her breasts made to jiggle and ripple with each new thundering pound of his bulging girth.

Romy quaked and shook atop her, giving a shuddering moan as he pulsed within her folds. The pleasure of being within her almost too much to bear.

He was like the best high, the one that she never grew tired of. Every time it was something new, different, and yet so spectacular. Her breasts had toppled free from her bra, and she went to grasp one in her hands. They were big and hefty, and she tweaked the nipple all while staring at him with an open mouth.

She was so horny, and each time he slammed into her body, she shuddered with need. Each thrust brought her closer to the edge, and her other hand slipped down over her dress and to her clit, rubbing it with a prolonged moan.

She could see the way his body writhed and contorted atop her, his eyes shutting as the pleasure of their fucking began to take hold of him entirely, losing him all thought and consideration for anything but how damn good she felt around his dick.

Romy let loose a deep, throaty moan as he bucked into her erratically, and she knew his end was nigh. Could read the pleasure etched in his muscle and flesh as he pounded into her.

Her pleasure grew with his, and every time he groaned, she moaned in return. Every time he shuddered, it sent an equal thrill through her. It was hard for her to keep her eyes open, but she was addicted to how he looked, the way his muscles gleamed with that thin film of perspiration.

She licked her lips and they tasted salty as her back arched and her fingers worked quicker against her clit.

And then the stars aligned, and she lost control over her body as her muscles tensed and then released in quick succession, her nerves alight with sensation. It was so intense, her pussy milked him so gloriously as she screamed his name.

Romy's spine arched and he followed her into that spiral of pleasure soon after. He let loose a shuddering cry that filled his apartment just as his seed filled her. It was a tumultuous, body quaking release, their groins mashed together messily as they rut one another through their final moments.

Though at last, Romy collapsed upon her, panting and exhausted as the last of their lust crackled through their loins, leaving them both sweaty and panting.

Her hands worked up over his back, clutching him to her, their sweaty and disheveled bodies writhing together. Her fingers still strummed over her clit, sending little shudders through her body and she gasped softly against his neck.

"Fuck," she hissed, licking at his salted flesh, kissing him there with a languid moan.

The final pulses of lust travelled through Romy and down to his cock as it remained lodged within her, spurting its last as he laid upon her, kissing at her pouty lips and face. He lifted a hand up and ran his long fingers through her hair, revelling in its feel.

"You have no idea how hard it was to keep from fucking you sooner," he confessed to her breathily.

"We were in public," she teased, but then silenced him with her mouth, kissing him with such intensity. Her slick digits slipped away from her slit to rest next to her as they both fought to catch their breath.

Her fingers scratched up along his back, feeling him shiver as she rubbed her tongue against his, the little padding so enticing.

After their long, passionate kiss, Romy broke from her lips with a moist pop and grinned at her.

"Like being in public would have been enough to stop me if I decided to," he remarked with a bit more husk than usual in his post-coital state. "Could've hauled you into a bathroom at the Tropicala and pounded you there."

Even though Angela's orgasm had come and gone, his words still sent a shiver down her back and a moan from her lips.

"Naughty boy," she purred so affectionately, her fingers running along his jawline. "I might have liked that."

"I know you would have," he responded, such self-assurance, such confidence in his voice as he kissed her, rubbed her side, stroked her hair. "Just like I know you're going to enjoy staying the night, and being fucked at least once more," he boasted, a big, toothy grin upon his handsome face.

"Do you know that?" she purred, and Angela knew. That was precisely what she wanted, what she needed. To hell with logic or control. For that one night, there would only be ecstasy.

# CHAPTER 14

Romy had been true to his word that previous night, Angela could tell distinctly, even if she couldn't remember entirely the details of it. The empty bottles and the pleasantly sore feeling in her limbs all spoke of the truth to that.

She stretched her stiff limbs with a groan, her muscles tense and dehydrated and turned her head to find Romy absent.

She frowned as she shifted from the bed, the room spinning a little as she groaned. She still felt drunk from the night before. They must have drank quite a lot after that first time, and as she stood on shaky legs, she desperately had to use the bathroom. She didn't bother grabbing her dress, which she couldn't even find, though her bra was scattered on the floor.

As she stepped out of the bedroom, though, she heard soft, quiet voices coming from the living room.

"No man, we need someone we can trust for this," came Romy's voice so soft.

"We don't have anybody to fit that bill. If we go to someone else in the family, they'll spread word and we'll be in shit. What else can we do?" the voice was hard to place at first, but Angela thought she recognized it as Romy's friend, Abel.

"So what do you suggest then? You can't just haul people off the streets for a job like this," Romy insisted.

"Well… what about that woman of yours? She'd be perfect," Abel offered.

"No way man, I'm not involvin' her in this! Shit, she's just comin' around to being my gal and you want me to ask her to do this? No man, she might dump me! She's a classy lady, got a real job and shit."

"There's no risk to it or nothin'!" Abel insisted. "And in the end she'd walk away with ten grand. Who would be able to say 'no' to that?"

Angela's heart raced and she moved quickly into the bathroom, quietly closing the door behind her and not turning on the light.

*Holy shit.*

She locked the door and sat on the edge of the bathtub, lowering her head to her knees.

*You can't do this,* her little subconscious voice

chastised her, and Angela shook her head. That only made the room spin more, though, and her breathing was heavy and ragged.

*Don't even think of it!* her inner voice screamed louder, and Angela put her hands over her ears as if she could somehow block it out.

Ten thousand dollars?

No, there'd be nothing good and easy that she could do for ten grand. Nothing she should involve herself in. But tears stung her eyes. She was going to be fired on Monday, she knew it. And, hell, they might not even pay her for time worked. She'd heard about some employers who did that while she was in prison, saying that because she got the job by lying, they refused to pay.

It wasn't legal, of course, but how hard could the unemployed ex-con really fight the charges in court?

*You're just going to land your ass back in jail.*

Angela wasn't even sure that was the voice or her, and the first tear escaped as she let out a soft sob, trying to quiet herself. She was so desperate. Not just for the money, or the companionship. She wanted the rush again. The quick cash, the fear, the excitement.

She wanted it all, and too quickly she moved from the ring of the bathtub to the toilet, finishing her business and washing her face in the dark. She couldn't stand to see herself then.

Her fingers trembled as she grabbed for the door,

trying to sneak back into the bedroom without them noticing.

"Just think about it, with her? All she gotta do is distract the guy, and she don't even need to be connected with us. And with a woman like that? Man, she won't have to try hard. By the time he gets back to find himself ripped off, she'll be long gone and there'll be no reason to even suspect her," Abel said. "She'll have just been the prettiest client of the day. The lone bright spot on an otherwise shitty day."

"I won't fuckin' ask her that," Romy said firmly.

Angela's heart was racing. All of the pieces were falling into place, and she was so dangerously teetering on the edge.

Ten grand.

Just conning some guy.

*You say just as if that's all it's going to be, Angela,* her inner voice chided. *But that guy's got enough shit lying around that missing a few dozen grand is just a shitty day. No guy like that's going to be just a guy.*

She threw herself down on the bed and immediately regretted it as the room spun into view, her stomach lurching and head pounding.

Ten thousand dollars was enough that she could pay her rent for a nice long time, though. And give her enough time and freedom to actually find another job.

All of the things that she could buy were spinning around in her head along with the hangover, and she took in a deep breath.

Just one job.

One time.

And then she could go straight. Find a job without being desperate and then just... walk away.

She laid there for a long time, mulling it over, her mind churning and her stomach doing even worse.

At last Romy returned to her, his talk with Abel complete as he came in, the shirt from the previous night on him, done up just enough to be decent, pants hung low from the lack of belt.

"Well look at this lovely sight," he said with such intense interest, enticed by the view of her voluptuous form splayed before him upon the bed. "It must be my lucky day," he remarked, undoing the buttons of his shirt again, to show his smooth, lean chest, so gorgeously shaped.

She smiled at him, watching him undress and her pains slowly started to be forgotten as she licked over her lips.

"Well, you did abandon me here to my fate last night," she teased, her heart racing and her skin flushing. Could she really go ahead with it? Just... jump right in, then jump back out?

Part of her, a big part, even, knew it was impossible. For anyone, let alone her.

But still she knew she would.

She was weak.

She needed the thrill.

Romy's gorgeous physique was on full display, that large young cock of his already stiff from the mere sight of her as he climbed up onto the bed over her. He kissed his way across her body, over her stomach, her breasts, across her shoulders and neck before finally he found himself at her lips.

"I was only gone for a few minutes," he said softly, clasping one of her large breasts in his hand and kneading its supple flesh.

"Felt like longer," she growled as her back arched so that her tit was pressed into his hand, her eyes heavily lidded as her mouth parted. He had a way of distracting her, and she was so eager for that distraction. To forget about her worries and fretfulness and just lose herself in his body.

Their kisses were noisy and unrestrained, Romy's friend undoubtedly gone as he settled in to enjoy her gorgeous flesh, to savour the moments of their bodies combining. He grasped hold of her thigh with one hand, tugging up her leg to bend her knee at his side, getting her into the position he wanted her in.

"You're gonna be my woman," he said as if predicting the future, slowly sliding his cock into her warm, wet cunt, a low moan escaping his lips as he felt her tight canal about his shaft.

He felt so good. So hard and strong and eager for her.

It gave her as much of a mental rush as a physical one, and she let out a low moan, her pussy muscles clenched around him. She shuddered beneath him, her arms wrapping around his back and dragging her nails down along his shoulder blades.

"Y'think?" Her green eyes were on him as she licked her lips before pressing them to his collarbone, teasing along his flesh.

He rocked his hips, pumping his cock into her at a slow, steady pace, but then he reached up, prying her arms from around his neck and pinned them back to the bed over her head. It was a slow, powerful sort of motion, and he rose up over her to watch her breasts rock and shake as he thrust into her pussy harder.

"I know it," he said more firmly, keeping her wrists pinned there as he grew rougher with each passing jab of his hard cock into her.

Her fingers twisted, his weight bore by her slender wrists as she squirmed beneath him. But it only served to excite her, her sweet moans filling the air. He was so damned sexy, and it was like every time with him just got better as he learned her body, those little things that made her tick.

She smiled up at him devilishly as she tried in vain to release her wrists from his grasp, though her struggles only sent her tits rippling and rocking as he pounded into her.

Romy pressed down upon her wrists tighter,

locking her in place with one hand as he brought the other down along her body, feeling out her curves, appreciating her flesh with a squeeze here, a squeeze there. Upon her breast, her waist, her hip, her thigh.

"Say it," he commanded her, fucking away the morning hangover as he thrust into her harder. "Say you're mine," he demanded.

She whined as she tried to resist obeying, but he felt so good. Was hitting all the right spots, and her body responded, coiling about him. Her legs wrapped about his waist as she tried to pull him in, to beg him in deeper.

But he resisted, and frustration claimed her.

"I'm yours," she whispered, her brows furrowed.

Romy rewarded her with the hard, deep thrusts she so desired, rocking her body beneath him as he picked up his pace. That hard, morning wood so rigid inside her as he slammed himself between her thighs, claiming her atop his bed so roughly.

"Good girl," he growled at her, sinking his fingers into her hip and waist so tightly as he groaned amid the noisy slaps of their flesh.

Her head spun, her body sung, and she was lost to the bliss of their coupling. He felt so good, and she didn't hold back her cries, her whimpers and the way she begged for more. She struggled to free her hands again as her wrists ached, but there was no reprieve as he fucked her so hard with that stiff cock.

That hand of his roamed in from her hip, his thumb brushed against her sensitive clit as he pounded her. His hand prodded her nerves to life as he bucked and moaned.

"Cum for me now. Be a good girl and cum for your man," he insisted, thrusting almost savagely hard as he kept her pinned. Her body forced to writhe around him as that throbbing cock swelled within her so thickly with excitement.

Her flesh bounced with each thrust, her legs pressed around him so tight just to keep herself from being pounded into the bed. She ground her hips, made him hit her just so with his thumb, his cock, her breathing quickly becoming stilted.

"Holy fuck," she hissed, and in just a few seconds more there was blinding light and the spinning of the room intensified. All of her nerve endings lit up and she screamed as she came, her pussy gushing warm around him.

By the time that the spinning and tingling explosions were at an end, her lover was panting and bucking atop her. Romy bent down, mouth hung open as his dick was spurting his seed into her cunt once more. Yet another reckless, crazy fuck that risked so much heedlessly.

His grasp upon her wrists loosened, and he kissed her slowly, languidly, basking in the trembling afterglow of yet another one of their passionate love makings.

"Every day should start like this," he panted out breathily.

It was hard to disagree as sensation slowly made its way back into her hands, which immediately wrapped about him, tugging him in close. Her lips pressed to his chin, then down lower over his neck as she moaned into his skin.

She enjoyed such times, basking in the warmth that followed passion, grinding against him in a subdued fashion, just to feel alive.

"I'd like that," she whispered.

Romy kissed upon her repeatedly, the young man managing to seem so worshipful of her body even without saying a word. Just the way he savoured her flesh, kissed and stroked her smooth skin. He did it with such reverence for her.

"How about I take you to breakfast, huh?" he remarked huskily, his manhood still lodged inside her as he only slowly softened.

She gave a nod against the hollow of his throat, blood rushing back to her brain and making her stiffen slightly beneath him.

She had to mention it. To bring it up. She had no idea how, but she licked along his salty flesh, tasting him with such desire before she pulled back.

"I... heard you out there," she murmured softly. If he was to take her to breakfast, she had to get it off her chest first.

Romy frowned a little and stroked her cheek.

"Aw I'm sorry babe, didn't mean to wake you. Thought we kept it quiet," he said, kissing her lips before pulling his hips back to slip his cock from within her cum-stained folds.

"Well, I woke because it's... morning. And I had to pee." Her lips quirked before the look disappeared off her face and she glanced to the side.

"And... I heard you, heard you."

Romy's face froze a while as the implications of her words sank in.

"Oh babe," he said, shaking his head slowly. "Don't you worry about any of that, I mean... you're safe. It's just work, and you won't be involved at all. I swear. I'm gonna keep you safe, and treat you right," he pledged, leaning in to place a kiss upon her lips, so soft and warm.

She moved in against his mouth, so tenderly, tasting him with such slow, delicate laps. He was so beautiful, so handsome.

And his job could solve all her problems.

She pulled back a bit breathless as she looked at him with lidded eyes.

"What... What if I want in?" Angela's voice was soft, meek. She wasn't used to sounding like that.

Romy's eyes widened with some innocent surprise, then a slow, crooked grin crossed his face.

"You don't want in," he said with almost a laugh before realization set in more completely. "You've got a legit job, right? Why... Is it just the money?" He asked, stroking back her cheek and hair softly. "I'll take care of you if you need help. You can be my woman. All mine. And live here even."

Was it just the money? The quick and painless way of getting herself out of the hole she'd dug?

Angela shook her head, not even fully aware that she was doing it.

It was more than the money. It was the rush. The thrill of control, of risk, of fear.

"What's the job?" she asked, swallowing anxiously.

# PART II
# THE NARROW PATH

# CHAPTER 15

The beat of the music in the club reverberated through the walls of the office, so that even though it was quiet, the feeling of the beat and energy below carried up into it. Javier sat upon the corner of his desk, a fine white suit upon him to contrast his dark skin and eyes, though he'd shed his tie.

"I see you out that window every night, and I can't help but smile," he said to Svetlana, who sat upon the edge of a one-way window that looked out over the dance floor below. His lips were spread into a broad smile as he eyed the dainty woman, dressed in a mix of fluorescent pink and black, a raver outfit if ever there was one.

She leaned back as she looked at him, all softness and affection in her every move.

"Vell maybe you should be coming down more

often instead of hiding away from all of us. Enjoy the life you've built." Her toes were pointed inwards, resting against one another in her high stiletto heels. They glowed under the black light, just like most everything else she wore.

She flicked her blonde hair over her shoulder, running her fingers through it idly as she glanced back to the crowd, a lingering look of enjoyment upon her face.

"I've got a lot of work to do," he said simply, then rose up from his spot upon the desk, the tall man towering over the much shorter woman as he made his way towards her.

"Besides," he continued, sitting himself down on the arm of the leather sofa next to her, reaching out to take her dainty hand in his large palm. "I can't be myself with others around. But you? You bring out something special in me," he said, his deep voice so soft and warm with her, in a way it never was with anyone else, matching the way he gently stroked the pale, smooth skin on the back of her hand.

Svetlana giggled, shimmying a little bit closer to him as her gaze met his.

"You're too kind," she protested with a little shake of her head. "But I'm glad, regardless, that you think so." There was such a reverence in her gaze as she bit down on her lower lip nervously. Not nervous of him... nervous of how she acted around him.

He made her head spin, all of her willpower

drained as she wanted nothing more than to make him happy, and it was etched all throughout her features.

Javier smoothly lifted her hand up to kiss at the backs of her knuckles, letting his dusky eyes meet her gaze as he took his time, revelled in that moment together. Until at last he lowered her hand again and reached out to rest his palm upon her bare knee.

"You're the most beautiful vision to walk through those doors down there, and there's just something about you," he said, his Cuban accent so rich. "You have a way of making me — and everyone else — more relaxed, more pleased. You've an aura of peace and serenity about you, dear Lana."

She blushed a bit brighter. For one in her line of work, she certainly took every compliment as if it were the first and only one, and her eyes descended to her lap.

"Oh Javier," she purred, her voice so soft beneath the hum of the rhythm of the Tropicala.

"I just like beink around you. Vhen that happens, it's just right, is it not?" She spoke into her lap, her skin so soft beneath his hand, her stockings only coming up to just below his grasp.

Javier nodded to her slowly, the two of them threading their fingers together, his long, dark digits knitted between her slender, pale ones. He squeezed her knee and leaned in, the two of them so close, his spiced cologne light and pleasant. Her bubble-gum scent so girlish and whimsical.

"You should come see me more often," he husked low, leaning in so that his forehead was nearly pressed to hers. "Here, or… we could go meet somewhere else. Just the two of us. For a meal, and maybe some quiet time alone."

She was so soft and delicate beneath him, those supple curves of hers enticing as she rubbed into him.

"I vould like that," she cooed, her voice so filled with nervousness and cheerfulness, the two combatting one another. She was clearly thrilled at his invitation, at his touch, and she moved nearer him.

Her eyes fluttered up to him, that sky blue so enchanting.

"You have my number, yes? Any time you'd like," she said as a bouncy and flirtatious smile crossed her features.

His own smile was wry and self-assured, contorting his handsome face as he eyed her, soaking in that youthful, charm. He gave a slow nod.

"You can count on that call," he remarked in a low, rumbly voice just moments before he leaned in, head tilted, to place a kiss upon her soft little lips, painted pink with a rim of carefully applied black to match her outfit. His tongue delved past them, into her mouth to taste her as he grasped her with both of his long arms.

She tasted like she looked, as if she'd just eaten a bunch of cotton candy before coming to his office. Her tongue pressed against his, all that shyness slowly slipping away as she very slowly kissed him. A sigh passed from her to him, her entire body arched and lifted so that she could meet his mouth with all her enthusiasm.

Javier pulled her to him, lifting her tiny form up and into his lap as their kiss only grew further entangled. He wanted her so badly, his two hands beginning to rub at her soft, supple flesh, slowly pawing at her form, feeling her curves along her hips and rear.

"You're so gorgeous," Javier said, breaking their kiss to breathe heavily and look in her bright blue eyes.

She swallowed, her eyes lidded as she ground against him so wantonly. Her arms wrapped around his neck, the party still thrumming behind them. Something about being able to see the crowd as they danced and writhed without them ever knowing she was up there, knowing what they were doing... it was a thrill.

Her thin legs spread about him, her bust pressed to his chest.

"Thank you, Mr. Hevia," she purred, her skin still flushed and dewy from his kiss, his touch.

He was so much taller than her, a giant next to her tiny form. He held her, cupped her cheeks in his palms as he moved in to kiss at her lips again, his excitement showing beneath her with a throb to go along to that beat below.

"I wish I could have you all to myself, all the time," he said in a low husk. Though something below began to catch first his eyes, then hers.

Looking aside, Svetlana could make out the curious sight of Romy and his new lady at the center of a commotion.

But Svetlana didn't want his attention to drift, her finger going to his jaw and trying to gently guide his eyes back to her.

"You can have me whenever you like," she purred, another grind of her hips following her words. Punctuating them.

Javier's eyes lit up at that, and he couldn't fight the grin that formed upon his long yet somewhat narrow face. His arm squeezed her so tight, the little beauty might nearly have popped.

"You don't know what you've just got yourself into," he nearly growled at her before lustfully kissing her lips once more.

# CHAPTER 16

*R*omy was more pumped up and full of himself than Angela had ever seen him. He seemed almost taller, his shoulders broader, his grin wider than ever before. His attractiveness only amplified as he held her to his side so snugly and walked through the crowd.

"Free drinks, on me! We're gonna fucking celebrate tonight," he yelled, to a resounding chorus of shouts and cheers in return.

Their heist was done, and the results had been better than anticipated. Even if Angela's heart was still pumping hard.

She couldn't believe it'd worked. She almost would rather just gone home and thrown up from the stress. Instead, she clung to Romy and siphoned off his energy, feeling that thrill resound through her.

"Get me a mojito?" she purred into his ear, needing something strong. Something that'd numb the rush just a little bit so that her stomach wasn't twisted in knots.

Her dark hair was pulled back into a ponytail, her black dress new and absolutely scandalous with how low it delved between her breasts, showing off her ample cleavage. Her heels brought her up closer to Romy's height, though he still had about half a foot on her, but she leaned up and kissed his mouth eagerly.

She could feel his heart pounding in his chest, and she pressed her fingers to him so eagerly.

Conning her mark had been one of the most exciting things she'd done since getting out of prison. That rush was addictive, she knew, but she'd promised herself it was just one time. Get the money and then that would be it. She'd go back to her dull day-job, and work her way up like a normal person.

Not that she had a day-job anymore. She couldn't clear a criminal record check and was quickly shown the door, and she hadn't heard back from any of her other applications. But at least the ten grand would go a long way to helping relax her while she looked.

Romy took her up to the V.I.P. section where he slapped hands with Daryl.

"I heard you had some good news," the towering

bartender said, though Angela had a feeling he was more than a mere bartender.

"You bet, my man. Now how about two mojitos, and make them doubles," Romy said cheerfully, stroking his hand along Angela's side so vigorously, revelling in her feel. Then he leaned forward and muttered low to the big, bull of a man, "And hey, any way you can hook me up with something special to celebrate with tonight?"

Daryl was already busy mixing the drinks, but he gave Romy and Angela a cursory look before casting his gaze up at the managerial officer, looming over the rest of the club.

"Nah man, I got nothin' on me right now. Check with the boss," he said, jerking his chin up towards the office.

Angela felt a chill go through her, but excitement was coiled in her belly and she knew that there were no rules. Just for that one, beautiful, wonderful night, she wanted to let herself go.

Completely ignoring the fact that every time she was with Romy, she let herself go.

Her mouth moved along his jaw, kissing at his flesh and licking him teasingly. Her hand worked over his chest, feeling out his muscles, as she ground her body against him in time to the music.

Romy seemed to forget what he was doing to kiss her back, his own greedy hands roaming across her body, feeling her up for all his friends to see. They were already drunk on their victory, and they'd barely had time to finish up the heist itself.

"Here you two, drink up before you fornicate all over the bar," Daryl said, part annoyed, part amused.

Romy took up his mojito, and before much could even be said about it, he'd downed the whole thing and let loose a cry of excitement.

"Damn baby, we did it," he said, eyes alight at her.

She was just as excited. More so, maybe. Perhaps she should have been more hesitant in the little bit of surprise to his voice, the fact that there was likely some doubt if they could pull it off.

Instead, all she felt was high on life, on him, on his hands and mouth as she took her own drink and downed it just as quick, the minty burn going down her throat.

"Fuck," she hissed, taking a step back so that she could better look him down, drinking in his gorgeous visage. His tall, leanly muscled form dressed in a tight black shirt, buttoned up — or more aptly buttoned down — to show some of his gorgeous, smooth chest, those pecs of his so wonderfully visible. A pair of dark pants to match his look, with a maroon blazer slung over one shoulder.

"What a rush," she purred.

"You know, if you're just going to down them why even bother ordering a mixed drink?" Daryl interjected on their fun time, topping off their glasses again.

Romy was all grins as he took up the topped off drink and drank it at a more relaxed pace, his eyes bright and twinkling as they roamed over Angela shamelessly.

"You wanna come with me to see the boss? I wanna get somethin' real special for this evening," he said in his charming accent, thicker with all that rum in him..

Her lips moved back to his neck again, moving along his flesh so lovingly.

"Whatever you want," she murmured as she took her drink, holding it in her hands at the chastisement. What she wanted was to drag Romy back to his place and fuck him long and hard, but Angela never minded a little anticipation.

Together they climbed the stairs up to the manager's office, only to be greeted by a burly guard that watched over the office door in place of a secretary.

"Hey Frank, can I see the boss man about somethin'? Was lookin' to get a little something for the evening's celebration." Romy said to the man, smiling.

"Can't do that," Frank said simply, a large man that appeared as if he might be related to Daryl below. "The boss man's busy right now," he said, eyes trailing to Angela casually, unable to resist her allure.

"You can appreciate his predicament, I'm sure," he added on pointedly.

"Aw shit," Romy muttered, downing the rest of his drink.

Angela frowned, but secretly she was a little pleased. Just the faintest bit, running beneath her disappointment. She wanted that celebratory gift, but was grateful that it was denied her. She had no self-control, that much was evident. Especially with how lewdly she fondled Romy's chest in front of Frank.

Her teeth nibbled Romy's ear, tugging the lobe away before letting it elastic band back into place. "We can still celebrate."

They fondled each other a moment as Romy shut his eyes, enjoying the feel of her teeth as he stroked her hips and waist.

"Yeah baby, you're right," he said, ready to turn around and leave.

Though the door opened then, and out came a rather flushed looking Svetlana. She looked surprised to find herself facing the pair of them, and tucked her face down as she adjusted her short skirt.

"Oh hey, Svetlana," Romy said, unaware of the awkwardness of the scene.

Angela gave the other woman a knowing, almost fiendish smile before she could stop herself, the rush of the job and the alcohol giving up some of her control.

"Hey," Angela said with a wave, nudging Romy a little bit in the ribcage.

Svetlana gave a quick, embarrassed look to Angela that was part pleading for her silence and part need to flee. Her blue eyes were wide as she chewed down on her lower lip before she forced a smile at Romy.

"Oh, hey you two!" she finally managed with a nod of her head.

Romy was drunk on their successful heist more than the alcohol, but both contributed. He smiled at Svetlana, not paying particular heed to the way the lovely young woman's cheeks were so flushed, nor even how her hair and makeup were just a little bit out of sorts until Angela nudged him in the shoulders and he took stock again.

"Hey Svetlana," he said, fighting a grin. "It okay to go see the boss man now?" he asked, squeezing Angela's side even tighter, giving her round ass cheek a pinch.

Svetlana looked to Frank, as if he held the answer, before smiling to the couple in a strained manner. It wasn't at all like her usual, chipper self, but then, after what she'd just done with her married boss, that wasn't too surprising.

"Give him a moment," Svetlana finally sighed as she took another step in those high heels, back towards the club floor. "Have a good night, you two," she said with a wave before quickly taking her leave.

Angela bit Romy's ear a bit harder, giggling in it with a purr as she ground against him, heedless of all else around them.

Despite Romy's insistence on getting them what they were after, they had no trouble passing a few moments outside the office door. Paying Frank little to no heed, Romy grasped a hold of Angela and pressed her against the railing, kissing her deeply and with such passion. He let his tongue delve deep into her mouth as he felt up her sides, her ass, every little place upon her body heedless of the lewdness.

It took Frank a few loud clears of his throat to garner their attention.

"He'll see ya now," he remarked, pushing open the door to let them pass.

Inside was Javier, looking good behind his desk. Angela had to give it to Svetlana, her time with the man had obviously relaxed him, made him look less stiff and imposing. Instead he appeared calmer, cool.

"What can I do for you, Romy?" he asked, reclining back in his seat as he cast a look to the security monitors.

"Was hoping you could hook us up with some of the good stuff, boss. We're celebrating tonight," he declared brazenly.

To which Javier arched a brow critically.

"The good stuff's very expensive, brother," he said, as if he didn't think Romy was aware of what he was getting into. Though when Romy pulled a roll of bills from his pants pocket and placed it before him... well, Javier still didn't change his expression. Svetlana did wonders, but she wasn't a miracle worker.

Instead he reached to a safe built into his desk it seemed, opened it up and produced several small packets which he tossed onto the opposing side of the desk.

"Don't overdo it," he cautioned, "I don't like to see our own lose themselves in this stuff."

Angela watched with a sense of quiet, growing dread. As if she could feel herself sinking into the quicksand, but that it felt... good, like being at a spa. She knew she was going under, but she couldn't deny herself the pleasure.

She clung to him a bit closer, that pit of excitement and fear working their way through her body as she licked her lips. Though her eyes went from the drugs to the money, widening at just how much Romy had tossed the man.

She leaned in to whisper to him, "It's too much, c'mon."

Romy simply gave her ass a shameless pat and kissed her on the neck.

"Don't worry babe," he said to her so full of confidence. He scooped up the packets and stuffed them into his blazer pockets before slinging it back over his shoulder.

"Thanks boss. We'll leave you be to your business, just wanted to get this celebration right," he said as he began to lead Angela out of the room.

"Keep up the good work though," Javier announced. "Some more work like that and you'll be indispensable around here," he said, in what must've been the most conciliatory terms that man ever gave before others.

"Oh, you don't need to worry about that, boss," Romy said with a grin back to Javier before he and Angela made their way out and down the stairs.

Angela was practically tripping up on him as they walked, so eager to be near him.

"What is that stuff anyway?" she whispered, though a whisper in a club like the Tropicala was more like a low shout. She eased it, though, with a kiss beneath his earlobe.

Romy gave a big, smug grin to her as he led her down the stairs towards the V.I.P. area again. Though when he opened his lips to speak, instead Angela's attention was drawn to the dance floor, then his along with it.

There some commotion was going on near the door as a large man made his way through the crowd.

"What's going on there?" Romy asked, though Angela's keen eyes made sense of it first. Though, how could she forget the man who'd broken her heart and left her to wallow in a life of crime all on her own?

Jamal Khalil. Tall, dark and handsome, and only more so since she'd last seen him. A neatly groomed beard upon his broad jaw, a tight shirt upon his broad, well-built frame. He looked more muscular and in shape than the last time she'd seen him those years ago. Before she'd gotten herself into jail.

"Jamal," Romy muttered aloud, much to Angela's surprise.

*Oh, fuck no*, she cursed inwardly, and those double mojitos couldn't even numb her anger and rage as it bubbled forth. She stood up straighter, her eyes fiery as she refused to run even though all she wanted to do was hide from him and his charms.

"You know him?" she hissed at Romy, her heart pounding in her chest and her stomach twisting into a million little knots. How dare he walk back into her life?

Romy looked to her with excitement in his eyes.

"Do I know Jamal? We've all heard of him!" he said with a loud exclamation, drawing the attention of Daryl over by the bar.

"Jamal's back?" the giant brute of a man said, coming over to lean upon the railing and staring off almost dreamily. "Damn… how time flies, huh? Felt like he'd never get out," Daryl said, shaking his head in mild disbelief.

A little sense of smugness came over her, that little bit of superiority. He was in prison too? Good. Serves him right.

But still, that didn't mean she was prepared to see him and be confronted with all that anger and pain once more. Not that night. Not after making so much cash and finding her way towards freedom.

"I should go," Angela said to Romy, all her willpower and determination quickly fading from her.

Romy squeezed her hip and grinned, tugging her towards the stairway heading onto the dance floor.

"Come on, I'll introduce you to him, he's a great guy I hear," Romy said.

"The best," Daryl interjected, the giant of a man sounding almost like a boy with a crush. "He did four whole years in jail just to protect us, never flipped on us even though he was on the outs with the chief at the time."

*Four years?* Angela thought. But that would've meant he went to jail almost immediately after breaking up with her.

Her nose crinkled as she shook her head, but she was already too tipsy to fight hard against that guidance.

"It's fine," she protested. She didn't want to have to get into a *thing* about it. About him.

Romy was drunk on more than rum, however; he was high on their recent success, that macho feeling that put him on top of the world. He pulled Angela along with him down onto the dance floor and before she could object any further they met the oncoming Jamal and the people around him who were fawning over the beautiful man.

"Jamal!" Romy exclaimed to the man, "Congratulations on getting out, my man!" He said reaching out to bump fists with him, though Jamal's attention was already turned towards her. And it was intense. "I've heard so much about you from the gang! Even my bro Javier wishes I were more like you I think. Hey, I want you to meet someone very special… my babe, Angel."

Jamal stood before her, in the flesh, the first time she'd seen him in four years. And he only looked better. His long, sleek black hair draped around his shoulders, his black and purple shirt rolled up past his elbows, and undone at the collar to show some of his smooth, dark chest. He was an Adonis. More so than ever.

"Angel," Jamal repeated, staring at her with awe in his voice and gaze. As if he hadn't ditched her so callously.

She tried so desperately to puff up her chest, to act as though she were better than him. To let that anger at him dumping her make her strong, but instead her hands trembled and she had to glance away. She tried to smile, to make it look coy, but tears glittered in her eyes before she blinked them away.

He was the reason she'd gone to jail. When he'd dumped her, that was when she'd gotten reckless.

That was when she started making mistakes, first little, then huge. She'd started using drugs seriously, and gone through such hell to heal her broken heart, to forget he'd existed.

It wasn't fair of him to come back, hotter than ever.

"Nice to meet you," she said, forcing her eyes back to his, her smile tight.

Somehow, that handsome devil had the nerve to look aggrieved by her greeting, but only momentarily before he forced a smile back to his broad, handsome face.

"Now that you're back, you need to get involved in the gang again, we could all use your help around here," Romy stated, genuinely excited for the man's return, though Angela suspected his already excited state had something to do with that.

"Well, we'll see once I talk things over with Javier," Jamal said with a casual shrug of his broad shoulders. "Hopefully he won't have an issue with that."

"Well I'll speak for you on your behalf, man. Daryl says you did a lot for him," Romy said with such certainty.

"Thanks," Jamal said with a slow nod. "I'll keep that in mind. You two gonna be around?" he asked, looking between them both. "Maybe we could have a drink together afterwards, or… are you two on your way out?" he asked, brow raised.

That was exactly what she wanted to do. Have a drink with her ex and her current lover, chatting about drug deals and prison.

Angela smiled broadly as she looked to Romy.

"We were just about to head out and celebrate in private," she said, every word a purr and intended to stab at Jamal's heart.

Though Romy's knowledge of him did give her a bit of a pause. How long had Romy been involved in the underbelly of society? She'd guessed he was only nineteen, maybe twenty at the outside — which, according to certain standards — made him way too young for her to date. Not that she cared.

Jamal gave a slow nod, though apparently had a hard time keeping his eyes from her.

"You two have fun," he said to them. "If you'll excuse me," he placed a hand on Romy's shoulder and went around him up towards the V.I.P. area, and much further acclaim.

Romy looked down to her and squeezed her tight with a grin.

"Damn, good times all around lately, babe," he said so fondly, both his arms coiling about her.

But Angela couldn't get over how hurt she was that Jamal didn't seem the least bit injured by her. At least not to her liking. She glanced after him as he walked away, though she wished she hadn't, and then quickly moved back into Romy's side, giving a nod.

"Yea," she murmured, frowning a little. "I'm... not feeling so hot. I'm going to go to the ladies room."

Romy looked down at her with a sympathetic frown. He rubbed a hand up along her cheek and gave her a kiss on the lips.

"You go take care of yourself babe," he said affectionately.

She stilled against him before moving away, through the crowds and towards the ladies room. There were two girls inside, talking in a language she didn't know. They stopped only to look her up and down as she pushed into the largest stall, locking it behind her.

Their chatter picked up again as Angela's face fell to her hands.

She wouldn't cry. She wouldn't let herself cry over him again. For four years, he'd left her to stew and writhe in her angst and sorrow. She'd gone to jail, gotten out, got a job, tried to get her life back on track.

It was only fitting that he'd return to her life just as it was spiralling back out of control.

She held back her sobbing, but her heart still raced and her stomach heaved as she struggled to get control over herself. He wasn't worth it. He'd broken her heart, shattered her mind, and he should not have any more control over her.

So why did she feel so horrible?

It was a long time before she moved, long after

the two women left the bathroom. But she couldn't leave the safety and security of the stall.

It was like the kick in the ass she needed to stop letting her life get out of control. To stop herself from following the same path once more. Slowly her sorrow dissipated and her resolve grew and by the time she finally forced herself up and out to the sink, splashing some cold water on her face, she felt hard.

She'd take her money. Go home.

And that'd be the end of it. Simple as that.

She pushed herself out into the crowd, the music still thumping through her skull and vibrating her insides as she looked about for Romy.

She found him after a bit of searching up in the V.I.P. area, nursing yet another drink as he spoke with some others. She worried it would be Jamal, but as she got up there, instead she found him nowhere in sight, just his usual friends chatting.

Romy's face lit up a bit drunkenly as he saw her.

"Hey babe," he remarked. "You feelin' better?" he asked.

She shook her head a bit.

"Naw... I think I better just head home," she said, her arm slung around her midriff.

Romy looked crestfallen with that news, but put aside his drink and came down the stairs.

"I'll take you back," he said, though she knew if he did that, he'd likely worm his way into more than her apartment.

"It's fine," she said as she leaned in, kissing his cheek. "I'm just gonna grab a cab. You celebrate with your friends. You deserve it." Angela ran her finger along his cheek and jaw, forcing a tight smile.

"Just... call me tomorrow," she added on.

Romy kissed her back and nodded, looking down at her concerned from his higher perch.

"You take care of yourself babe, I'll check in on you tomorrow, you bet," he promised, offering a warm, reassuring smile.

She was so grateful he didn't fight her as she walked back into the cool night air, sucking it in. She moved just beyond the door, enough that she could still hear the music, but she was shrouded in darkness. She settled onto the pavement, a chill going through her.

She let the cold air cleanse her lungs, her body, and took a few minutes before finally punching in the number for a cab company.

Instead a deep, husky voice broke the quiet she enjoyed.

"Let me drive you home," Jamal said, sounding sympathetic in his own way. He extended a hand to her, that thick, exposed forearm lined with jutting veins as he offered to help her up. "I owe you that much at least, right?" he said.

She startled as she ended the call just as the dispatcher picked up, brushing her finger under her lower lashes instinctively.

"You owe me a lot more than that," Angela hissed, a tremor in her voice that she loathed. He was her first love, and just broke it off as if it were nothing. As though she didn't matter.

"Yeah, I do," he said simply, his hard, masculine face etched in sympathy. An expression she just was not used to seeing upon that handsome face of his. He tilted his head to the side, gesturing to the road. "Lemme give you that ride, and anything else you might want too. I owe you after all," he said apologetically in that deep, gravelly voice.

And despite herself, she was tempted, moving towards him just a little as she looked up at him with wide eyes, tucking some dark hair behind her ear. She felt just like she did when she'd first met him a decade ago when she was so young and naive.

Ten years of fast living, of prison, of redemption and pain, and still he made her heart flutter.

"Fine, but it doesn't mean anything," she finally said as she stood.

"Of course," Jamal led her along the sidewalk just up the road, to his black car. It was a nice vehicle for him having just gotten out of prison, though not exactly mind blowing. He unlocked and opened the passenger door for her.

*Still a gentleman*, she thought, inwardly rolling her eyes as she sat herself down on the leather seat. She rested her head back against the seat and let out a sigh as he slammed her door shut and rounded the car to slide into the driver's seat.

"Corner of Dundas and George," she said, not in the mood to talk. If he wanted to apologize for how he'd wronged her, he could go ahead, but all he was doing was saving her the cab fare.

Jamal took his time pulling out of the parking space and onto the busy Toronto streets. Silence reigned between them for a while, the man quiet as his thick arms moved the steering wheel, until finally…

"I'm sorry you're still hurting," he said at last. "I never thought you'd cling to what we had for this long." He stated it all so simply, his voice a little softer than usual.

"Oh fuck you," she hissed, all venom, her words slightly slurred.

"I was so fucking over you. I *am* so fucking over you," she corrected herself quickly. "So get over yourself."

His handsome, stoic expression never showed a flinch at her verbal assault. He just looked so damn cool through it all. So damn unfazed by her—

"I never could get over you," he said firmly. "Never went a day without thinkin' on you. It made prison both easier and harder," he remarked, turning the wheel and taking them down another road.

*That* was unexpected, and she glanced towards him, her eyes narrowed as if he were pulling the wool over her eyes. Trying to trick her into admitting things she'd long ago settled.

The well of tears in her emerald eyes threatened once more to overflow and she instead looked back outside at the neon glow of Toronto at night as they went through the busy entertainment district.

She didn't know what to say. What could she say?

She swiped along the lower rim of her eye once more, begging herself to hold it in just another couple of blocks.

"Just got out?" she managed through a mumble.

"Just today in fact," he responded with a slow nod. When last she'd seen him, his hair was short and styled in an intimidating manner. Now it was long and luxurious, framing his broad face so wonderfully. "Had to pick up some of what I was owed. Then I was intending to track down someone I missed. See if things might be okay again. I guess not."

"*You* broke up with *me*, Jamal. I'm not sure, like, how this was supposed to somehow be okay. You just left me, and dropped off the face of the planet. You don't—" she had to stop herself, her voice cracking dangerously. It took her a few breaths to calm herself down, to make her voice cold once again. "You don't know what I've gone through."

"I know I don't," he said to her calmly, driving her towards her place. "But I was going to have to do some time, and I didn't want you to have to pay it with me. I know you better than you know yourself, or at least I did," he said, pulling up to where she told him to take her. "You've got needs. And I didn't want you feelin' obligated to me, holdin' on to a love for me while I was away. I wanted you to go out and fuck your pains away guilt free."

"And besides," he added, putting the car in park, "if you knew I was gonna take the fall for someone else, you'd find a way to talk me out of it. And then we'd both be on the run from the consequences forever."

He laid out all that information so plainly, but it still seemed to take him some effort to look her way. That handsome face fighting against the emotions that awaited beneath the surface, yet a knowing glance from her was enough to show the emotions that bubbled up beneath.

She couldn't fight the tears forever, the fact that she'd lost him over something so stupid. He was right, she would have talked him out of it. And she would have gone on the run with him, without a second thought, and probably been happier than the four years she had spent since.

Fucking her pain away? Sure, but it never went away. It only grew, her anguish and self-loathing never lessening. She looked up towards her apartment, leaning towards the door as if it'd protect her, hold her as she trembled just like a school girl.

"And how much did you get, huh? How much

was four fucking years of your life worth to those jackasses, huh? A few pats on the back and a wad of cash for your silence?" Anger and anguish mixed, her voice still slurred from the drinks.

"Not enough, you're right," he said to her, but she could see him shift uncomfortably, clearly the desire in him to reach out and comfort her was high, but he kept himself in check. "But the alternative was rattin' out the only people I had connections with. And then what? We go on the run? Yeah, okay. And do what? Not exactly a big country when it comes to my line of work. Gettin' hooked up with new suppliers and—"

He stopped abruptly, and looked at her with concern, lifting one thick arm to reach out and rub at her shoulder tentatively.

"I didn't wanna burden you with this shit back then," he said as if that was final.

Her head jerked at him with such force her hair slapped across her face as she glared.

"You don't even know what you did to me!" she cried out, the alcohol loosening her tongue. Her fist connected with his arm, though not enough to hurt. "I went to prison too, asshole! What the fuck was I supposed to do without you, huh? Fucking *two years* gone. And you know what I've gotten since? *Nothing.* You think you can ever walk away from that shit, you got another thing coming."

Her punch against that hard muscle did nothing

to faze him, but her words… they clearly cut to the bone. His expression melted instantly, and he looked devastated by the notion of her in jail, destitute.

"I thought you'd just go back to dancin' when I was gone," he muttered dumbly. "Shit, I mean… fuck, how'd they get you?" he asked, then shook his head. "Fuck I'm so sorry Angie," he said, looking away and down, sounding crushed by that revelation.

"I got *fired* from dancing because I was too fucked up for the fucking coke-head owners and all the asshole bouncers," she hissed, her mascara running as she desperately tried to fix it, to regain some control. But it was futile. Her life was a mess, and she was right back on the same path that got her there in the first place.

Jamal waltzing back into her life, talking about trying to protect her, that was just the last straw.

"Dammit, Angie," he said, not condescendingly as he might've done years ago, but so regretfully. "I owe you for this, I'm so fuckin' sorry," he said, his strong fingers rubbing into her shoulder as he leaned over to wrap both arms around her and pull her into his embrace.

She couldn't resist him, or how good it felt to have another person care about her. Someone she didn't always have to be 'on' for. Someone who had seen her at her best and her worst and could bring out both of them in her.

It was just so nice to let herself *feel* all of the

things she'd been trying to hide, to suppress and deny.

"I'm sorry," she whimpered, trying to push him away. "I should go."

Jamal resisted that push at first, still squeezing her form in his thick arms, but he relented, and loosened his grasp as he looked at her with wounded eyes. More sadness in him than she'd ever seen in all their years together before.

"I mean it, Angie," he said to her in a low, strained voice, "I've got so much to make up to you. And I intend to make good. You're due a share of all I've got for my time," he said to her, unlocking the doors from his side for her.

"I don't want your money," she whined, fumbling with the door handle as if something within her wanted so desperately to stay. Finally she got out, looking up at her apartment building, at the peeling paint around the windows, the buzzer that was hanging off half broken.

She couldn't even feel happy about her own score, the money she'd 'earned' that night.

Not now.

But as she turned to slam the door shut, the momentum sent her off balance and she stumbled backwards, falling rather unceremoniously on her ass.

From walking bombshell to stumbling fool, all because Jamal had come back into her life.

He was already climbing out of the car then, and made his way to her in a hurry.

"You okay?" he asked with concern, his brow furrowed as he reached down, taking her arm in one hand and scooping her up with the other arm. He lifted her with such ease, his prison-built-body able to hoist her with no issue. He was hard and warm, cradling her against his chest.

"I'm fine," she said as she reached down to take off one of her too-high shoes, then the other, lowering her a half foot and making her have to stare up even higher at him. At least she was stable on her feet, though.

"You don't just get to waltz back into my life after four years and expect everything's okay," Angela cried, her green eyes glossy as she stared at him, her lower lip trembling. "I can't handle this right now. This week..." She rubbed her forehead then shook her head.

"I know," he said to her, his voice sounding wounded but understanding.

"I'm fine. I'm home. Just go," she said, trying to move away from his warmth and inwardly begging him not to listen to her.

He stood there, letting his hard fingertips trail along her arms as she began to move away from him, his grasp not loose enough to let her escape entirely without more force.

"I never thought it'd be easy," he said to her in a

low husk. "But know that I didn't spend four years longing for you to give in easily either," he said to her with a stubbornness that fit his new, towering masculine form. "And know that I know I owe you even more than I thought, I'm not about to ever let it go unpaid."

His broad face was contorted with pain, his brows furrowed, his dark, almond-shaped eyes glimmering in the street lights as he released her fully at last, only keeping his hands positioned in case he needed to catch her.

"I'm with Romy now," she said, though she didn't know why. It wasn't something that could ever go anywhere. Sure, she burned hot for him. But she'd already resolved that she'd have to end it — more than once — and that she couldn't get caught up in his world. She so desperately wanted to, but the things she wanted to do for him were dangerous.

So stupidly dangerous.

"For now," he said, as if agreeing with her. "But we both know boys would never hold your interest for long. And Romy's just that: a boy." He reached a hand up to lightly brush his thumb over her cheek, gazing at her so lovingly as he let it graze her lower lip. "We had somethin' special, Angie. I was able to keep you happy like you'd never been before. And I owe you that and more now."

He spoke with such certainty, as if everything he said were absolute truth.

The worst part was that she knew it was. For four years, she'd been searching to fill that void he'd left in her heart. Drugs, sex, and prison had all done more harm than good, though, and she looked up at him with wide eyes as she pushed herself away from him.

It killed her to do it when all she wanted was to feel his mouth against hers, for them to find what they'd both lost so long ago.

But she couldn't, and she forced her gaze downwards. Everything within her was so frayed, rubbed raw and exposed.

"We can't take it back," she said, trying to sound strong but that little quiver gave her away.

"I was never the type to worry about takin' things back, regrets are not my deal," he said to her. "I made a bad choice years ago, yeah, but all I can do now is make up for lost time. And I intend to do just that," he stood his ground, refusing to retreat, but not advancing either. Not without her say so. She knew well enough from when they first fell in love he'd not be the one to cross that line unbidden.

"I love you more strongly now than I did before it all went to shit," he professed in the cool night air. "Four years were spent thinkin' about you. Thinking of how I'd mend the damage I'd caused, and how I'd make you happy again. I hope at least I had a few good ideas."

Tears stained her cheek and she wiped them away. Her entire body pulsed with such life.

Everything she'd been searching for, everything she'd been so desperate to feel, stood before her in one package of messy, terrible, amazing love. She'd never gotten over him, not for a second. No matter how enraged she'd been, no matter how off the track she'd gotten, she still thought of him in the dead of night, wondering what she'd done wrong. How she'd chased him off when things were going so good.

She stepped in towards him once more, drawn like a magnet to her first love, her tear stained face raised towards him.

"This isn't fair," she whispered.

Jamal lifted his arms and went to embrace her, but their moment was interrupted by the loud, loathsome roar of a motorcycle. No, several. The rumble tearing through the street, echoing off the buildings and making all sound die except for their cacophonous racket.

As the three hogs pulled up nearby to a halt, Jamal pulled her into his arms and leaned down. His deep, heavy voice piercing the air only by virtue of being so close to her ear.

"Lemme escort you to your door," he said, a suspicious eye upon them.

She leaned against him with a nod, their beautiful, sad moment torn away from them by those assholes once more.

"You're not coming in," she whispered as they moved.

"I know," he said simply, no judgment in the words, no bitterness or sense of loss. He was focussed on the big, leather-clad thugs just down the road as he led her to her door. There he even stood between them and her, as they watched from beneath their helmets, as if blocking her from their view made all the difference.

"They're always around," she said with a sigh and a shrug. "Welcome to my glamorous life, Jamal."

He gave them but one final look before offering her his sympathetic expression and resting his hand on her shoulder.

"We'll work somethin' out," he promised her as she unlocked her building door. "You deserve much, much better."

"Yea, well, tell that to all the people who won't give me a job because of my criminal record. Just got fired, too, so it's pretty much been a slam dunk of a week."

"Meet me tomorrow for dinner," he said bluntly over the purr of those bikes. "A simple dinner. Just you and me, and we'll solve your problems," he said to her, so confident and sure of himself. Just as he did when he'd solved so many of her other problems in the past, relieving her of all responsibility so she could just be… herself.

"Nowhere fancy," she said, her arms folding

beneath her chest as she looked up at him, her eyes still wet with tears. "And only so we can figure this out. Are you done with that? With them?"

He never used to lie to her, that time he broke up with her was the only point he'd ever told a falsehood by her accounting. So when he took a moment to think about it, she knew his shrug meant that he'd not decided.

"I wanna work for nobody but myself goin' forward," he said to her with firm certainty. "So how about I pick you up tomorrow here, at six?" it was a question, and that was peculiar for him. In years long ago he'd just set the agenda, and she'd keep to it. Relieving her of having to fuss over it. But they'd become estranged. And everything was starting anew.

So she nodded, opening the door further and slipping inside, her eyes working their way up his body. Finally, she bit in her lower lip and when she let it pop back out, she said, "I'm glad you're okay."

Jamal gave a gentle, warm smile, that one comment making his face light up with that usual handsomeness, washing away the dour expression and all its remnants. It left his sandy-brown complexion smooth and lovely again.

"And you," he husked. "Take care of yourself."

The sound of the motorcycles broke the moment again, revving so loud that any conversation became fruitless between that door crack.

She rolled her eyes as she shut the door to the lobby and turned to the stairs, her shoes still dangling in her hand as she made her way up to her apartment.

It was going to be impossible to sleep.

# CHAPTER 17

The midday sky was bright and blue, and the sun shone on through the glass walls of the upscale bistro, helping add to Svetlana's beautiful smile. The young woman was dressed up in a lovely pink skirt and pearlescent blouse outfit for her lunch time date.

Javier, for his part, was dressed in another well-tailored suit, a thick European cut tie that contrasted the dark maroon paisley of his vest. His hand reached out to stroke along her knee and up her slender thigh.

Their meal sat before them, finished but for a few bites and a little wine.

"This is how I wish to spend all my lunches from now on," Javier declared in a smooth, deep husk to the younger woman. "Gazing upon your bubbly, effervescent face," he declared, leaning in with a tilted head to place a soft kiss upon her lips.

She giggled, the sound like twinkling music as she gazed over him with her bright blue eyes.

"You're too much," she teased, enjoying every moment of their time together. She shifted closer, nudging the chair over so he could better stroke her soft flesh. "But I vould like that. Very much."

A grin crossed his face, and he leaned in, kissing back along her cheek towards her ear. He teased that soft lobe with a graze of his teeth and murmured to her lowly.

"I have a suite nearby we can visit. Someplace we can be ourselves, yes? No need to be secretive in there, just enjoy our time before we have to return to the world outside. How's that sound?" he asked, letting his fingers slip under her skirt to crawl up her soft inner-thigh.

She nodded, her blonde hair bouncing along her shoulders as her smile widened. She smelled of sweet cotton candy, and her flesh was so soft as her fingers touched his hand, guiding him up her thigh lewdly. Her legs parted for him, that light pink material bunching up around his wrist.

"Now, sir?" she asked softly.

His dark brown eyes began to light up and his head nod before his gaze was torn away to look worriedly at someone else. Svetlana followed his gaze, her head tilted and blonde hair cascading over her shoulder.

Jamal strode up to their table, the newly released convict dressed in a sleek grey vest with a black shirt beneath, rolled up to the elbows again.

"I need a moment of your time," he said to Javier firmly, grasping the back of a chair across from him.

For his part, Javier gave a hard look up at Jamal then glanced at Svetlana who looked fairly shocked at the interruption. She flushed so pink as she pulled away from Javier's lewd touch.

"She can stay," Jamal said, as he pulled out a seat and sat down. "I won't waste a lot of your time."

"How'd you even know to find me here?" Javier asked, brow raised.

"Did you forget? I was always good at findin' folks. For you," he added somewhat pointedly.

Svetlana did not often see Javier like that, so clearly perturbed but not willing to show it. It wasn't quite like he was afraid of the man — although, perhaps a little — it was more like he was indebted to him, and afraid to act.

"So what do you want?" Javier asked.

"Simple," Jamal stated, resting one hand upon the edge of the table before shooing away a waiter. "You owe me, and the car was a nice gesture," he said simply, "but I want something more."

"I've already arranged a sizable payment for you,"

Javier insisted. "Like I said last night, you'll get it the rest of it soon."

"No no," Jamal said, shaking his head. "I want something more substantial."

"It's a lot of money already," Javier said, gritting his teeth, though Jamal held up a hand defensively.

"Not money. In lieu of money, I want a business of my own," Jamal stated.

"I thought you wanted out of the business?"

"I did. And I still do," Jamal insisted. "I want a legit business. A club of my own, like yours perhaps."

"Dance clubs aren't exactly the most profitable of businesses, and they come at a heavy cost," Javier stated. "But…" he trailed off, looking back to Svetlana then to Jamal. "I was preparing to buy a club. A strip club. I could make you co-owner."

"Full owner," Jamal insisted. "I don't wanna answer to anyone."

Javier bristled, but only for a second.

"On one condition," Javier said.

"Name it."

"Appoint Lana here as day manager," Javier said firmly.

Svetlana looked to Javier, her eyes widened though her smile was so genuine and pure. She was clearly touched by the offer, glancing towards Jamal with renewed interest.

Jamal took a moment to consider it, eying her over closely before nodding to Javier.

"Done. But I'm the boss, and I wanna run it my way, she answers to me."

"Just treat my girl with respect, and we'll be fine," Javier insisted with a smile, squeezing Svetlana's hand beneath the table. Jamal got up to leave but Javier insisted, "What made you change your mind?"

"Well," Jamal said, arching a brow and peering back at the two of them, "turns out I've got more of a debt to repay than I thought. What you offered won't be enough. I gotta think long term."

Then with that, he simply strode off.

Svetlana squeezed Javier's hand back, her entire body vibrating a little bit. She could not be more excited, and when Jamal finally left, she let out a little squeal, almost knocking over the table as she went to hug Javier.

"Oh my God!" she purred, a little ball of energy rubbing against his body.

Javier put his arms around her, squeezing her tiny form in his long arms.

"Now I've got the perfect excuse to come check up on you every day," he remarked with a grin and a low chuckle.

"And take me out to lunch, yes? How far is your secret hideaway from the new club?" she asked, though never did she stop or slow bouncing up and down against him. Svetlana was an open book of purity and joy, and it shone through.

Javier picked her up out of her chair, kissing her

on the lips before putting her back down, feet to the floor after he stood up.

"Yes, and come on, I'll show you," he remarked with a sly grin.

$\mathscr{A}$ngela woke late, to match the late night she had had. Tortured by both the troubling emotions that stormed within her and the roar of the motorcycles outside, it wasn't until Romy called her that she awoke at last after lunch.

His name flashed on the phone and his voice carried out quickly as she answered.

"Hey chica, how are you doing today? Better I hope," he said with that charmingly boyish concern in his voice.

She felt hung over, her head pounding, but she knew that wasn't it. She'd been drunk, but not hang-over drunk. It was the tears that still burned beneath her lids, the way her head felt stuffed with cotton.

"I'm just getting up," she admitted, her voice harder with the sleep, her body aching everywhere as she pushed herself up from the bed. "How was your night?"

"Oh, alright you know. Not what it could've been had my lady been there with me," he said somewhat cutely. "Thought of you the whole night through though. And conversation. Even with the gossip of Jamal returning hot on people's lips, your ass was ever a fond topic."

She laughed as she made her way to the bathroom, looking in the mirror at her tired, makeup stained eyes. She grabbed her makeup remover, dabbing it beneath them as she spoke.

"Well it's good to leave an impression," she purred. "I'm just sorry our plans got interrupted." Though secretly she wasn't. She knew what she was like on drugs, and it clenched her stomach when she thought about how close she'd been to throwing it all away.

Jamal had saved her from herself once more.

"Well if you're feelin' up to it, how about we hook up this evenin' and pick up where we left off? I could come get you around… five, six maybe?" he offered, his voice on the other end, sounding anxious. Eager for her even. Though something about it had lost its appeal.

Was it in his voice or was it something that had changed in her? Did the arrival of the older, wiser and more capable Jamal change her opinion of Romy?

She wasn't sure. She pulled her hair back into a ponytail, washing her face free from the debris of the night before, trying to cleanse herself of more than just the old makeup.

"I don't think I can, lover," she said, sounding more upset than she felt. "I'm still not up to partying. Rain check?"

"Of course, chica," he said, trying to sound cool, but she could detect the hint of disappointment there in his voice. "You take care of yourself, and I'll be sure to check in on you real often. In case an opportunity comes to slip on in over there and spend some time with you," he said it in a teasing voice, but it was easy to tell what he had in mind for her and him together.

"Don't worry, sexy. I still got your number," she said with a purr. "We'll talk later," she added efore hanging up and putting both her hands on the sink.

What on earth was she going to say to Jamal that night?

# CHAPTER 19

*A*ngela took the hottest bath she could, but that still didn't make her feel clean. It wasn't even just seeing Jamal for the first time in four years, or being given the bombshell that he'd been in prison for that time. And he'd broken her heart to protect her.

No, it was the ten grand burning a hole in her pocket, and the fact that her feelings for Romy had instantly fizzled down to something more tepid and less exciting. She hated herself for the sudden change, and felt as if she'd used him just for the cash, but she knew that wasn't true.

She'd burned hot for him. He'd made her feel alive. As if she had purpose once more.

But that couldn't compare to the flame that Jamal had lit in her heart when she was so young and tender. She'd been around Romy's age when she'd fallen for Jamal, and long years apart had apparently done nothing to dim that fire.

She curled her hair into ringlets. He'd always liked her hair when it was curled, the long tendrils bouncing over her shoulder as she pulled on a more modest blouse and a skirt. At least her old work clothes weren't going to waste, and maybe the itch of the pantyhose would distract her from those feelings she'd long denied.

She kept her makeup light, and by the time she finished, she looked almost modest. When the clock struck six, though, she made him wait. After four years, there was no way she was going to be prompt for their reunion.

Jamal didn't know what apartment she was in, so all he could do was wait. Or cause a scene. But when she took a peek out at him, she found him waiting patiently by his new car. A fine vest and tie on, even though his shirt was still rolled up around his elbows, letting those two thick forearms show.

He didn't come with flowers, but she knew what he was like. He only showed with as little as he did because she'd asked him not to make a big deal of it.

Jamal felt deeply for her, if any bit of what he said was true. But like in those years past, she had to give him consent to let that flame burn free before he scorched her with it.

Relaxing outside against his car, he kept his arms folded over his chest, one foot rested back against the side of his vehicle as he studied the area, her building. Everything. She recognized that look on him, it was business. He was studying her area with the same intensity he put behind his work, all those years ago. Learning every little detail. So he'd never be caught at a disadvantage there.

Angela finally made her way out, fifteen minutes late, more due to her own boredom and the way her stomach twisted. Maybe some decent food would sort it out, though she knew that to be a lie.

She had slung on her leather jacket, her purse over her shoulder as she left her apartment building. For a second she hated how damn good he looked but she quickly brushed it aside as she waited for him to open her door.

"Lookin' so good as always," he said to her with a smile, lifting his sunglasses from his eyes to appreciate her as he opened the door. "Crazy how little you've changed in the past four years," he remarked, helping her in before making his way around to the driver's seat.

"Can't say the same for you," she said, though she was more appreciative of his changes than not. Prison had been strangely good to him. Fuck, most of the time she felt like she barely made it out alive, but there were always ways of making friends for someone like her.

He took no apparent insult over her words, either inferring her true meaning or letting it slide as another deserved jab for leaving her as he did. Instead he pulled his car from in front of her building and began to drive.

"Prison was a learning experience," he said simply. "I've found a nice place to eat, I think you'll like it. Not romantic or nothin'," he assured her.

"I trust you."

The words slipped out, unbidden, and she didn't have time to take them back. They simply floated away from her, out of her control. She glanced out the window to try to pretend like nothing happened, as if it were just three meaningless little words, but she knew he was smarter than that.

He let the remark go untouched, the two of them driving along in quiet. Though it wasn't so much an awkward pause, because in many ways it felt so natural. Like the long drives and walks they'd taken together years ago.

"I hope you got to sleep alright. Those fuckers made a ton of noise last night," he remarked. "Would've done somethin' about it, but they saw you. And even if I got them away no problem, they might've taken it out on you after."

That was Jamal. A macho man to be sure, but one who at least used his head a little.

"It's fine," she said evenly, grateful for his respect of her vulnerability. "They're always out there. I've almost gotten used to it. I think they run the bar by my place or something."

And besides, it wasn't like they were what was keeping her up last night.

She knew he wanted to say more on that. Probably wanted to remark on getting her out of there, offering her this or that to make it happen. She could see the tension in his face as he restrained himself.

"I suppose the place we had shared years ago had its own issues like that. We were just too busy making ruckuses of our own to notice, huh?" he remarked, slowly cracking an amused grin.

Oh, they'd had such times. From the two of them exploring every kink they could think of to the big parties and loud music.

It was like college that was always shown on the TV, always midterm break every night. All of the people in their building were young and wild, just like them, with no apparent jobs or fear of retribution. Every day was a party.

She smiled a little at the memory, the wonderful things they'd learned in one another during those more carefree days.

Though she knew now that there were deeper concerns than she wanted to admit, even then.

"Yea, well, when you're up 'til five every night..." she finally said.

"Yeah, was different when we were kids," he said, his deep voice so much harder than she remembered it, yet still so familiar. "All that time away gave me time to think on it though. To realize what we did wrong, what we could do better. But I guess you know a bit about that too, huh?"

She let out a dry laugh. "Something like that. Mostly thought about getting out. About what I was going to do to turn my life around. No more guys. No more partying. I'd be safe and clean, and wouldn't have to worry about anything." She knew her tone made it obvious that it hadn't worked out as anticipated.

More so since he found her at the Tropicala.

"That was smart thinking," he said, no irony, no mockery in his voice. "Came to a few similar conclusions myself. Except for the guy's part, y'know I can't lay off them pretty fellas," he remarked with dry humour, looking over at her for a moment before he cracked a wry smile and pulled them into a parking spot nearby some quaint shops along a park area.

"Yea, it's been working out great for me so far," she said, not in a hurry to get out of the vehicle, looking over at him. He was so damned cute with his little jokes and she forced her gaze away. "Except for the part where I got fired from pretty much the worst job to exist because of my record."

Jamal put the car into park and took the keys out. He reached out to touch his hand to her arm, right at her elbow, that warm, familiar feeling coming back to her.

"It's a setback, but it's more my fault then yours. It's because of me you got mixed up in shit you shouldn't have. And then you had to crawl your way out. But don't worry about shitty jobs you were too good for in the first place. We'll fix all that," he said with that certainty and authority he always had, undiminished by his time in prison.

He got out of the car without further fuss, rounded about to open her door and help her out.

"It's just over here," he said, pointing to a quaint little spot on the corner that looked more like a historical site than a restaurant.

She resisted the urge to lace her arm into his as they walked, her heels more modest than the stripper heels she wore the night before, and she only came up to his mid-bicep.

"What's it serve?" she asked, though it was just idle chatter. She didn't really care, and had never been a picky eater.

"Homey kinda stuff, or that's what I'm told. I only got outta prison yesterday, so I haven't had a chance to check it out myself," he stated, opening the door for her and letting her go on ahead into the restaurant.

Inside it had a classic, old style charm, with carved wooden pillars and etchings around an old pub-style bar, and quaint booths.

"Khalil, reservations for two," he said, and the smiling little waitress took them to their seats, a lovely booth in the back that was sheltered from the rest of the place, but had a window looking out directly onto the trees in the park.

Angela slipped into the seat, relaxed back into it and crossed her legs. The waitress handed them their menus and quickly poured them some water.

"I'm Lucy and I'll be your server today. Have you been here before?" she asked, not for the first time that day.

"I hear your specials here are to die for, Lucy," Jamal said firmly. "Tell us what it is you've got goin' on today in that department," he instructed, smiling over at Angela the entire time.

Lucy gave a nod back to them both, her eyes gazing thoughtfully at the ceiling.

"The chef's special today is homemade chicken pot pies. Everything's from scratch, and it's served with fries, rice or salad. We also have a steak and lobster dinner for two, and all our high balls and pints are two for one until eight," she said with a smile, taking out her notepad. "Did you want a few?"

"We'll have the steak and lobster for two, rare," Jamal said without hesitation, tapping the menu against the table before gathering up Angela's as well and handing both back to the waitress. "And bring us a bottle of merlot. Somethin' with a good year on it," he stated, paying the waitress only a momentary look before turning his attention fully to Angela.

"Right-o!" Lucy said, not bothering to write it down and taking away their menus.

Angela relaxed as the other woman left, glancing around at the interior before finally settling her eyes on Jamal.

"I guess we'll keep making small talk 'til our wine gets here?"

Jamal took his sunglasses off and tucked them into his vest pocket as he smiled over at Angela, that look upon his face one of rather sublime happiness.

"You know, I fantasized about those curls every single fucking day in prison," he said, folding his hands in front of him. "Remembered their bounce. Their smooth, rich feel. The many times I ran my fingers through them, grabbed a hold of them..." he shook his head, as if recounting the experience of his first time having sex. "Seeing you like that does somethin' to me like you wouldn't believe." He laughs wryly, grinning. "Oh but I guess you do."

Her finger grazed against one of the curls and glanced aside. She should have known he'd have seen what those curls meant despite her simple makeup, her chaste dress. It was a sign of something they'd shared, something that she refused to give up after all those years.

And the idea that he'd been dreaming of them for four years was flattering beyond belief. She knew how it went in prison, how she'd longed for those touches, those days dedicated to nothing but sex and touching and pleasure. Those had always gotten her through, though she'd have denied it to anyone.

"I imagined you out here, fucking your brains out, and having the time of your life, y'know? And you'd think that'd make me jealous," he remarked, shaking his head slowly. "It didn't. Made me happy. The only thing about it that makes me upset at all is knowing you didn't get that freedom, that fun. Knowing things didn't go as I'd planned," he remarked, his handsome face, so beautifully framed by his thick, sleek black hair, contorted in displeasure at the thought.

Her gaze went downwards, taking a deep breath in to try to balance herself. To try to find that center she needed so that she wouldn't simply float away.

Her stomach twisted and turned, but it burned lower.

He knew just what to say to make her pussy throb and she was grateful when Lucy returned with their merlot.

She poured it up with a smile, glancing towards Angela's rouged cheeks for a moment before the waitress excused herself.

Angela lifted the glass to her lips, grateful for the excuse not to speak as she just ruminated over his words, trying to find some response that wasn't completely inappropriate and finding none.

Jamal helped himself to his own wine too. It was flavorful but not the finest, after all, the restaurant was more homey than upscale, though clearly catered to a higher class of clientele anyhow. The type who paid a lot of money for good food rather than the pomp of a pretentious joint.

"I'm going into business for myself," he said to her, voice a bit raspy after drinking the wine. "Legit business. Gonna run a club of my own, clean. No drugs, nothin' illegal. All above board," he said to her firmly, folding his hands atop one another, letting the one ring he wore rest above the others. An old one she'd gotten him in ages long past, dark and not terribly expensive, but sentimental.

She glanced down at it, trying to remember if he'd been wearing it last night as she inhaled.

"Good for you," she replied with so little enthusiasm. What was she supposed to say? Congratulations on so easily finding a way to slip back into reality?

She couldn't bring herself to fake that, not with how rotten her own life had been since leaving prison. One day out and he was already making big plans, taking over the world.

"It's gonna be a strip club, like the old one we worked at together, long ago," he said to her. "I need someone to help me run it," he said firmly, as if he had the whole world figured out, not just that club. "Someone I can rely on, that I know. Someone who'll work with me to keep the business clean, so I don't risk landing my ass back in jail," he said firmly.

Her eyes went back towards him, thoughtfully,

taking in his words. It was easy to read between the lines.

He wasn't being too subtle, after all. And most of her wanted it, more than anything. A clean, easy job that wasn't boring, that she would be good at.

But it'd also mean that something would happen. She had no impulse control around Jamal, and that was the biggest consideration. If she wanted something to be rekindled.

"I don't know," she said softly, rolling her glass between her fingers thoughtfully.

"It'll pay well, hell," he remarked casually, shrugging his broad shoulders, "you could even be a partner in it with me. Co-owner. If you're up for it," he remarked cautiously, looking across at her. Offering her not just a part in his dream, but a whole slice for herself so easily. Just like that.

Though accepting his help — letting him repay that debt — carried its own risks.

"It'll mean more work," he said. "More risk. But we'll be clean, clear and in charge of our own futures."

She watched him as he spoke, noting every bit of his posture and the way he moved. It brought back such intense memories. She knew the way those muscles moved beneath his shirt so intimately. It was hard for her to even fathom that he was back, in the flesh. He'd been gone from her life for so long and then had just waltzed back in.

But not like nothing happened. Some of the ways they acted was as if those four years hadn't happened, but there was a chasm between them as well, something that was hard for her to understand.

"I've never been afraid of hard work," she said softly. "And I know it wouldn't be boring. But that's not why I'm hesitating, Jamal, and you know it."

He bobbed his head slowly to her in understanding. He got it, he got it completely. Of course he did. That handsome bastard, so strong, so capable, so in control so soon after being in a place where he lacked all control.

"I'll be in charge of the business side of things, managing the books, and keepin' everything safe. That last part just like it used to be. And you can manage the women, promotion, events. That'll be your turf."

He understood her reluctance, but he was intent on breaking through it.

And she couldn't deny that she wanted him to. She wanted him to break down her defenses, to make it impossible for her to say no. She reached across the table, slowly touching his hand.

"Who's giving you the club, Jamal? Javier? Is that how he's repaying your debt for going away for him for four years, by giving you more work?"

Jamal gave a derisive sort of laugh at the idea.

"He's paying a debt to me, that's all. The club is going to be mine. One hundred percent mine to own, that is…" he said, reaching out to cover her small hand with his large mitt. "Unless you want to join in with me. Partners," he made it sound so enticing. "There won't be any coke in my club either," he said pointedly.

He knew. Somehow he knew what she'd been on her way to do that night?

Her hand retreated, her gaze averted as she sucked in a breath.

"What's that supposed to mean?" she asked, never one for subtlety or not speaking her mind, and her emerald eyes moved back to his, brows furrowed.

"It means with me you won't repeat old mistakes," he said firmly, his tone more patronizingly fatherly than the smooth, even tones of before. "Means I'm old enough to know better than my younger self. And I won't let either of us get mixed up in shit we both know better than to do."

He reached out across the table for her hand again.

"We've had time to think back on where we went wrong, Angie. We let the money go to our heads, the wild life. We were young and foolish, and that's fine, what's done is done. But now we're wiser. And I'm gonna keep us from failin' ourselves," he said firmly. So authoritatively. As if she didn't have a choice in that, unlike all the rest.

And she recognized that tone. It sent a chill through her that was electric and warm and so welcome. It opened parts of her that had been closed off for years.

He'd been the world to her for so long, and it was that tone that made her always come back to him. Felt safe with him. It was one of the many reasons why she'd stayed faithful to him for so long. He understood her better than any other, and accepted her for who she was. Flaws and all.

"I can't go back to working in an office," she said, her voice trembling a little. She'd put out countless resumes and hadn't heard back from anyone. It was hard enough to explain a two year gap, let alone make up for it with no relevant experience.

"You won't even have to set foot in our office if you don't want to," he said with a wry smile. "The changing rooms could be your office."

The waitress arrived with their food then, an array of trays for a fancy and expensive meal, steak and veggies on a plate for each of them, then the giant specter of a lobster on its own, looking over them.

"Can I get you two anything else?" she asked, and Jamal shook his head and dismissed her.

The aroma from the food was delightful, it all smelled of real, home cooked sort of ingredients, rich and flavourful, not artificial. Jamal reached over and broke off the lobster's tail with his bare hands, then placed it upon her plate.

All of the stupid things, he remembered.

She looked down at the tail, and it was so much more. It was a show of how much she'd been on his mind, how much their years together had clearly meant to him. For so long she'd felt like she was nothing, that she couldn't even make it work without him.

He'd been the one that had built her up and made her whole, and then shattered her into a million pieces. After he'd left her, it was as though all the life had been drained from her, her soul sucked out and her body in a wreck.

But he still remembered she loved the tail, and sacrificed it to her.

It was almost too much, though she began eating it slowly, if only to hide how much it moved her.

"What were you going to say when you first saw me? How'd it go in your mind?"

Jamal was cutting into his steak, those thick fore-arms of his bulging with veins from every little motion. He'd grown harder in prison, physically speaking, but he'd lost none of his softness for her it seemed.

"I'd run through a dozen scenarios each day," he said casually before chewing on a hunk of red meat. "It all boiled down to what you were doin' when I found you. If you'd stumbled upon someone you were really entangled with. But… the gist of it was, I'd get out, get my payback. Then with that money in my pocket, I'd come find you."

Jamal looked straight across at her, his vision never wavering.

"I figured it'd be tough, you'd have a strong guy or two you were attached to. A new life. But I'd settle in near wherever you were, start a new life with my spoils. Run across you casually on the street at some point. Figured it'd take a while, I mean… I knew I'd hurt you. I didn't figure you'd be up for talking to me right away. But every day I'd stumble into you again, on purpose, and eventually I'd coax you into coffee or somethin', some excuse to talk things out. But the first thing I'd say? The *very* first?" he stressed, before cutting into his steak again. "I never meant it, I'm sorry."

"You could have told me. After. Just... a letter or something, saying it wasn't me. Anything," she breathed out. Her voice didn't quiver as she spoke, her eyes stuck on his as she lifted another bit of lobster meat to her lips. "I've spent four years going over what I did wrong to make you hate me so much that you'd cut me out, cold turkey."

"Until I was able to be there with you," he said evenly, not flinching from her stare, "I didn't think it would make anything better. So what if I sent you a letter? Convinced you I loved you? I'd still be in jail. We'd be apart. I couldn't do anything to make it better, it'd just be words. And you know I'm not about words. I'm about doing."

Part of her knew it was true. That instead of

spending four years loathing herself, she would have spent four years feeling pity for herself. Either way, they wouldn't have been a blast.

She leaned back as she took another sip of her wine, looking at him with such interest and curiosity. The man that knew all the ins and outs of her mind, her body, sat next to her and was professing… what?

That he'd thought about her every day, that he'd do anything to make it up to her?

Angela licked over her lips with a sigh.

"And what is it you wanted our happily ever after to be, Jamal?"

He smiled at that, the thoughts of his plans bringing such joy to him so easily.

"I was gonna talk you into runnin' off with me. Take my reward, go off and move to some place where the rent's cheap, the sun's hot and we can live a nice, quiet life." He said, though he returned his gaze to her and looked serious once more. "But after what you've been through I saw that wasn't gonna cut it. I needed more long term plans. Somethin' practical."

Angela's lips curled into a smile, sorrow hidden there behind her gaze.

"So you wanted to tempt me back with a strip club, a clean strip club, so I can, what, get back in touch with my roots? Feel I have some purpose again?" she asked, her head slightly tilted as she looked at him.

He gave a casual shrug.

"You wanted a job. A more normal life. And you were still mixed up in that kinda life. I thought it was the way to go to repay you my debt. And to get you back in my life," he said simply, as if it were all so obvious. "If I asked you to run off with me, would that have been more likely to work?" he asked, brow raised at her.

"No," she stated simply, leaning forward on the table. "But not because I wouldn't want to. But because it'd be easier to turn down."

He knew that of course, he understood it fully. That's why he switched his approach. He knew her too well to gamble on that proposition.

"So what concerns me now is you," he said firmly. "Righting my wrongs, making up for lost time. Making you happy. And secure. Because regardless of what happened, and how much I fucked up, I know we're right for each other. Too right. We belong together, and more so than ever. I can look out for you now better than I could when I was a younger man, still full of myself, still addicted to the thrill of that life we led, outside the law."

Her wine was gone, her food pushed around on her plate more than ate, and she could do nothing more than look at him. Hear that raw emotion in his voice, letting it resonate through her body. It was as though he was speaking to her soul, that hidden little part of her that she kept smothered for so many years.

She wanted to argue. To remind him how easy it would be to get caught up in old habits, but she trusted his words more than her inner voice. He didn't say anything he didn't mean.

Except, apparently, when he said he didn't love her.

"What about Romy, huh? What about Javier?"

"That kid's your concern," he said simply with a shrug of his broad shoulders. "As for Javier, like I told you, once the club's mine, he's no longer my business." He flicked a hand dismissively, "I did more than enough for him already. And if he thinks he can ask for more, he's in for a rude awakening."

That harsh voice he took said he was serious. And while the prospect of one man standing against a mob seemed unrealistic and foolish for most, with Jamal she could start to believe it. He'd make enough trouble to put a whole gang on alert.

Besides, four years of his life was nothing to shake a stick at.

"What do you want for us, Jamal? To go back to how it used to be, except we get a cute picket fence and a dungeon in the basement instead of the living room?" she asked, her shoulders so heavy. It was hard to swallow, and she looked at him with such a mix of desire and disbelief.

"We'd go to work every night, trying to make a living and yelling at each other over bills?" Angela shook her head. "What we had worked because it... fit. But now we're not even talking about being different people, but living a completely different life. And you want me to put all my faith and trust in you when you couldn't even tell me how deep you were into it before?"

"I was different then," he said in a confessional sort of tone, his own food left alone, hands folded in front of him after he pushed his plate away. "I knew what was best for you and that was that. I didn't want you getting as deep into it as I was. Didn't want you going to those people when I was gone, looking for... whatever. I thought I was doing what was best. I was wrong. I'm wise enough now to see that."

He looked across at her, brow furrowed as he looked so serious.

"We'll make that life work together. I'm a better man now. Most men get worse in prison. I used the time to make myself stronger. Wiser. Better. I will keep you clean, keep you safe, keep you secure. Keep you happy." He listed off those things with such firm certainty. "We'll run our club, our lives, a far sight better than any of those fuckers we knew together back in the old days. You have to know that at least."

She crossed her legs beneath the table and nodded, her eyes skirting to the side.

"I know we won't have a problem with that,

Jamal. But... you're asking me to put all of my life in your hands. Again. My everything would be entwined with yours, even legally."

"Yes," he said, not equivocating, not arguing the point, but granting her that. "And you can trust me with your life. You know it. You told me so your very self on the way here," he said, pointing out that very slipup he'd let slide so very recently. "I'll put your life before my own, you don't need my word on it, you know it. You saw me do it. I'd do it again, and again. A thousand times if I had to. You're the reason why I came back ready to throw everything else away. So I could give you a life closer to what you deserve. Something stable, something secure, something happy."

His eyes were intense then, boring through her as he stared across the table.

She couldn't hide the way he made her feel. It was just as plain to him as it was to her, etched along her face and body. That flame that burned within her, hidden and protected for all those years...

She wanted him so bad. Not even what he offered, his protection, the stability.

He could have come in as a ragged bum and she still would have been tempted. The reminder of the way his hands, his body felt around her, atop her... It was like muscle memory. Even after all those years apart, just talking to him again reminded her.

"And what if it all goes to shit?" she forced herself to ask.

"You've told me it's already gone to shit," he said with a helpless gesture of his hands. "I found you at a mobster's club, with some young man who had you drunk and was gonna get you high. You said your life was a mess and you couldn't keep a job. I don't know the details, and you don't need to tell me, but I do know that the only thing we can do when our lives are shit, is try to build 'em back up. That's the only option in front of us, Angie. The only option."

He looked across at her, tender concern in his dark, hard eyes. He had such depth of care for her, she could feel that in his gaze. Even when he was being so serious on such a dark topic.

"How'd you know he was gonna get me high?" she asked, her eyes narrowing even as she felt such longing. Such desire.

His brows furrowed and he looked disappointed in her.

"That's what you're hung up on? How I know? C'mon," he said with a bit of a scoffing tone to his voice as he looked around the restaurant. "You just went and saw one of the biggest suppliers of the stuff in the city, you were walkin' with some cocky young prick, drunk off his own ego. And," he looked back to her, "he mentioned it to me casually on my way out of Javier's office. Not exactly the secretive type, that one."

She let out a soft sigh and shrugged her shoulders.

"I'm hung up on that because it's the easiest thing I can ask, Jamal. Everything else…" she lifted her hands into the air as she looked at him. "Everything else is complicated and terrifying. Because I still fucking—." She cut herself off. She would not tell him she wanted him. Not then.

"I need time to think on it," she finally said with a sigh.

Jamal nodded his head to her in understanding, his fingers knitted together in front of him.

"I understand that. I didn't expect an answer right now. But come with me at least when I inspect the club. I want you to be there with me. Even if there's only a chance you join in, you should have a say from the get go," he said, that point stressed to her.

"When?" she asked, looking up at him curiously.

"I'll let you know," he said, reaching back into his rear pants pocket, then pulling out a newly bought phone and sliding it across to her. "Put your number in there and I'll let you know as soon as I do," he said firmly.

She picked it up, hesitating as she ran her fingers over the screen, making it come to life.

"This'd be the most elaborate way to get a woman's number in the world, by the way," she said, lifting her eyes, teasing a little before finally adding her number to his phonebook and handing it back. "Should make sure to lock it."

Jamal chuckled deeply as he took back his phone and stored it once more.

"Well now that I've got somethin' of value in there, I know to do just that," he remarked with a wry smile at her. The expression highlighting his strong jaw and smooth, handsome face. He was older than her by a few years, but he'd taken care of himself while away. Four years of clean living and working out had maintained that look. Enhanced it even.

She opened her mouth, thoughtfully, but then Lucy returned, all smiles and wondering if they wanted the dessert menu.

Angela leaned back in the bench, watching Jamal. Waiting for his decision.

She still expected him to be the one to set the pace, to take control of the situation. To relieve her of the need to worry and fret about doing the right thing.

She'd forgotten how nice it felt to be able to trust someone with all the mundanities of her life.

"Naw, we're good," he said before reaching into a pocket and forking out a large sum of bills. "That should cover it," he remarked, and the waitress' eyes went wide, a happy grin upon her face.

"Thank you so much! I'll give you two some peace if you wish to linger, just lemme know if I can do anything else for ya," she said before chipperly making her way off.

Jamal looked back across at her, an intense gaze.

"There's nothin' more I'd like than to spend the night with you, Angie. But I know it's too soon," he said simply in that dark voice of his. "I can just give you a ride back now, or… we could take a trip down memory lane. Visit an old haunt or two. I'm gonna do it anyways at some point, but I'd rather do it with you."

She shook her head no.

"I have a lot to think about," she said, looking up at his face. She was so tempted, so horribly tempted, but there was no way she could rekindle that. It was too quick, too soon, and she needed time to deal with her feelings for him. For Romy.

She thought back to the young man, his dapper charms, how passionate he was for her and felt bad for blowing him off. He deserved better than that.

Angela tucked some of her hair behind her ear, the curls trailing over her shoulder.

Jamal nodded in understanding and slowly slid out of the booth to stand.

"I'll give you a ride back to your place then," he said warmly.

The ride back was fairly quick, and Jamal got out of the vehicle to help her out and walk her to the door. As they stood there beside it, the towering man leaned in so close, almost too close. But he never tried to move in for a kiss.

"More beautiful than ever, even when you try to hide it beneath these stuffy clothes," he remarked, and with one hand he reached up to brush the backs of his fingers over her dark curls.

She looked away, shaking her head as she sighed.

"I just don't know why you had to come back right now. Just... when I need you the most."

She felt so warm beneath her blouse, the itch of her pantyhose mildly successful in keeping her libido in check. And yet still, her gaze slowly went up to his.

Jamal's face showed the procession of emotions, the worry, the relief, the love. He let his fingers brush over her cheek, stroking her smooth, unblemished skin on her back, then on to her sleek, dark curls that he loved so much.

"I'm never goin' away when you need me again, not if there's anythin' on this earth I can do to prevent it," he pledged in a low husk, finding himself nearing her. Those lips of his so achingly close they were nearly kissing.

But Angela pulled away. She wasn't ready for that. Wasn't even sure if she wanted that. Not yet.

"Jamal," she whispered, and loved how that name sounded on her tongue, but she couldn't let it go further yet.

He nodded slowly in understanding, and

retreated from her casually as he let his fingers graze along her curls one last time.

"I'll be thinkin' of you," he said, and a promise from that tall, dark giant was solid. He backed away, went to his car, but refused to go until she was safe and sound inside the building.

She made her way up, slowly, filled with that gnawing sense of pain and loneliness and uncertainty. She didn't know what to do, and could only pray that a good night's sleep would help her see more clearly.

# CHAPTER 20

Romy stood off in the distance, just down the road. He'd just come from the dank bar, and was keeping an eye upon Angela's place when they pulled up. He'd hoped to catch her coming home, after he'd finished his business, but what he saw instead…

The young man seethed.

His fists clenched and he reached for a jacket pocket that bulged with something heavy inside. He hesitated though, as Angela went up into her building.

Quickly, Jamal blew a kiss at her building and got in his car.

It was all over like that.

Though seeing the two of them so cozy, him leaning in to kiss her…

He couldn't see that their lips never met. Jamal had blocked the view too much.

So all Romy had in him was that jealous anger.

# CHAPTER 21

Angela had tried to give Romy a call that next day, but she got no answer from the man. It frustrated her, in part because she desperately needed to hear his voice, as well as the fact that it made it harder for her to figure out what to do.

She'd planned on coming clean about knowing Jamal, but didn't want to do it so impersonally.

Instead, she sent a text asking him to call her before going to the pile of money she'd hidden beneath her mattress. She had no idea what to do with it. It had been so long since she'd seen that much money, and Jamal had usually handled it for her. All of the bank accounts, the convoluted way of making sure everything seemed legit.

So she did the only thing she could, and counted it, let it feel real. It was the only thing in her life she felt certain about at that point.

But even that couldn't distract her for long, and she tossed one of the rubber band wads away, hearing it thunk against the wall. It was just another representation of how desperate she was, how unhappy she felt. A physical manifestation of something she hoped would calm her mind, but instead it only added stress.

She stood up, padded barefoot towards the bathroom. Pulling back her long, dark hair, she looked into the mirror and saw herself staring back.

"What am I going to do?" she asked it, as though her reflection would hold the answers she needed. As if it could help her sort through her tumultuous emotions, and how Jamal had said all the things she so desperately had hoped he'd say over the course of those four years without him.

Seeing him again made her realize just how much that breakup had fucked with her head, how desperate she'd been to prove to herself she wasn't useless without him. But instead, without him as an anchor to keep her safe and protected, she'd almost drowned.

She was still almost drowning.

How close had she gotten to getting completely fucked up again? A few minutes away, at best?

She shook her head at her mirror, tears blurring the vision and making it seem fragmented. Her fingers reached out for that reflective surface, simply needing to feel it and know she was still solid.

Jamal would protect her from herself.

243

The obnoxious roar of the motorcycles' engines were a constant disruption to Angela's life. Though that day they were particularly bad. She supposed it was the fact they woke her up at 4AM that really did it, hearing them again in the middle of the afternoon was just salt in the wound.

With a bitter expression she was drawn to the window to look out and… do what? Scowl at them in private, most likely. That was about all she ever did, or would dare.

For once, though, she saw a surprise. There was Romy talking with the bikers again just down from her place outside the bar.

The guy who hadn't texted or called her back.

Her eyes narrowed but she didn't linger at that window to stare out at him. Instead she grabbed a pair of jeans and a t-shirt, pulling them both on with complete disregard for her undergarments. Bringing her fists to her hair, she pulled it back and glanced in the hallway mirror as she pulled on her shoes.

She certainly didn't look glamorous, having just woken up, but she was in a hurry.

She couldn't understand why Romy was, all of a sudden, avoiding her and her stomach was tense with worry about what could have happened.

Grabbing her keys she quickly ran down the stairwell, sprinting towards him for a second before remembering she wasn't wearing a bra and slowing to a trot.

When she emerged from the building she received a sharp whistle. The three men on their motorcycles all appreciated the view of her bouncing bosoms at the very least.

Though as she looked around in the mid afternoon sun, she could see no sign of Romy.

"Hey babe, come bounce those over this way," said one of the bikers, short and stocky, greasy looking asshole. Though the tall one smacked him in a quiet sign to shut up.

It took her a moment to recognize that one, his hair sleek and slicked back, but he was the hard looking man she'd seen threaten Romy before. His aquiline features not quite as weathered as the last time she saw him. He continued to smoke and eyed her up and down.

"Lookin' good," he called to her, his gaze intense.

Everything about that man spoke of the fact he was a guy you didn't fuck with. Even Jamal knew better than to mess with him and his fools upon first glance, after all.

But she wasn't in the mood, her brows narrowed and her arms folded beneath her breasts, though that did little to reduce the attention given to her large chest.

"Where's the guy you were just talkin' with?" she asked, trying to sound calm and unbothered by their threatening presence, and their crass assessment of her body. She might have been flattered, at another point in time, but she was irritable from the lack of sleep and the fact that Romy was avoiding her.

The leader leaned back against his bike and blew out a cloud of smoke as he eyed her. He wore the typical sort of biker gear, though since the last time she'd seen him, it looked sleeker, more expensive. A high collared leather jacket that fit him snugly, cowboy boots that even sported some spurs.

"That pipsqueak?" he said, his voice so deep and gravelly it made Jamal sound downright soft. "What's a real woman like you want with that kid anyhow?" he asked, head tilted back just a bit as he looked her over shamelessly.

"I just need to talk to him," she said, avoiding the question, but meeting his gaze. She could look hard when she needed to, and she hoped she did then with her narrowed eyes and downturned lips. "Just let me know, huh?"

The towering man tossed his cigarette to the cement sidewalk and stood up. He ground it out beneath his heel, taking his time, then very casually strode over toward her. He was an ominous sort of figure, not built like Jamal but lanky, though with all that leather he looked bulkier.

He got within distance of her, looking down his angular nose. He licked his lips and looked at the sidewalk over her head then back to her.

"You'd do yourself a lot better if you talked with the right sorta man," he stated in that hard voice of his, smelling of fragrant smoke.

It was a stupid idea to rush down to find Romy, but she needed to talk to him. To figure it out. It hadn't yet occurred to her that maybe he'd simply lost interest, given her up in favour of a new toy. He seemed so into her, it was hard to conceive that.

Yet there he was, up and about, and in her neighbourhood, and still avoiding her.

Angela's stomach churned as she looked up at the biker.

"I have all the men I need in my life right now, thanks. So if you could just tell me where he is, I'd appreciate it."

"A lady like you?" the biker said, stepping up closer to her yet again, looking her over shamelessly. "I wouldn't think you'd get enough that easily.

Would figure you'd need a dozen fellas like that punk to keep you satisfied," he stated lowly, his voice so dark and low, the other thugs couldn't have heard it.

Angela couldn't hide the fact that his words caused her to feel a bit hot under the collar but she forced her eyes away. Licking over her lips she swallowed, feeling suddenly so small and vulnerable under the afternoon sun.

"I just really need to talk to him is all," she finally breathed out, her emerald eyes going back to his blue.

"Shame," he said, his gaze upon her as he rolled his broad shoulders. "Because I'd love to spend some time talkin' with you myself." He tongued the middle seam of his lower lip. "I bet we'd find out we have a whole hell of a lot in common, you and me," he stated. "Intersecting interests, at least," he added with a wry grin.

He reeked of trouble. Yet up close and personal with him, it was undeniable that he had an air of calm control, mixing with that imposing, ominous nature.

She ran her hand along her ponytailed hair, looking at him intently.

"I'm taken," she said simply.

Romy had lured her in with his boyish charms even though she thought he might be shady.

But the biker? Oh, she'd only go at it with him if

she had a death wish and a lust for trouble. He was the guy she would have gone with after Jamal left her broken hearted. The guy that'd be the cause and solution for all her problems.

"Guess I was wrong about you then," he stated simply, tilting his head to one side, giving her that cocky once-over as if seeing her anew once more. His first glance clearly wrong. "Didn't think you were the type of woman to settle down with anyone. Let alone just one guy. One wimpy guy. Yeah I seen where he went," he stated.

Her frustration was rising, the man somehow finding his way under her skin so easily, with each passing word.

"Where, then?" she asked. Already so much time had been wasted.

"That's it?" he said, holding his hands out to the side in a display of how little she was offering for her side of the bargain. "Just a demand for an answer. No offer of exchange? No pretty please?" he said, giving a wry, smarmy smile.

"Pretty please?" she said, trying to pout though she would put money on it coming out as closer to a sneer.

Whatever it looked like to him, he smiled. A genuine smile, not the sort of smug expression he bore before. And the damn thing had the effect of making him look significantly more handsome.

"You're a gutsy lady," he said to her, not coyly.

Not in some playful manner. But a genuine, honest confession of her daring against a man who clearly could've made her life hell. Or simply ended it.

But she wouldn't give him the satisfaction of looking proud at his words, though something within her shined a bit brighter.

"You missed 'em," he said simply. "The kid had to hop a cab. Guess he's lucky mom and dad gave him enough change that he doesn't have to take the bus."

Her lip quirked into a sneer, not at his jab at Romy, but at the fact that her lover was clearly avoiding her.

"Right. Thanks," Angela said, anger roiling inside her veins.

"Don't let the look and the thugs confuse you," he said to her, and for once she noticed the curious accent about him. He looked like he could be a typical, white-bred sort of fellow, albeit a particularly special one. Instead there was that slight hint of something else in his words...

"I'm not some thug," he said. "You should spend some time with me yourself and figure that out."

"You the one revving your bike down here at all hours of the night?" she asked, none of that bravado having drained from her the more they spoke.

He eyed her up and down again, a hard sort of inspection one might give a potential criminal about to rob them.

"Not anymore," he stated simply. "I'll make sure the boys keep it to a minimum."

Angela nodded, flicking her eyes up at his two big guys, before she looked back to the man in front of her.

"Got a name?"

"Vitaly," he said simply, then jerked his chin in her direction. "You're Angela," he pointed out. "But I think a name like Anj would suit you better. What do you think?" he asked in that hard voice of his, though his harshness seemed somewhat alleviated with their more familiar conversational turn.

She stared at him, arms tightening about her ribcage.

"How'd you know my name?" she asked. Curiosity was getting the better of her, and she knew she should take off, but she didn't want to be alone just then.

"I just think it's a sleeker, hotter name, for a very sleek, hot woman," he stated, tilting his hip to one side as he stood before her, so cocksure and in control. He avoided her question though. The man seemed ever to be directing the conversation *his* way and not hers.

He was infuriating, but she did her best to hide it.

"Well, Vitaly," she said, "I'd appreciate it if I could get some sleep tonight."

"I will do my best," he said to her frankly, one brow raised. "As you can likely tell, however, we have business here at the bar. So it can't be avoided altogether. But no needless revving," he said to her firmly. "I hope this will make you more amenable when next we meet."

"We'll see," she said simply, glancing to his buddies before back at him. "Until next time." She turned on her heel, walking more sullenly back to her apartment.

Why was Romy avoiding her?

wo calls came in quick succession, and they left Angela dazed.

First was Romy.

"We're over," was all he said, and the tone of voice he used was so flippant and cool as to be suspicious.

There were a hundred things she could've said then, among them: we were never officially a thing. After all, despite her fondness for him, their many times screwing, she'd never actually agreed to his many propositions to be his girl.

Though mostly she was left confused by it all, the sudden shift. The change in his demeanor.

She tried to find out what was going on, but he had hung up the moment her lips parted.

That left only the silence. And she went to call him back, but before she even had the chance, her phone rang, coming to life with Jamal's name across the screen.

She answered, her mood soured and hard.

"What'd you do?" she asked, for though he said Romy was her problem — her responsibility — she didn't have any other idea of why Romy would suddenly turn cold on her with no reason.

Unless Vitaly had threatened him.

Her lips curved into a sneer.

Her tone of voice and demanding question immediately set Jamal off, but he recouped quickly.

"I've got us an opportunity to go look at the club, help make our decision. I can swing on by and pick you up in an hour if you're free," he offered, though clearly the man sounded confused and doing his best to make up for it.

She took in a deep breath.

She wasn't even that upset about Romy, but the idea that someone was meddling in her life had set her on edge.

"Fine," she finally exhaled. It'd been another long few days with no response to her gap-filled and inconsistent resume, and she couldn't live off ten grand for an eternity.

"Everythin' okay?" he asked, and despite his apparent confusion, there was genuine concern in his voice. Where Romy had treated her with such casual disregard, he'd only shown consideration for her since they'd reacquainted.

The text message that popped up on her screen then reaffirmed it.

*I've got no time for a loose whore.*

It was all Romy said.

She stared at it for a second but then her anger turned into an eye roll. Of course. He only wanted her to be a loose whore for him. As if a girl that goes home with him after just meeting could ever be dedicated to him and him alone.

She put the phone back to her ear, her jaw tight.

"It's nothing," Angela managed.

She hadn't even been with another man since she'd met him; that fact was just salt in the wound he made though. Their relationship was a wild ride, it'd been fast and intense. But short it seemed.

"I'll be right over," he said to her in that deep, masculine husk that was especially soothing. Jamal at least had made it more than abundantly clear he'd hold no such thing against her. Not that he had any right to.

She hung up the phone and let out a loud sigh. She didn't know what had happened to make Romy change so quickly, but it barely mattered. The fact was that if he wasn't willing to do anything more than fuck her and put her on a pedestal, he was not going to be the one for her.

Especially since she's turned down the man she'd loved for so long. All out of consideration for Romy.

She threw the phone on the bed as she got

dressed, her skin still boiling and flushed with her anger.

Jamal arrived right on schedule, this time buzzing her door through the intercom.

"Your ride awaits," he said.

"Be right down," she said grabbing her purse and walking downstairs.

She didn't want to be overly dressed up so had pulled on a pair of dark jeans and stiletto heels, a white blouse and pulled back hair. She walked up to Jamal, waiting for him to open the door, before slipping into the passenger's seat with little more than a smile given to him.

Jamal for his part was looking infuriatingly good again. All that time in jail had undoubtedly messed with him in many ways, but by all she could see, he'd only come out stronger, wiser and a hell of a lot better looking.

He climbed into the driver's seat wearing a sleek pair of black jeans and a button up shirt, both of which hugged his physique nicely. He wore a black blazer over both, indicating he was likely treating the whole situation seriously as a business excursion.

"You're lookin' great," he remarked simply, pulling out of the parking spot.

She stared out the window again, trying to avoid looking at him, though she didn't know why. She was free. There was no more Romy to worry about.

Angela bit in her lip briefly before tasting her lipstick and rubbing her tongue over her teeth to free them from its taint.

"So, what, we meeting with the former owners or...?"

"Nah," he said to her. "Just their representative who should be waiting for us when we get there. He'll give us free reign to look around, make our decision. The sale's in the bag really, all it needs is our approval," he said smoothly.

Though, of course, what he really meant was *her* approval.

That it was something she wanted.

Her fingers traced along the door idly as she watched the world whip past before she finally tore her gaze away, meeting his.

"I just got dumped," she said simply. She never could keep secrets from him.

Perhaps it was the fact that he'd never treated her lesser for being her whole self. Not just the idealized version of herself.

Though Jamal was a stoic man who did not show surprise easily, the little twitch upon his face, the way his eyes widened in that tell-tale manner said it all.

"You should've dumped him. You're too good for that punk anyhow," he said in that dark husk of his. "I mean, other than a quick fuck what's he got to offer a real woman like you?" he asked, his arms moving upon the steering wheel.

"He's been avoiding me," she shrugged. No matter if what he said was true or not, it still damaged her pride to have been dumped.

"What a little shit," Jamal nearly growled the words out. He took a deeper offense to her dumping than her almost. "Could tell he was a little shit the moment I saw him," he said just before pulling up outside a club. What it lacked in class it made up for in size. It was a huge strip club, Angela had to give it that, though the sign was busted. Easy to estimate why, as big as that sign was with its giant lights, it must've cost a small fortune to repair.

She shook her head free of the thoughts of Romy. She had to get her head on business. Had to do it right.

She took in a deep breath as she waited for Jamal to open her door, then stood up straight and, hopefully, imposing. She was a short woman, but in her heels she was middling height, and her dark hair and intense eyes often gave her a serious air.

"We'd have to fix that," she said, stating the obvious. "Make sure that's accounted for in the price." Not that the price mattered. It wasn't his dollar.

Jamal escorted her to the front door, where a man in a business suit got out of a silver Mercedes while he spoke on a phone. He gave Jamal a nod in between authoritative "yeah's" but otherwise said little. He unlocked the front door and said to them at last, "take your time, I'll be waitin' out here." Then went back to his phone conversation.

Jamal placed his hand upon her lower back and guided her in. The place looked even bigger on the inside. Much larger than the club the two of them worked all those years ago.

With red carpeting and walls, it had the appearance of a real house of debauchery. Shiny metal poles and mirrors, a dark wood bar at one side. It was old, but in surprisingly good shape. The interior far exceeded the exterior.

Angela gazed around, feeling all of those old memories well up in her. When she'd stripped, she felt alive. It was a constant rush of emotions, and not all of them were good, but looking up at the 20 foot pole, she couldn't help but smile.

Stage shows were her life. Swinging around the pole, stripping for dozens or hundreds of eyes, manipulating the audience into wanting her. She could almost hear the beat of the music thrumming through her body and she had to force herself to see it as something more than just a way to relive her youthful indiscretions.

No, she was going to be the manager she'd always wished she'd had back when she was dancing. One that understood the realities of being a stripper and not just some skeezy guy who wanted to make money off of the dancer's hard work.

She walked away from Jamal, going towards the bar and inspecting the fridge, the washers, all of the little corners that she could see. It was clean, she had to give it that, though the carpets would need replacing. They were worn, and the shelves would be a bit cumbersome for any short bartenders to reach.

She walked into the champagne room area and instantly approved. The dark purple curtains were transparent, a little table in each with benches all about. They were in surprisingly good condition, as well, with cute little pillows.

Definitely workable.

Next was the lap dance sections, but they were less well kept, and needed to be reupholstered. It was an excellent start, though.

Jamal came out from behind her, having been inspecting the back rooms.

"There's change rooms back there, actual ones. Not just one big one either, there's a couple of individual ones for feature dancers I guess. Oh, and two offices even, in case you change your mind about ever wanting one of your own," he remarked, smiling down at her. "I don't know about you, babe, but… this place looks damn workable," he said, sounding genuinely excited for the whole venture.

"I don't want us just to have any girls. If we're gonna do this, we're gonna make a reputation as being the best — not just for clients, but for dancers too. If we can attract some big names, some real stars..." she trailed off.

She was excited.

It could work.

Jamal stepped up to her, and like old times he put his arm about her back, rested his hand upon her shoulder as he peered around the place. From the upstairs where they were, they could see down from the railing over the club below. The two mini-stages and poles, the main one, and all the tables and seating about.

"I can feel it too," he said to her in his low voice, so full of optimism. "This could be big. Real big. Not like any of them clubs we worked or saw before. Somethin' with a name that people know, far outside the city. It's got the layout, we just need to fill it and use it right."

"Didn't seem they were doin' that great before. I mean, not bad, but," she glanced around. "For a place like this I'd expect the lap dance couches to be immaculate, but they've been letting it go. We're going to have to do some retooling to get the right clients in here. Get the right clients, we'll get the right girls."

Jamal's large hand rubbed at her shoulder and he leaned into her, his hard pecs pressed to her arm as he spoke in a low, gravelly tone.

"Been speakin' with some folk who owe me favours. Seeing about gettin' some big spenders in here, make it their club of choice once I take over. I did a lot of good for 'em before I went away, least they can do is spend some of those fat wads of cash they made while I was gone on our club and girls."

It caused her to hesitate, but she slowly nodded, despite herself.

People that owed Jamal favours would be inviting trouble back into her life, and yet she had no other ideas. She couldn't convince the whales of the city simply to come to her strip club just because she wanted it.

"And what do we do if they get out of hand?"

"That'll be my area," he said to her with a hard edge. "I'll keep the club clean and safe. Keep the books balanced. I'll leave the girls and everything else to you. Anyone that gets in the way of business will be gotten rid of in turn."

He reached out to take hold of both her shoulders and bring her to face him entirely.

"We won't be pulled back into that life. And I'll defend us against it with force if it becomes necessary. I'm only gonna invite along those ones I trust to behave themselves. No hard cases, no thugs."

He had a serious look in his eye as he stared down at her, his thick strong arms holding her securely as he stressed his point.

He never broke his word.

She let her gaze fall between them, looking at his

tailored shirt, eyes tracing along the buttons as she slowly nodded.

"I know you get it. That I can't go back there. But I can't be a nobody eeking out the rest of my years in tedium. Trouble follows me, Jamal." It went unspoken that he had been the only one that had been able to protect her through it all.

He knew anyhow.

Which was why he pulled her into an embrace then, pressing her into his hard, muscular chest as he wrapped his arms about her and placed his hand alongside hers. That raw, masculine comfort so pleasing in the face of all that upset her.

"We'll stick it out," he said in a low husk. "Make a life for ourselves. Full and complete. We'll be players, determine our own course. But we'll not get sucked into that dangerous life."

He felt so warm around her, like cuddling into her favourite blanket. Familiar. Safe. And like armour, he made her impenetrable.

She let her face press into his chest, inhaling his scent as her arms hugged around his back, holding them together.

"We'll give it a try, but I'm out if anything happens."

Jamal pulled back and let his strong hands roam across her back up to her shoulders, then to her face. He cupped her two cheeks and leaned in to place a kiss upon her forehead.

"I'm gonna protect you from whatever might come," he said firmly, such determination. "All I've dreamt about these years is giving you a good life, security and love," he said, his dark eyes alight with conviction for what he said. "I'll be the man you need, Angie. The one I should've been all these years. I got a lotta time to make up for."

An excited chill went up her spine at his words.

He kept saying all the things she so desperately wanted to hear, and she couldn't hide how much it pleased her coming from him. Couldn't deny what he made her feel.

All that anger that had been built up over the last four years wasn't just being chipped away anymore, it was crumbling, a demolition of those walls she had built up.

"I don't wanna change you, babe," he said sincerely, "I worked hard to change me to be the man you need. All I ask is you give me that change, and I'll not disappoint you," he professed, and holding her face between his two hard, dark hands, he leaned in to press his lips against hers. It was an intense, passionate, spur of the moment thing. And even she could tell he hadn't planned it.

He'd tried to restrain himself, but just couldn't any longer. He was helpless against his desire for her.

Her mouth opened against him, and just like that, it was as if those four years hadn't happened. Her tongue brushing against his, fingers digging into his shoulders as she leaned into him, off her stilettos, hungry for his affection.

That attraction had never waned, she just did her best to push it to the side, to get over him.

Jamal let his hands dip down, releasing her face as they kissed. His tongue wound about hers as he delved into her mouth, and he moved his two hands along her sides, down to her waist and then coming to rest his palms upon her hips. He squeezed her there, pulled her in against him tighter as he gave a low, lusty groan that reverberated between them.

She'd done her best to move on and get over him, but he'd had years of nothing to do but pine over her. To think about the woman and the life he'd lost. No distractions, except self-improvement and the danger of prison. Just longing for her that bubbled over, and swelled the fabric of his dark jeans as their bodies pressed together.

She lifted her arms from his back, curling them instead around his neck, tugging herself close to him as she jumped up, legs wrapped around his hips. She knew he'd grab her, hold her there, and it was what she needed to do. What she desired to do.

Put her body in his hands, entrust herself to him once more, and let the broken pieces of her heart mend.

Jamal's strong upper body made holding her easier than it ever had been. He cradled her ass cheeks in his palms and held her up with relative ease. Their two pairs of lips smacked moistly as he moved to the wall and pinned her back to it.

"I missed you more than life itself," he growled between smacks of their lips, his insatiable hunger for her irrepressible as he found himself rocking his hips so that immense bulge of his all-too-familiar cock ground into her loins. The strength behind that sexual motion so much stronger than when last they'd made love.

She could still remember it. She'd gone over it in her mind so many times, trying to figure out what it was that she'd done wrong.

But since he'd come back, it had taken on a renewed replay, looked at through another lens. He hadn't been disinterested, he'd just been defeated.

Her hips rolled against him, her mouth hungry for his as her breathing quickened, her body wound so tight.

With her up against the wall his powerful hands moved across her body, up to her breasts, to feel that supple flesh, sink into her two supple mounds through her bra. He was intensely hungry for her, and she could feel without him saying that she was the first woman he'd had since his return. The first he'd had in many years. For a virile man like Jamal, who had kept her sated for many long years? That had to have been agony.

"I missed these thick tits of yours so bad, baby,"

he growled and she let out a whimper in return, arching her back into him.

He only relinquished his hold upon those large breasts to reach down, reluctantly moving to undo her jeans in his hungry need.

They were in the middle of a strip club, but it wasn't like that had stopped them before. They'd never let practicality stand in the way of their fucking, and she pulled back just slightly. Him working her jeans, her fingers working his button down shirt, polished nails pushing them through the buttons so quickly. Her hands then snuck beneath his blazer, feeling his built up heat.

She was breathing so hard and fast, so caught up in him, her mouth going to his so desperately.

As she raked her nails over that stony chest of his, felt his hot, bulging abs and pecs, he tugged open her jeans and began to pull them from around her sumptuous ass. She couldn't have picked a worse outfit to get out of on the spur of the moment, but there had been no planning involved. There never was with them.

He lowered her down from around his waist, and worked to get her jeans off as she popped his buttons open to reveal that mocha brown chest of his.

"I've never needed anyone or anythin' as bad as I need you right now," he groaned in desire, pawing and groping at her in his mad lust.

She kicked off her heels, headless of the worn carpets as she tugged her pants down the rest of the way, stepping out of the clingy material rather carelessly as her fingers went to the button on his jeans.

"So quit talkin' and help me," she said, her eyes flitting up to him so daringly. She needed him just as bad, even if it hadn't been so long for her.

She'd had other men, but they didn't compare to Jamal.

When they rid him of his jeans, she found his lewdly sized dick swelling through his boxer-briefs. Such a behemoth of a man, he'd certainly lost none of his size in the intervening years. If anything, she swore that bulge was bigger, and when she pulled his dick free of its confines, to see its immense, veiny shaft, throbbing so full of life, she felt she was either going mad or simply it'd been too damn long since she'd last been with him.

But as she found herself enraptured by that glorious manhood of his, he was groping at her ass, rolling his thumbs along the waistband of her panties then peeling the garment away as he tried so desperately to get at her femininity.

He unveiled that shaved pussy, already slick and rouged with her arousal, and she quickly stepped out of her panties as well.

She looked at him, almost in disbelief, as her fingers went to his member, wrapping around him so gingerly as she stroked back his foreskin.

"I'm on the pill," she said, as her feet went back into her heels, leaving her bare except for them and her top, and she turned to face the wall, legs spreading as she looked over her shoulder at him.

Jamal had always been a careful man. They'd partied and done wild things in their younger years, but he always made sure she was safe. Never going bareback with anyone but him. Always clean and protected.

The old him would've made sure she'd kept to that first before he did anything. At the very least. But four years apart wore away any worries. Or perhaps he simply committed himself to throwing all in with her regardless of any other possibilities.

He merely took hold of her hips and waist with one hand, then grasped his dick with the other.

The tip of his cock was a deep, dark purple, and gleamed with pre-cum. He pressed the bulbous crown up against her folds, and without any hesitation, any doubts, he speared it up into her, thick and raw.

He let loose such a deep, loud moan of pleasure as he felt those walls close in around his cock, and the mighty man was nearly felled by the incredible pleasure of her body.

She didn't hold back either, her ass pressing into his hips as she let out a loud growl, her entire body prickling with need and lust. Her flesh was so warm, her pussy so very wet.

"Jamal," she hissed, and even saying his name made her quiver and her pussy throb.

He grasped a hold of her hip tighter, but with the other hand now free, he reached up her top and pulled down the cup of her bra to manhandle that breast of hers. He squeezed its thick, supple flesh and began to pump his cock into her. Nothing else mattered anymore but the grind and thrust of their two bodies.

He was loud and unrestrained, filling the empty club with the sounds of his deep, husky moans as he began to pound against her ass, making those thick cheeks ripple with each thrust in. She could feel the incessant throb of his manhood. Again and again it stretched the walls of her cunny wider than they had been in years.

Her screams and cries grew as all that tension worked its way out of her shoulders, filled instead with such absolute lust and need.

He simply felt... right. Good. He was what she'd been seeking for so long, finally returned to her, and she nearly trembled with climax instantly. Instead, it built within her, growing more and more intense as her nipples stiffened, her cunny throbbed around his large, stiff member.

Jamal was unable to hold back as well as her, so many years without the comfort of a woman's flesh, he was bent over her form, pounding her cunt and then... he came hard. Though he was wild with lust, and he hammered his dick into her without interruption, spurting his seed deep inside her as he felt his balls tighten and disgorge their essence.

He never stopped, never missed a beat. Years of long, unresolved desire for her pushed him with a deep fanaticism and he plowed into her pussy with more vigor than a young man half his age.

"Oh God," she screamed, that pounding driving her wild as his hips smacked against her ass. He felt unreal, and all of their history, all of that buildup, sought to raise her up higher and higher.

For a moment, she thought that perhaps her orgasm was ebbing, disappearing from her, but then it struck out with all the power of a lightning bolt. It would have made her fall, helpless, to her knees if she wasn't being held up by his powerful grip, hammered into the wall.

Instead her legs trembled along with the rest of her, throwing her head back in a scream.

Yet her beloved Jamal refused to relent, he kept her there, his two strong hands grasping her tight, commanding her to stand still before him as he pummeled her. Even with the aid of her stilettos, he had to bend his knees to really hammer his manhood into her. The wet sounds of their loins slapping filling the air.

He bent over her back, panting and moaning into her ear as his dark, gravelly voice tickled her eardrums.

"I came out of that prison with an ache in my groin like you wouldn't believe," he growled, "but I knew no woman out there could sate it. Not as long as you were out there with this tight little cunt of yours, waiting for me to come back and fill it."

That dark whisper sent another electric shudder through her. Her fingers dug into the wall, and every part of her body felt so alive. Her throat warbled, rubbed raw from all of her moaning and panting, but she wouldn't succumb or pull away from him.

She wanted him. She wanted what they had before.

Jamal was bent on rekindling all they had before and then some, if she were to judge by the way he hammered her pussy. How he squeezed and groped at her thick, round tit with the enthusiasm of a boy who'd just got a hold of his first real one, and the expertise of a man who'd fondled and sampled many of the very best.

He groaned and roared loudly, jolting her whole body and pounding her to the wall tight and hard. His rock solid body was all about her, keeping her increasingly pinned to that wall as he pounded her.

"I wanna feel this lil' pussy of yours cum for me again," he growled, and she felt his hand move from her hip towards her mons. "I wanna remind it of all its fuckin' missed these years," he said before biting her ear and suckling her lobe into his mouth as his long finger reached down and began to circle her sensitive clit.

She was still spasming with the aftershocks of earlier, and that hand touching against the pulsing, pounding nub was almost too much. She was so slick and he was able to glide over it so readily, and her entire body shivered, harder and harder.

And then she couldn't hold back or resist any longer, her pussy throbbing and milking him as his cum squelched against her reddened labia. She twitched and jerked, her scream warbling.

Then remarkably he toppled into that blissful state with her for a second time. That thick, dark shaft spurting its seed yet again, filling her up as he let loose a bellowing moan of sheer pleasure. He was lost in rapture inside her, gone wild with his lust, his love for her.

Time lost all meaning, and they were sweating, panting messes, bent over against the wall, bodies intertwined. Jamal kissed at her neck with such fond devotion. No, lust hadn't betrayed them, neither had love. Each of those kisses was laced with his devotion.

She had no idea how she could pick herself up after something like that. It had been so intense, leaving her entire body a quivering mess. She wanted the freedom to just roll over and bask in the afterglow, to feel out his body and get reacquainted with the harder muscles, the beefier limbs, his gorgeous face.

Yet there was no part of her that regretted what they'd just done.

Jamal took that time after their tryst to feel out her body, to reacquaint himself with her as she wished to do with his. Those strong hands groping, squeezing, fondling her. And just as she felt him pull back and thought it was over, he pushed back in again, starting up a slower pace.

The moment, however, was broken by the man clearing his throat loudly. And though Angela couldn't see him, she could feel the awkwardness in his voice.

"I've been waiting over half an hour," he called out, his voice echoing through the club. "Not to rush you, but… I have other appointments to make."

"Fuck," she hissed, anger in her tone more than embarrassment. She wanted to stay there forever. Just her and Jamal, worshipping each other once more.

She couldn't move, pinned between him and the wall, and she took in a deep breath.

"Yeah," Jamal called out, his voice hoarse and gravelly as he reached down to cup at her cunny, "we'll be takin' it." He pulled his thick, long member from out of her, that sleek, glistening shaft leaving her so empty. Yet he considerately cupped her pussy, collected the thick drool of his seed on his palm instead of letting it splatter onto her jeans and panties below.

He pulled a kerchief out of his blazer pocket and used that to help tidy her if only a little.

"We'll be down in a minute," Jamal added, leaning in and kissing her lips lovingly.

She kissed him back, eyes fluttering open as she looked at him with such affection. She took the kerchief from him, and did her best to quickly tidy herself up before kicking off her heels and pulling up her panties and jeans.

It was so unexpected and inevitable at the same time, and she rolled her shoulders as she very nearly blushed at him.

After doing up his own pants and shirt again, he cupped her cheek with his clean palm, stroked his thumb over her smooth skin and smiled at her. So much fondness and love etched into that stony, stoic face of his in a way that was pure Jamal.

"Come on," he husked lowly. "We've got a club to buy for ourselves," excitement edging into his voice once more.

She looked up at him with so much love in her gaze she thought she might break. Instead she stepped into her shoes, fixing his shirt a little bit.

"I can't believe we're really doing this," she said softly, excitement warping her lips into a smile.

"It's just the beginnin', babe," he said to her, somehow looking even more cool and in control than ever since he got his rocks off in her. "C'mon, I wanna see your name on the dotted line," he stated with a wry smile just for her as he reached down and took hold of her hand.

Her fingers laced into his, her shoulder pressing into his bicep as she squeezed his palm excitedly.

Fear and excitement wound within her, but she trusted in the decision.

# CHAPTER 24

There it was; her signature right next to Jamal's on the contract. Co-owners. One hundred percent official.

Jamal handed her a copy as the broker left them to the club. It was theirs entirely, keys in hand and everything. Throughout that brief exchange, she felt her phone vibrate a few times, but she didn't want anyone or anything to ruin her special moment, and had shut off the phone without so much as seeing who it was calling and texting.

"She's ours now," Jamal said, looking around the big empty club with a smile, then back to her with an even bigger one.

Yet they both knew that it meant, more than anything, work. Somehow they had to push aside their lust, find time for it amidst their new business.

She took a step inwards, towards the pole. She

was tempted to try it out, but resisted, turning back to face him.

"Now to hire some contractors," she grinned.

His own full lips crooked up high into a grin in return, and he stepped in towards her, nice and close. He reached out, took her hands and squeezed them in his.

"Right to it," he said in a low voice. "Not even a night to celebrate?" he asked, head tilted just so, a singular brow raised as if in challenge to her. Daring her to do anything but cave in for the night. Let their tryst upstairs become something a little longer, deeper.

"The foundation is going to be the thing that sets us on track," she said, her eyes avoiding his. Everything in her screamed to just take him home, rediscover his gorgeous body, but she didn't want to already toss away her new responsibilities as if they were secondary.

He was disappointed. There was no denying that. It was plain to see.

He stepped in, put his arms around her, held her against him as he leaned down and kissed her dark hair.

"We'll call the contractors, schedule things," he said firmly, as if it were his idea and not hers, "but then you'll come with me. We just started a new life together. Right after finding one another again. There's nothin' I've ever experienced more worthy of celebration," he said in a low husk, holding her supple body in his arms tightly.

"I don't know how to celebrate this, Jamal," she said, looking up at him almost demurely.

She didn't know what she was worried about. Her love for him... it had never waned apparently, and with his return, it had flared up into a nova.

Perhaps she was simply afraid of losing herself in him again, allowing herself to trust him. He'd been her lover, yes, but he'd been so much more. He'd been the one that had taken care of her, made her decisions, saved her from her worries.

And then he'd left her, filled with uncertainty and how to handle life on her own.

Yet something in her called out for her to go back to exactly how things used to be, to let her worries go and just once more submit to him utterly.

He lifted a hand up to cup her cheek, stroke her fondly with his thumb as he smiled down at her. His other arm went around, cupping her round ass and kept her against him snugly.

"One night," he said to her with such authority, as if it was not a question but simply the reality. "We'll make our calls here and now, make appointments with contractors, go over the place one final time. And when we're done all that business? I am going to take you away from here, show you a great night. Take you back to my place, where you can forget everything. Forget the years we had apart. Forget all the bullshit you've had to deal with. And just let me take care of you. Just one night," he reiterated.

It was like a siren song and she was helpless to resist.

It was as though her entire body simply responded to his words, like a puppet on a string, and her head was nodding before she could control it.

She looked away, embarrassed at just how easily she found herself obeying, and tried to hide her growing smile.

"That's my girl," he said fondly, a broad, warm smile on his face for her as he stroked her cheek, gave it a tender pat and guided her towards the bar. He pulled out his phone as he went, "I know a guy who owns a company that should be able to do most of the renovations for a decent price."

# CHAPTER 25

Romy paced along the sidewalk outside of Angela's place. His calls had all gone unanswered, yet that didn't stop him from leaving another. His voice carrying out loud, as he hoped that maybe she was in fact home and could hear him.

"Don't ignore me!" he shouted to her voice mail. "I'm sorry for reacting quickly! Just talk to me and we'll work it out! Just fucking talk to me!" he said before ending the call in a rage.

He was normally so smooth and suave, and the fracture in his disposition was leaving him looking lost and frazzled. He paced back and forth, his normally sleek hair a bit messy from running his hand through it in stress.

Truth of the matter was, he was far more into the older woman than he'd let on. They'd met so randomly at that bar, had a whirlwind of a relationship, but she'd sunk her nails into his heart. The theft they'd pulled together was the clincher. He had thought he'd finally found a woman — a partner — he could rely on, trust in. They'd done this dangerous thing together, and pulled it off. What said more about a couple's bond than that?

Yet to see her pressed up in the corner with Jamal?

His hands clenched into fists with anger. Yet…

Even if it were just like he saw, and she had been kissing with that old thug… they'd never talked about exclusivity. He'd never told her he expected loyalty. They'd hooked up in a damn bar and had what seemed like it'd be a one-night stand. If things had gotten more serious, they should've talked about it. Revisited the nature of their relationship.

So he'd do that. But first he had to talk with her, and she'd not been in communication for hours.

He tried calling again, but as he did, he saw in the street lights the look of some other nasty sorts. Dressed in old, worn clothing, they loomed about. And while that itself wasn't out of the ordinary, the number of them was. They tried to space out, but he was noticing that they were far too attentive to be the usual types of vagrants and brutes.

They were a rival gang.

There came a roar down the street, motorcycles. Romy knew it had to be more of Vitaly's guys, those obnoxious bikers who he did so much business with.

He was relieved because there was just the one of them 'on duty' at the club nearby, and that wouldn't be enough to deal with the number of men that seemed arrayed against them.

Romy's relief faded, however, when he saw it was just the one bike. Vitaly, all by himself. Which was odd in and of itself, as he never saw the old mobster travel alone. Stranger still was when his bike pulled up to stop next to him, rather than the club.

Vitaly never paid Romy much mind except when it was time to do business. No patience for Romy's charm or personability.

"Hey man we gotta talk," Romy said, trying not to look suspicious, but wanting to get them both off the street then and there.

"I understand you have been screaming at the ladies place all day," came that hard, Russian accented voice of Vitaly's. The topic of his words threw Romy for a loop though.

"Yeah, so what man? She's my— never mind," he said, trying to refocus, his temper flaring up there for a second as he was reminded of his romantic woes.

"No, you never mind," Vitaly said, climbing off his bike, that towering man, so tall and lanky making a heavy thud with his footsteps upon the sidewalk. "I do not brook interference with her, you hear? I made a promise," he stated, resting one hand at his waist, thumb hooked into the belt hoop, nudging back his leather coat just enough that his handgun could be spied.

Romy was outraged, his mind running hot with anger at Vitaly daring to tell him what he could do about his own girlfriend. Though more pressing matters were at hand, as the thugs began to move in their worn, winter overcoats. Those big garments enough to hide some serious weaponry.

"Fuck man! Let's get inside!" Romy shouted angrily, the two of them looking ready to fight when Vitaly's man in front of the bar pulled out his gun.

"Get back!" he shouted, but a gunshot rang out, filling the streets. Vitaly's henchman went flying back, his chest exploding in a bloody mist.

Vitaly reacted instantly, and was ducked down behind his bike with his gun out before Romy could get over the shock.

Shots came at Vitaly, ricocheting off the asphalt around Romy, but he sprang out of the way, hiding in the nook of Angela's doorway. Neither of them had a great spot for avoiding the shots, but they bided their time. Seconds feeling like hours in that situation, their hearts pumping so hard.

Vitaly knew what he was doing though, and at that exact right moment, with but a fraction of a second to spare, he rose up and fired three shots with precision at one of the gunmen. All three struck home, and the man fell to the middle of the road dead.

That was all the opportunity he got, though, before the rest of them were reloaded and shots rang out again. Vitaly instead dashed behind a car nearby, and with little time to spare as Romy watched his motorcycle topple over from the bullet spray it had already taken.

While the shots came, Romy got himself together enough to look to the building door. It was locked, of course, but he tried pressing the buzzers. All of them, shouting frantically into the intercom.

"Let me in! I'm being shot at down here! Please help!" over and over, as the shootout behind him carried on.

Romy's tension mounted. He had no gun on him, instead relying upon the Russians for their protection when he worked their area. That was part of the understanding their two groups had. But bizarrely Vitaly hadn't had any more of his men around, just the one who now lay dead or dying against the bar.

Finally the electronic lock buzzed and someone let him through. Though as Romy pulled open the door, there was Vitaly barreling in past him, shoving them both inside the hallway.

The door slammed shut behind them and they ran behind another recess as Vitaly checked out what was coming. Their time was short, even Romy knew that. The door wouldn't stop hit men like them for long, they'd just blast it open.

"What do we do?" Romy shouted at Vitaly.

Fighting was not his skill he had to offer to Javier's operation.

"Is there a backdoor?" Vitaly asked roughly, then repeated himself with a shout when he didn't get an answer immediately.

"I think so!" Romy responded, and immediately Vitaly rose back up from his crouched position and they headed back through the apartment's halls.

Before they got far, however, a bullet fired through the window on the door and struck a wall in the hall. Vitaly ducked out of the way, then took a shot. He didn't hit, or so Romy assumed, because another retaliatory bullet went whizzing down the hall by them both.

"You can't kill 'em all!" Romy shouted at Vitaly, pressing his back against the wall as best he could as Vitaly calculated his next move.

"Shut up," Vitaly said simply, his aquiline face hard and focussed as he leaned out just enough to fire another shot.

The sounds of someone crying out in agony said to Romy it was at least a hit.

"Let's go," Vitaly said to Romy again, leading the way on down the hall, through the corridors.

"What if they rounded about to get us?" Romy asked, a bit of panic and worry in his voice. Though overall, he was doing a good job of holding it together, considering it was his first gun fight.

"Shut up," Vitaly growled at him again and they ran on towards that door to escape.

It was a fire escape, and the moment they opened it up an alarm blared in Romy's ears. It was so loud that he didn't even really hear the shot that rang out from the other side of the door.

The feel of Jamal's lips still lingered upon her, the whole night being something surreal. Her fantasies come to life. The thing she dreamed about in his absence despite not wanting to, but made real.

Jamal, sweeping in to rescue her from mundanity. From herself. From responsibility for her criminal actions. Making it all right, and making her feel so damn good.

It had been so perfect, that she had to take a breather. She'd turned down his offer of a ride, repeatedly. Not because she didn't want it, not because she didn't want that extra moment with him, just to take a moment to think.

That felt like a mistake in retrospect, as she listened to the calls Romy left on her voicemail.

Then saw the police tape along the sidewalk outside her building.

The concrete was still stained with blood. It managed to steal her mind away from those thoughts of Romy. His apologies, his upset voice, so hurt, but so desperate to make things good with her.

It had broken her heart to hear them on the way over. He wasn't a bad guy, just a bit young and impulsive, but her stomach felt caught in her throat as she looked over the scene before her. She'd never seen so much blood, and she could almost taste it on her tongue.

Her eyes immediately went to the bar down the street, knowing instinctively that there must have been something that started there.

Right outside its doors there was another big blood stain, perhaps the biggest of them all.

Panic set in immediately, and she whipped out her phone. Romy's number was called. It rang. Rang.

It went to voicemail.

She tried again.

The same.

Her eyes were filling up with tears when from down the road the roar of a motorcycle drew her attention, the familiar, reverberating noise drawing her gaze. Blinking away the misty eyed moisture, she could see the familiar silhouette of a man sat high upon the bike. Looking at her from down the road.

She found herself walking forward, towards the

figure without thinking about it. Hoping there were some answers, but as she got to him… she saw it wasn't Vitaly as she'd hoped. It was one of the big, brawny thugs who hovered around him.

Still, he plainly waited for her, resting one foot on the sidewalk.

She should have felt more afraid, with how quickly embroiled she was becoming in the mob's world. She should have felt more afraid, approaching a burly biker, who was waiting for her. Only her.

"What happened?" Angela managed, trying to act calm, strong. To hold back the panic, the fear in her voice.

"Hop on," he said to her simply, his voice gruff and low, so very brutish with that harsh accent. He revved up his engine, ready to take off at a moment's notice as he waited for her.

It wouldn't have been the stupidest thing she'd done, but it was pretty high up there on the possible winners.

"I don't even know your name," she sneered, unlocking her phone and sending a quick text to Jamal as she made the biker wait.

*"Something went down at my place. Looking into it. If you don't hear from me in an hour, call the cops 'bout the bikers near my place."*

There. That wouldn't freak him out at all.

"It's not me you want to talk to," he said in that

coarse accent of his, giving her but a brief, pointed look of exasperation. "I've been waitink here all mornink for you. Come and I will take you to him," he said impatiently.

She should have been more cautious, for certain. Though she recognized him as one of the regular thugs that accompanied Vitaly. Knew that Vitaly worked with Romy…

It all seemed to add up.

"I've just sent a text to a friend. If I go missing, there's no way either of you'll escape jail. Got it?" she asked sternly.

The big Russian man looked rather unimpressed by her statement, even as her phone vibrated with Jamal's response.

"Was very stupid of you to want to involve police at all. But it makes no matter. You hop on if you wish to see him. Or don't. And I ride away, and he is very annoyed with us both," he said, putting it all so simply in that gruff voice of his.

Angela rolled her eyes.

"God, I'm hopping on, obviously, but you only got an hour," she said, hopping up onto the back of the bike, phone still clutched in her hand.

When the motorcycle revved up again, she could feel it reverberate through her, the tremors so powerful as they carried through her body.

"You may wish to hold on better than that," he warned, but gave her no more time. Instead, he simply pulled away from the curb and away from the club.

It wasn't long however, before he stopped, and delivered her right behind another motorcycle. The figure this time far more familiar.

Vitaly looked back at her simply, revving his motor as he left space for her to hop on. The roar of the engine said that it wouldn't be a conversation with him just yet either.

All she wanted was some damned answers, and by the time she was seated behind Vitaly, her arm around his waist, her eyes were narrowed and her face was red.

Sorrow had been replaced with annoyance and anger, and there was nothing she could do about it but wait.

Vitaly's motorcycle pulled off and away, the roar of it was felt through her like she was riding a freight train. She felt like she might vibrate off if she didn't cling tightly to the man's hard torso.

He took her through the city, off down street after street, until he finally came to a park where he led her down a road to a quiet little nook that was hard to see, hidden by a copse of trees.

With that, the engine was cut off and he put the kickstand down. Silence reigning once more.

She wasn't in the mood for waiting, and she quickly went to her phone, sending another text to Jamal.

*"Still okay."*

She didn't have time to read through his numerous questions and concerns, safe to say, she knew he was troubled.

"So what is it?" she said to Vitaly, no longer in the mood for waiting. "What happened at my place?"

He climbed off his bike, his long legs lifting up over it before she too was pressed to climb off, her body feeling odd from all that vibration, leaving her limbs a bit like jelly.

Vitaly reached into his pocket and pulled out a cigarette, offering one to her in turn as he looked her over.

"Was a rival gang. Looking to move in on mine and the Cuban's turf," he said to her in that deep, gravelly voice of his, so edged with authority. "They tried to take as many of us out in that one hit as they could."

Angela felt her stomach go like lead, swallowing down cotton balls as she shook off his offer of a smoke.

"Where's Romy?"

Vitaly lit up his cigarette and then tugged open his jacket. She could see a handgun holstered beneath the leather as the towering man tugged his shirt out of his pants, showing his lean, rock-hard abs and then… a bandaged wound.

"You know that punk was outside your place screaming his head off at you for hours? I came over just to tell him to fuck off and leave you be," he said to her in a low voice, his accent not nearly as heavy as the other Russians she'd met. "That is why I took this wound."

"I was out," Angela explained, as if she had to. As if there was any requirement for her to have to justify not being at home.

"But that doesn't answer my question," she said, even as her eye twitched at the wound.

Vitaly tucked his shirt back into his jeans, looking her over curiously, his head tilted back, the dangerous man scrutinizing her intensely.

"I get shot doing this thing for you. But you worry about a man who shouts threats at you?" he said, finding some dry amusement in that, laughing out a cloud of grey smoke. "You are a strange lady."

"Well I *know* you're fine. All patched up, and tough as nails," she said, her face turning redder at his insults. "And all you were doing was helping my neighbours out so they didn't have to listen to him anymore. I can handle Romy."

"Very well," Vitaly said in that gruff, ominous voice of his. "You will have to handle him your own self then. Because I do not know where he is. I led him to safety in the gunfight, but when I was shot, he ran off on his own." With a shrug of his broad shoulders he looked her over. "It is my bet that they have him. Or he is dead."

Angela had no idea how to feel about that. It felt

like she'd been kicked in the chest, and she even staggered back. She'd never known someone who'd gotten in this deep before, and her eyes widened with fright and rage. Maybe it was just hearing the words aloud.

"Who was it?"

His eyes narrowed at her and he reached up, plucking the cigarette from his mouth as he stared at her, hard and serious. The moment dragged on long before he finally spoke, his voice gruff.

"I can help you find out. Work with me," he said.

Angela stared back at him, and even in her grief, she remained stoic as she wondered how far down the rabbit hole she was willing to go.

# CHAPTER 27

"What's your name again?" Angela asked, rubbing at her temple. After all that had happened, the last thing she wanted to deal with was the police. Between juggling mobsters, hiding her own ill-gotten gains, and the loss of someone special... she didn't know if she had it in her to bullshit the cops too.

"Detective Luke Crusher, ma'am," he said, standing there tall and built. His uniform did little to hide that fact. He had a squared off jaw and bright eyes. Looked too damn handsome for his position. "But we were talking about your friend," he said, shifting things back to the topic at hand.

"Yes, yes of course," she said, tiredly confessing to knowing the missing man. She couldn't decide if that was carelessness or just pragmatism.

"Can I come in?" the officer asked.

She didn't know what to say, but part of her just shuffled out of the way a little and before she knew it, the officer was in her dinky little apartment. And she knew she'd made a mistake. After all, wherever he went in her place, he wasn't that far away from her own stash of ten grand.

"So you two knew each other?" he asked her again.

"Yeah," Angela let out a sigh, tucking some of her dark hair behind her ear. The past week had been exhausting, and the last thing she wanted to do was talk about it with a cop.

"Did you want some water?" she offered, going into the kitchen and already grabbing her own glass as she looked over her shoulder at him. She'd been sucked into the vortex and there was no going back. Not after what had happened.

"Sure," he said to her, casually pacing about her living room, those eyes of his scanning the place. Such a cop, she thought. Studying her, the place. Everything.

She kind of regretted the baggy sweater and jeans she was wearing, though at least she'd put on some mascara.

"Were you two close?" he asked as she poured up the water.

She thought back to the phone calls, the last words he'd said to her, and gave a slight nod as she offered him his water.

"Thanks ma'am," he said with a smile.

"I guess that depends on your definition of close," she said, and it did. What they had...

She sipped her water.

"Though I don't think I'll be of any help to you. I don't know what happened," she added on.

"So you know about what happened to him?" he asked, his circling motions coming to a close as he studied her place, his blue eyes upon her again as he awaited that answer.

Angela shook her head.

"I've not been getting any answers. I think the only reason I knew anything at all is because it happened in the lobby of my building."

"I see," he said, looking patient as he thought over her words. "So you weren't here at the time it happened, I take it?" he asked, sounding ever so patient and calm as he went over the whole thing with her. He helped calm her nerves at least, that much she had to admit.

But she knew that was dangerous, too. One misstep with him and there was no going back.

"No," she said, her eyes falling down. "Half of me thanks God I wasn't, the other half thinks, if I was, maybe..." she trailed off.

"I doubt there was much you or anyone other than an armed party of officers could've done," he said compassionately. Actually sounding like he wanted to reassure her. "Are you aware of any...

criminal connections he may have had?" the officer asked, not content to solely console her however.

Her brow furrowed and she hoped her confusion looked authentic.

"He must have just been in the wrong place at the wrong time," she said earnestly. "It's... not the best part of the city." She looked around at her sad apartment, her meagre existence, as if to prove her point to him. "Bad stuff happens around here all the time."

The officer didn't look convinced by her statement, however. Had she oversold it?

"Not like this it doesn't," he said to her, tapping his stylus against the touch screen pad he held. "Even for the criminal element in this city... this is a big deal, ma'am," he said to her, looking a little more stern now. "Which is why we're looking into this so seriously. The building's security camera showed him — and sometimes you and him — entering the building to go to your apartment. Now, I know you might be concerned about saying something to get yourself in trouble but... I'm really just concerned with finding out who would shoot up a neighbourhood in this city."

He made his case so well, his smooth, deep voice so convincing. He just wanted to help.

Angela sipped her water, doing her best to hold back her tears. She'd spilled so many, already, and was exhausted over it. She sat down on her ratty couch and let out a long sigh.

Detective Luke Crusher moved over, sitting himself down on her couch beside her, placing his glass of water on the coffee table. All the equipment dangling from his belt making it seem so awkward for him.

"This isn't the sort of city where we see gunfights in the streets, ma'am. And certainly not the kind of city where we see murder en masse, right out in the open. Your friend was a victim of that attack, and even if he was involved in something criminal… either way, anything you can tell us would help us track down the perpetrators."

Angela looked up at the officer, her emerald eyes glittering with her unshed tears, her face looking more mature than her 30 years, her lips drawn into a tight line as she considered the detective.

# PART III
# PATH TO RUIN

# CHAPTER 28

The club was only recently opened, but still the place was packed. The handful of dancers they'd taken on were kept busy, and the money was big for them. Yet that left Jamal and Svetlana rather swamped.

Jamal did not expect so much business so fast, and he certainly didn't plan to be facing off against it with so few staff. His connections had sent more patrons to his new strip club than he'd reckoned.

But Angela was nowhere to be seen.

Again.

Jamal was a big man, with a commanding presence, and that alone helped him keep some semblance of order in the large, crowded club. He was behind the bar, adjusting the cash in the register when a loud cry broke out.

A man, clearly drunk, stood up from his bar

stool, angry and full of venom for the beautiful dancer that had been at his side, but was now cautiously several feet away from him.

"Did you steal my fuckin' money?!" the balding old fella shouted, glaring at her angrily. Though her gaze travelled to Jamal's.

Petty little fucks like this guy made Jamal loathe humanity. Though thankfully they were usually easy to handle.

Jamal slammed the cash register shut, and only turned half-way towards them when the older man looked his way.

It took but a drunken moment for the man to soak in the scope of Jamal's mighty form. Suddenly, all that scorn and condemnation for the woman wilted. The little man, ready to play the part of a tyrant with the dancer, instead backed away.

"I'm goin' somewhere else," he said irritably.

Jamal strode down the length of the bar, still glaring at the man as he backed away to the exit. His words were intended for the dancer.

"He pay all you were owed?" he asked simply, that voice of his gruff and hard. Jamal was ready to leap over that bar and drag the man back if need be.

"Yeah, he did," she responded, sounding a little shaken as she adjusted her lingerie. "Was pissed 'cause he didn't have no more cash for drinks," she stated, a wry look upon her pouty lips.

The red outfit fit her nice, showing off her

tanned skin. She was a cute dancer with light lipstick and eyelash extensions, and she, just like the rest of Jamal's girls, hadn't caused him trouble yet. The patrons, well, that could be another story.

"Thanks, Jamal," she said before palming him over a share of her tips. "He was scary."

Jamal gave but a simple nod before he turned his attention back to work. He made his way out from behind the bar, leaving things there to the bartender. He'd been banking on Angela's assistance, but she'd been flaky and preoccupied as of late.

Svetlana should have gone home already, but Jamal knew the little Russian woman would be working still. Helping pick up the slack.

He rounded the back halls through the employee's only area. He could hear the sound of feminine voices chatting, and he found little Svetlana helping preen and push some dancers into getting ready, keeping them on schedule.

He'd been surprised. She was a devoted worker and, despite being Javier's kept girl, she didn't give him any sass or attitude. Didn't try to throw it in his face at all.

It was a relief, honestly. At least he had someone he could rely upon.

"Mr. Khalil," Svetlana said, pushing some of her own blonde hair out of her blue eyes. She could've been a dancer with those wicked curves and that sweet smile, and he knew she had to have been able to handle herself, dealing with Javier.

"Jamal is fine, Lana," he reminded her in that deep, smooth voice of his that did so much to calm and seduce women. "And you are supposed to be gone already," he reminded her, a patronly tone to his voice as he arched a brow and looked down at her. Those thick forearms crossed over his chest.

He was an imposing man, but he never so much as raised his voice at one of the employees since the club opened.

"Yes, vell, you are short staffed, no?" she said, more than asked, in her accented voice. Seeing he wouldn't accept that as an answer, though, she added on, "And it makes my job easier in zee day vhen things go smoothly at night."

"Yes, but now it is officially and severely night, and if you're going to open up in the morning, you need to be rested," he explained to her in that calm, assertive voice of his. "Head on home, get some rest," he told her. "We'll handle things here, and then you can pick up the pieces come opening."

His tone was smooth and gentle, but his face said he was serious and it was an order.

She let out a small sigh but gave a nod of her head. She was obedient, there was that, and she reached around her waist, untying her pink, fuzzy sweater from around it and instead tugging her arms through the sleeves.

"Okay, Mr. Khalil, but if you need me, please call."

"Don't worry, just get some rest," he said, unfurling his arms and reaching out to pat the petite woman upon the shoulder as he passed her by.

Truth was, though, he could definitely use her help.

*Where's Angela?*

# CHAPTER 29

The bang of the handgun firing even managed to get through her noise-cancelling headset, or perhaps that was just the reverberations of it coursing through Angela's limbs and body. Either way, looking down the barrel of that gun… left her feeling powerful.

But then, each step of Vitaly's training had that effect.

The tall man plucked her headset from her one ear as he stood directly behind her.

He had been training her with guns for close to a week. From the beginning, when he had to cup her hands and entangle his body about hers, to now, when he just stood behind her and watched.

"Well done, you are doing very good," he said approvingly in that deep, gravelly voice of his. She'd graduated from the firing range some time ago, and Vitaly had taken her outside the city for some practice on moving targets in the countryside.

"But do not get too cocky," he caution, his strong, calloused hands turning her slowly about to face him, as the sounds of nature eked back into the environment around her after being scared into silence by her gunshots.

"Your new self-defence moves will likely serve you better than this. If you find yourself resorting to a gun, you know things have become most fucked up," he stated in that voice just lightly tinged by a Russian accent.

The woman stared up at him, her emerald eyes taking him in as she gave a nod. Her dark hair was pulled back in a ponytail, and she was wearing simple pants and a fitted sweater. It was much more casual than her usual attire, but then, what else could she wear out in the middle of the country?

The sound of her firing the gun didn't startle her as it had in the past. A week ago, when news that Romy had been shot first reached her, she'd spent days agonizing over it. Every time she pulled the trigger, she pictured Romy there, in a pool of blood.

But that was what this was all about, wasn't it? Preventing something like that from happening again.

She'd changed, and looking over her tutor, so had Vitaly.

When she'd first run across him in that dive of a bar, he was lanky, haggard, pale. He looked like death, to put it frankly. Yet in the short time she'd known him, she'd watched him go from that deathly-sick look, up through several wardrobe changes, into a filled-out, muscular man. A hunk even.

His hair was grown out, but it was thick, rich, and styled nicely. He had a lustrous head of thick, silvery hair, and yet he didn't look old. Not any longer, anyways. He looked as fit and healthy as some young stud at the gym. She got to appreciate that more fully during their hand-to-hand training.

She realized they'd been so focussed on her training, she'd learned almost nothing about him personally.

"It won't be easy infiltrating their gang," he said to her, but when he looked her over he gave an approving nod. Just a hint of something more in his aqua eyes. "You can do it, however. No doubt about that."

She had her doubts in the past, but not any longer. She felt ready.

Yet there was one thing holding her back from all of it.

Jamal.

He'd come back into her life after spending four years in prison, offered her a job as the manager of his strip club. When he'd told her that, she thought it would be enough. A thin enough line for her to walk, with him keeping her in line.

But then she came home to find there had been a shootout in her apartment building, and another of her former lover's had been a victim of a rival shooting. So her perspective... shifted. With Vitaly's help.

She wasn't sure if it was revenge driving her, or just that it was her calling to misbehave, but whatever it was, she was motivated.

She put the safety back on the gun, tucking it away as she looked at him, arms crossed beneath her generous breasts. Even in her outdoors clothing, thirty years old, she looked good.

They were both banking on the fact that the rival gang would think so too.

Though she had to admit she was curious about his reasons. He hadn't even liked Romy, and she got the impression he didn't care for his business partners either.

"When do we move?" she asked in her honeyed voice.

Vitaly stepped back, a wry grin upon his face. The towering man clearly got a great deal of satisfaction from her enthusiasm for the mission. He pulled his headset off and gave it a toss into their equipment box.

He pulled off his sharp leather jacket, revealing beneath the tight maroon short-sleeve that was stretched taut about his broad upper body. It left little to the imagination, accentuating his bulging pecs and hard abs.

"Right away," he said. "You can make your move to get into their club starting tonight. But you can't be over anxious," he said as he reached into the supplies and pulled out a water bottle and drank. "Hurry and you will be obvious."

Angela rolled her eyes.

"When have I ever seemed over-anxious to you?" she asked, though she could clearly recall more than a couple of occasions where she had been eager to get on with it, and didn't want to give him time to remind her.

"So what's in this for you, huh?" she instead said.

Vitaly was a strange one. Came off as a pure thug, some Russian Mafioso out to rip what he wanted from the world. Yet in his training with her, he'd displayed a wide array of knowledge on self-defence techniques and a military style precision.

"For me?" he said, looking back to her, his eyes glittering in the sun. "I get to spend time with a gorgeous woman. And together we will take out the man who tried to have me killed. Why would I not enjoy this?" he said, holding out his arms in a helpless shrug.

"And that's it?" she asked, an arched brow raised.

She was risking a lot for him. For their mission.

Lying to the cops, infiltrating a gang... She'd done four years in prison for running drugs, but never had she been in so deep.

"What more could there be?" he asked, looking her over as he stepped back up to her closely. He loomed over her, so much taller than she was. "Do you suspect me of something?" he asked, that hard wall of muscular chest before her.

She should have been intimidated by him.

She knew he was into something deep, and keeping her in the dark about it. Someone didn't just order a hit for something small. Not when it was so public.

He'd lived through more than one bullet wound, was hard, huge, and strong. He knew all her tricks now, too. Taught her everything about self defense, pressure points, weak spots.

But she wasn't afraid of the towering Russian.

"Could be some profit in it for you to shut down a rival gang."

"Obviously," he said so casually, looking her up and down. "But more importantly it gives me pleasure to see you come to my side. If only for a bit," he raised up one hand and gingerly brushed back a stray hair that had gotten loose of her pony tail. "Why are you so committed to this? The boy was a mongrel," he stated so flippantly. "He did not treat you as well as you deserved. Did not give you the freedom a lady of such exquisiteness needs."

There was a way he spoke about her that made a chill go up her spine. When she first met him, it creeped her out. After their time together, and how he'd changed, not so much.

She had to admit it was a good question, and one she'd been afraid to answer.

Afraid, because she knew that any answer she felt in her heart to be true would only have said things she wasn't ready to confront about herself.

How could she admit that she was drawn to the rush? To the thrill?

It didn't even make sense to her, those strange, muddled reasons that swam in her mind.

"Because it's the right thing to do."

"So guilt then," he said to her casually, slowly pacing about her, his heavy footballs loud even upon the dirt and grass. "I'll take it," he remarked before making his way over and sitting down upon a large rock next to their supplies. He reached in and pulled out a couple sandwiches, offering one to her.

"When I first saw you," he said, "I thought to myself: there goes a dethroned Queen. Knocked from her high horse, but still a queen."

She joined him, accepting the sandwich as she looked at him warily.

"Dethroned queen," she muttered under her breath. "No, I've never been a queen. Just a spoiled princess who thought she was."

He eyed her from the corner of his view as he

peeled away the wrapping from his sandwich and bit into it. He took his time with it, his packed with meat and stacked almost absurdly thick.

"Missed your due coronation then," he amended his remark. "Either way, I saw a woman of some prominence, just waiting for circumstances to help her thrust herself back up."

She tore a bit of her own sandwich off, not failing to notice that hers was much less stacked and looking a little anorexic against his, before putting it into her mouth thoughtfully.

She shook her head.

"I was just a dumb kid, mixed up in things I didn't understand. Once I got out, all I knew was I didn't wanna go back there. But living a straight life is just a different type of prison."

Vitaly listened attentively as he leaned forward onto his knees, his legs splayed open as he looked out across the rolling grassy fields, away from the forests behind them.

"The rules of society keep us chained. They are not meant to benefit us, but to bind us by the rules of those with power. To keep them where they are, and us where we are," he said with certainty. "They do not want you or I rising up, attaining wealth and influence. Because that would take from them, if only relatively speaking. So they make laws, say you cannot sell drugs. But only certain kinds of drugs.

Others you can sell, some much worse, like alcohol. But you must pay them their fee. Fund their own hitmen, the police. Keep power in their hands. Out of ours."

He laughed dryly and looked to her.

"It is but another feudal system. Nobles playing at games, administering their fiefs," he said derisively.

She listened to him, quietly agreeing as she ate.

He looked like a dumb thug on the outside, but she knew he was more than that. Better than that.

It worked to his advantage. Keen minds stay alive.

"Yea, well," she said as she polished off her sandwich and leaned back, dusting off her hands. "It's their world, but they're just as hemmed in by their rules as we are. You think they woulda got the shooter? With all their police and all their do-good attitudes? There'd be money in their hands and it'd be the low level guy that takes the time."

Vitaly looked back at her again and shook his head as if she didn't get it.

"They do not care so much that we on the outside kill each other. They do here, but only because it interferes with their control. They said: no killing, at all. Unless we do it. But someone broke that rule, and for it they would punish them. But because it was nobody important, they are none too worried."

"Were it someone important to them?" he said,

arching a brow at her curiously for a moment. "Someone like a lawmaker, a rich business man… they would have the shooter by now. One way or another."

Angela looked at him, her keen eyes narrowed a bit before they flicked away.

"Whatever. We'll make it right," she said dismissively. Truth was, she wanted to hear him keep talking, but it made her nervous. The way it flamed a fire within her heart, making her want to rise up and take action.

It made her excited, and that was just what she couldn't afford to be.

"So, what, was that bullet your wake-up call to get clean?" she said, turning back to him, eyes roaming over his filled out chest and face.

Vitaly looked to her sharply, as if she'd just said something she shouldn't have known. Yet that made no sense.

"What bullet?" he asked, scrutinizing her hard with those blue-green eyes of his. "What are you on about, woman?"

She stared at him like he was suddenly speaking Russian.

"…You were shot. We're getting revenge for it."

He looked confused for a moment, as if he had forgotten being shot, then realization dawned.

"I am no junky. Never was," he said firmly, giving

her a pointed look. Yet she was no fool either, and when she spoke of him getting shot, it wasn't this recent time he was thinking of. There had to be another.

"So what happened the first time you got shot?"

He gave her a hard look, seeming almost irritated for a moment that she'd deduced something.

"Been shot several times," he said plainly, finishing off his sandwich then downing some more water. "First time was in Chechnya," he said, and suddenly a lot of things made sense. He'd been Russian military, fought in an actual war.

She watched him evenly, not fazed by his annoyance in her.

"And is that the time you didn't want me to know about?" she pried further.

He gave her another sharp look, but this time he laughed and shook his head.

"No," he said firmly, wiping his mouth and brushing his jeans down, though there were no crumbs to begin with. "But suffice it to say, it took me a while to recover from the last time. You saw me when I was first released from hospital."

With that, Vitaly leaned in closer to her, the large man's scent masculine but clean, his gaze so piercing.

"If you wish to know more, you must purchase the knowledge with a kiss," he said, crooking an uneven grin as he touched two fingers to his lips then blew her a kiss so nonchalantly.

She stared at him, her eyes dark and stormy as she slowly grinned.

"Oh, is that how you're going to play this game, Vitaly?" she said, taunting him. "Because I'm sure I can figure it out all on my own. Not used to working for someone else, having to take shit deals from guys like Romy who keep you waiting. Clearly more skills than you need to work out of a dinky bar. They'd have guys beneath you doing that level of run-around. My guess is the last fall from grace was a lot further than this one."

He gave her a dry chuckle, but she saw in his stoic face no signs of denial. No signs of her being wrong either. But a slight glint of admiration lit his eyes.

"Takes a fallen monarch to notice such things, hmm? What is the expression? 'Takes one to know one'?" He grinned at her, the moment of appreciation shared as the large, hulking man bent forward, his biceps bulging, his forearms thick and criss-crossed with rigid veins.

She looked at him, and she couldn't deny there was attraction there. Interest shared along with appreciation.

But she couldn't let herself get emotionally attached. Not so close to something so important.

"Same guy?" she asked softly.

The question somehow seemed to turn out more complicated than she thought it. Because Vitaly took some time to think about it, taking a deep inhale of breath, his broad chest swelling before he finally gave a sigh.

"We shall find out," he said.

# CHAPTER 30

Angela stopped off at the Tropicala, not because she was in the mood to party, by no means. Amid all her other waiting messages on her phone was a text from Abel, Romy's friend and their accomplice. He'd helped pull off that job she'd done, and she knew Abel and Romy were close.

The club itself was filled with the upbeat rhythm of the hip new Cuban beats, and even though it was early for the night crowd, the club was open and not exactly dead.

Climbing the stairs to the back area where Romy's crowd hung out, she noticed that their faces were still more than a little less excited and jovial than usual. It was comforting in a way to know that she wasn't the only one affected by Romy's disappearance.

Abel came from a supply room around back,

holding a box. The tall, lanky man looking surprised to see her. He went to her immediately after putting down the box at the bar for Daryl, coming to her.

"Hey, you came!" he said, sounding excited — or more likely surprised — even though he spoke quietly for how loud the music was.

She looked him over before giving a nod.

"Of course I did," she said, not bothering to force a smile.

It felt like it was ages ago she'd first set foot in the Tropicala in her skimpy dress and high heels and teasing laugh, making out with Romy on the dance floor as if nothing else mattered.

Now she felt a lot darker, and her jeans and blouse were more business than flirty.

"Over here," he said, the tall fellow a little mousy despite his size. It was easy to see why Romy had been the one to take the lead with him. Abel did not affect the disposition of a leader. But all the same, he brought her off into an employee's area in the back, a quiet room full of bottles and boxes of liquor and wines. He even waited for her to enter in before he shut the door behind them.

Things had to be pretty serious, yet she didn't have a bad feeling about him.

She instead stood calmly, looking at him with an even expression.

"What's up?" she asked casually.

Abel ran a hand back over his hair, looking rather stressed out.

"Have you heard anything about Romy?" he asked first, and with his shoulders slumped, his posture slumped, he nearly had to look up to her. His eyes were glassy and worried, and it was plain to see the young man was strained with anxiety.

Her shoulders slumped a little. Part of it was compassion, but it was also marred with disappointment. She had been hoping that there'd been word, and she shook her head a bit more gently as her gaze softened.

"No. I was hoping you had."

Abel's expression fell, and it was easy to see he had been hoping for something from her. Anything. Any little tidbit.

"I'm troubled," he said, running his hand back through his hair again, tugging it a little, an obvious betrayal of his anxiety. "The boss ain't been doing much to find him, or to have… whoever did this to 'im paid back."

Abel was stressed, Angela could've found a hundred little signs in him to show that. But the suspicion seemed to run even deeper.

What type of boss — what type of family — wouldn't be looking for one that put a hit out on their own people?

Angela'd already had some suspicions that Romy's so-called brother, Javier, hadn't been doing much to help but Abel's words made her rethink just what that meant.

Her voice lowered in kind, though she didn't figure anyone could have heard. Still, the fact that they were talking shit about Javier in his own club was asking for trouble.

"What've you seen?" she asked.

"That's the thing," Abel said, his voice quiet but strained by worry, "the Boss has been keeping everyone busy. Busier than ever. He let Frank and Daryl go look into what happened to Romy at first, but quickly put 'em to work elsewhere." He was wringing his hands, and Angela could tell the man was wearing dirty, unwashed clothes. "I asked Javier about it, and he said the wheels are in motion."

How he said that indicated to Angela that Abel thought that meant anything but.

She nodded as she exhaled, straightening her spine.

"But we just did a good job. Why wouldn't he want Romy back?" she asked. That was the one thing that really got her. When she was with Romy, Javier had even let him borrow his ride, seemed to approve. They'd been like brothers, as Romy told it.

That only said one thing to her. The person who called the shot? He must've been far more powerful than Javier.

"I don't get it, don't none of it make a lick of sense to me," Abel said, his hand still lingering in his hair, tugging at the follicles. "I mean… Romy could get on Javier's nerves now and then, but they was like family. And Romy was on the fast track to bein' the Bosses right hand man."

"Have you told anyone else you're worried about this?" she asked, her green eyes intense as she watched him.

"No, I mean, not exactly," he said, swallowing, sounding frustrated with himself, the situation. He felt powerless, she could tell that from him. "I spoke to Frank and Daryl about trying to find out what happened to Romy, and they was both really gung-ho about it at first, y'know?" he said, looking up to her with wide eyes. "But then the boss kept givin' 'em new work to do, and before I knew it… they was callin' it quits."

She exhaled, reaching out and placing a hand on his shoulder, squeezing him reassuringly.

"Listen. We're going to keep hope alive, alright? He's out there. I'm sure of it," she lied. "Keep it between you and I, don't draw attention to yourself. We'll figure it out."

Abel perked up a little at that, and she could tell by the hopeful look in his gaze that he'd not gotten much in the way of any comfort for his missing friend in the past week.

"Alright. What should we do though? I don't wanna just sit on my ass if he or the son of a bitch who did him in is out there," he said, swallowing anxiously, trying not to think of the possibility Romy was gone for good.

"The first thing you gotta do is calm down, okay?" She nodded up towards his hair. "Stop pullin' on your locks. Stop looking so nervous. Believe the boss has it under control, and look relieved next time you talk about it. And then you listen, and you tell me everything you hear, and we'll make sense of it."

Abel took a deep breath, and slowly she watched the man seemingly inflate before her eyes again. Her control of the situation, her calm, just radiating out through his limbs.

"Okay," he said. "I'll report everythin' I find out. And what about you?" he asked, looking to her.

She realized he just wanted more of her reassurance.

"I'll be okay," she said with a smile, though there was no way she was going to be giving away just how she was going to help.

"I have some leads I'm looking into. Just... trust me."

Luckily that was enough for Abel, the young man just needed a leader who'd act. This time, that meant Angela.

# CHAPTER 31

Angela slipped the black thong up over her tanned thighs, letting the lace delve between her soft ass, over her hips.

Her push up bra in place, it made her breasts look larger, the clean skin smelling a little like French vanilla ice-cream. She looked over at the slutty black dress she'd picked out and shimmied into it, looking herself over in the mirror.

Her hair and makeup was already done, her eyes smoky and her lips a bright pink that was slightly too young for her. Her hair was straightened and down past her shoulder blades, the dark tresses teasing her bare throat.

Vitaly knocked on her door, drawing her back to reality and out of her perpetual planning. His rich, gravelly voice breaking the silence.

"Are you ready?" he asked, having been waiting

for her in the living room. His towering presence somehow seeming so out of place in her home. He stood larger than life in many ways, like a man out of time and place.

"Just about," she said, casting him a glance back to the mirror. "How'd you track these guys down anyhow?" she asked as she put in her silver hoop earrings, smacking her lips as she went over to the foot of her bed and grabbed her shoes.

"There's only a few other gangs I figure have the balls to do something like that to me around here," he said casually, watching her through the crack of her door casually, her back turned as she stepped into the platform shoes.

"I got a good look at some of them. Knew they weren't Cubans. Only one other outfit around here has that kind of muscle to spare. Had my men look into a few things for me this past week. And so they tracked down the bosses club, where he hangs out most often."

Angela still wasn't close to his height, even in the heels, but she felt invincible, like she was wearing armour, in that outfit. Even if she had to crane her head to peer into his eyes up close as she stood before him.

"How will I find him?"

Vitaly made no effort to hide how he looked her over, appreciating the shape of her body in that scandalous outfit. There was no hiding how much he enjoyed her in those clothes, even if he tried.

"You are asking me?" he said, giving an exaggerated shrug as he stood there before her in a sleek black jacket over a curious shirt that hung loose about the neck. It looked European in style, she thought.

"I would think you are a professional at finding the most powerful man in a room."

Her lips quirked a bit at the compliment as she took her small clutch-purse.

"Some help you are," she teased as she pushed past him into the living room, grabbing her phone and tossing it in her bag.

"I'll find him," she promised.

"Wait," he said, coming up to her as he reached behind himself. He pulled a small, compact gun out. "Here, this one is small, light, will probably go unnoticed. And even fit in your little purse," he stated. "But more important than that, give me your phone," he offered the gun over to her, his other hand waiting expectantly for the phone.

She looked at the gun with a feeling of dread in her belly before her emerald eyes went to his aqua gaze.

"Why do you need my phone?" she asked as she handed it over. She'd upgraded, spent a bit of her criminal spoils on something that wasn't out of the last decade.

Vitaly worked her phone, searching something.

"Downloading something," he said. It took him but a few moments and then he flipped the phone around, to show her what he'd installed.

"Should you get into trouble, the gun is an absolute last resort. Your first defense is this," he stated, showing three buttons that were marked innocuously as 'Dismiss,' 'Sleep' and 'Shut Down'. "Every ten minutes you will get a message from this program. Hit dismiss if you are okay. Sleep if you need me. If anything comes up before then, hit 'Shut Down'. I will be there to haul your ass out ASAP."

He explained it all so clearly and patiently, but the look on his face was deadly serious.

She knew better than to believe it'd be suspicious of a young woman checking her phone every ten minutes, but it still made her feel somewhat uncomfortable. Still, she tucked both the phone and the gun into her purse with a growing sense of dread.

It wasn't as though she didn't understand the risks. He had spent the last week teaching her how to fight and shoot for a reason. She didn't even know why she expected him to send her in without a gun in hand.

It just made it seem so much more real.

"Thanks," she said taking in a deep breath to steady her nerves.

He smiled to her approvingly and touched his

large hand to her shoulder, giving a reassuring squeeze.

"Just find the man in charge. Get his name, get invited back with him some place private. Preferably a hotel room. Then send me the alert. I will wring the information out of him from there," he said firmly, guiding her out the door.

Her stomach was in knots as she waited for the cab, and all throughout the drive. Her hands in her lap, touching along her purse nervously.

She was an ex-felon with a gun on her. Even though her prior was drugs, she knew the cost of someone finding the piece in her purse. She knew she had to still her nerves, but she felt like she was going to throw up.

Especially as she looked up over the seedy club, its neon lights flashing.

*Girls, Girls, Girls.*

She handed the driver a twenty and slipped out, feeling so tiny in her slutty dress, her too-high heels.

But the second the guard at the door gave her the once-over, she immediately felt more in control.

Dealing with attraction, with men, that was something she had an intimate understanding of. There was nothing she was more at home with, and so as the bouncer inspected her, she knew she was safely in her element.

"You lookin' for work, doll?" the big guy asked,

though despite his gruff voice, Angela couldn't help but notice the tinge of interest to those words.

Thank God for push-up bras and good genes.

"Yuh-huh!" she said in a bubbly way, her eyes glancing inside, then back at him. "I was told to, like, come and audition or something?" she said, adopting a persona younger than herself, her flirty smile not leaving her full lips.

One of her fingers trailed down her chest, the vibrant pink nails nearly glowing.

The man's eyes followed her fingers, just as intended, and he swallowed.

"Normally we do auditions in the afternoon," he said as they stood there in the dark evening air. "Come on in," he said, and stepped out of her way. "Tell the lady over there at the coat check that you wanna speak to Ernest," he told her, shamelessly giving her another once over.

Though he didn't stop there, he leaned in and murmured to her privately.

"And if you want a hit of somethin' before the nights over, just come back and see me. You and me could party afterward," he said, smiling at her unevenly.

Angela smiled so wide, as if she couldn't imagine being more flattered than being hit on by a twenty-something year old bouncer.

Hell, part of that wasn't even fake. But the best

lies always have a kernel of truth, and she touched her hand to his chest lightly as she nodded.

"Thank you," she murmured back. "Wish me luck!"

"Good luck," he said diligently, staring at her ass as she walked on into the club. He was slow to get back to his work, and it was exactly the kind of confrontation she needed to get herself off on the right footing.

The lady at the coat check took her request and picked up the grimy old phone in her booth. It wasn't long before the call was over and the woman was pointing her off in the next direction.

"Up the stairs, on your right. You'll see a bar there, Ernest's the man at the end in the flashy suit," she instructed none too excitedly.

Climbing the stairs into the din of the club, the neon flashing lights were hypnotic. All about were dancers, the place was packed, and she was reminded of her new club with Jamal.

And how it was going neglected by her. She'd have to deal with that later.

She pulled out her phone, hitting 'dismiss' on the alert that had just popped up. Ten more minutes before the next reminder.

This place wasn't as nice or as well cared for as Jamal and hers new club. It was skeezy, first glance told her that. In some of the booths around, Angela could see some dancers already pushing the bounds of legality, and that was on the main floor. Whatever went on in the back rooms had to have been worse.

Before she could get down to Ernest, however, the man found her. His pinstripe white and black suit lit up under the lights as he looked her over. He had long hair, kinda stringy, and the man himself looked a little strung out. On coke judging by the gaunt look in his face.

"Damn," he said with a whistle. "Not often a girl like you comes waltzin' in here lookin' for work." The lascivious grin said it all.

She smiled coyly at him, her nerves soothed at his response. Though she wasn't an idiot. The manager was never the owner of these places, and Ernest looked like he was a shitty front at that.

Her hand rest on his bicep as she smiled.

"I just got in from out west," she said into his ear. "Hoping for a way to make some cash."

He stroked this slick goatee and leaned back, sizing her up. Though unlike the bouncer there was no kind of wholesome attraction about it all, this guy was a skeeze. A skeet. A total slime ball. But he was a rung on the ladder.

"Oh yeah? A quick buck, is that it?" he asked, and she realized she'd have to tread lightly. He was greasy enough to turn things into an awkward sexual proposition that there'd be no graceful way out of if she wasn't careful.

She nodded as she removed her hand from his

arm, clasping her hands behind her back and thrusting her chest outwards.

"Yea, I used to dance at one of the no-contact clubs out in the oil sands," she said, shifting her weight to the other leg. "I'm real good on the stage."

That shifted his demeanor, and for a moment she thought he might've lost interest. But instead it became clear she'd just triggered something else in him instead. He looked more business-like, and eyed her with some smaller amount of lust. Though the glint of a challenge-accepted lingered in his eyes.

"Well if you wanna stop by tomorrow we can do an official sort of interview with some of the girls," he said, though Angela was hoping to not have to drag this out longer than need be. It'd already been a week since Romy disappeared.

She glanced to the stage, at the woman lazily shaking her ass with a dour look on her face before pointedly returning a look to him with a raised brow.

"Give me one song. If I don't make the customers cheer and tip, I'll come back tomorrow."

That got Ernest grinning at her, and he plucked a drink off the bar, downing it as he eyed her over. He seemed to ponder her challenge, but she could tell right away... she'd got him.

"Alright," he said and started walking, brushing on past her. "One song, and we'll see how you do."

He took her on around to the backstage, and she

could see the women there, rushing about to get ready, the club in a complete state of disarray even there. The change room was cluttered with boxes that gave the women a hard time.

"Summer," he said to a woman that looked anything but a summer. "Take a break, this lady's up next," Ernest said, smiling back at Angela. And though Angela worried there might be some dispute about that point, instead the woman looked her over and wearily gave a nod.

"I could use a break anyhow," she said tiredly, going over to sit atop a stack of boxes that cluttered the hall as well.

"What's your name then, darlin'?" Ernest asked her. "I'll go get the DJ to set you up."

"Roxy," she said with a smile. "Something techno," she added on as she went to the mirror.

Her eyebrows were perfectly arched, her dark hair framing her tanned flesh and her large, emerald eyes. She dabbed a bit more red lipstick on her lips before giving herself a dangerous smile.

It was show time.

It had been a while since she'd got one of those calls from Vitaly's security app, and there was the risk of her not being able to respond in time while on stage, but she had to chance it. Then the DJs voice rang out.

"Up next we have a special appearance, and a club first! Everyone give it up for the foxy Roxy!" he said, giving the announcement more flair than such a dingy club and such a dull crowd deserved. In all honesty, he was the one person seeming to put much verve into their job at all.

But that was all she needed. Just one person to bounce energy off of, and as she flounced to the stage with a confident swagger, she felt the eyes burning into her.

She was hard to ignore, after all. It wasn't just her body, the hourglass figure, the raven locks and high cheekbones. It was the fact that she radiated something special, something that demanded attention.

At heart, she was a diva, and there was nothing more that she loved than having the spotlight.

She let the beat go through her, her heart finding its rhythm, her legs finding their stride as she took the stairs up to the stage and went towards the pole.

Her gaze went across the crowd, seeking them out, drawing them in with that devious, flirtatious smile. But she was looking for someone special. It wasn't all fun and games.

The club was dull and lifeless when she came in, the guys none too excited for the lethargic shows by the city's bottom rung dancers. Even the DJ with his pep couldn't talk them up for each dance, but once Angela was working the pole, it was like she'd cast a spell and resurrected the lot of them.

Though with that crowd livening up, the men sifting closer to the stage, dangling money in offering, trying to lure her close, it grew easier to note the few that weren't drawn in. And any man of power wouldn't be elbowing his way to the stage like a dog in heat. He'd have too much respect.

There along the wall were some large, spacious booths. One in particular was elevated above the rest, up a small flight of stairs. That was an obvious one to begin with, and there flanked by two women, sitting with two big beefy guys opposing him that were clearly thugs, hired muscle, was one man, cigar in mouth — despite the no-smoking ordinance — who looked her way.

Bingo.

When she sucked her lower lip into her mouth, her eyes smoldering and her fingertips trailing down the center of her chest, she met his gaze.

Though she didn't stare. No, instead she gave a seductive smile before her gaze went to the ravenous men clamouring for her attention.

She couldn't act too desperate, nor too aloof. He had to believe she wanted only him, without drawing suspicion.

Luckily for her, that was what she was good at. Making the big spenders want only her, and never giving too much away.

She turned her back on the crowd as she glanced over her shoulder at him. The man with the cigar. As her fingers hooked into the bottom of her dress, drawing it up over her shapely ass, she winked at him, exposing her sumptuous cheeks beneath.

The black lace thong delved beneath, and she tugged the dress up higher and higher 'til it was over her head. Throwing it away, she turned back to the crowd and took a few steps away from the ravenous tippers. She was a tease, a high class woman, and she wasn't going to beg for their fives. They'd give them up freely and thank her for it.

Especially as she took a few long steps towards the center and, using that momentum, began swinging herself around the brass pole. She spun elegantly, her hair whipping behind her before she started the climb.

The pole wasn't as high as some, only about twelve feet, but it was enough to make her stand out from the lazy floor shows she watched the previous women do, and the crowd went wild for it as she dipped herself upside down. Her hair didn't touch the ground as her body was on display, large breasts almost toppling from the bra.

It'd been a while since she was on the pole and she thanked God for muscle memory.

The crowd was likely more lively than they'd ever been, lots of talk, hooting, hollering, men leering and grinning with jaws agape. Yet it was the change she'd caused in the ritzy man up top that mattered most. His was a more subtle shift, but he subtly indicated for one of the big men to lean over.

Words were exchanged, and then for a moment everyone there was staring at her before the guard nodded his head and got up.

She had him, she knew it. The big, burly man in his tank top came down the stairs and made his way across the floor where some other eager men awaited her walk off stage.

The three and a half minutes passed in a rush. She'd never even gotten to take off her bra, and she felt dewy and alive. Like she had all the power in the world. Especially as she gathered those tips up.

She grabbed for her dress and her purse, praying she didn't miss the call as she took the phone out. Even then, she was on task, moving towards the big man.

The safety message was waiting for her, but she had no idea how long it'd been. She hit the 'Dismiss' in a hurry. The last thing she needed was Vitaly barging on in ruining everything from the start.

There was a gaggle of eager men all eager to have her for a private dance, but the big one stood out. In large part because he'd shoved his way to the very front.

"Hi," she said with a small tilt to her head, letting her dark hair tickle her cleavage, her dress slung over her purse. "You lookin' for a dance, sexy?" She knew why he was there, but she wanted to hear what he had to say.

"My man over there," he said with a gesture of his

head, "wants to get to know you some." He looked her over, "Just him," he clarified, not wanting her to think she was being solicited for a group thing, she realized.

She made a show of it. Letting her skin darken into a flush, tucking some hair behind the shell of her ear as she glanced towards the man he pointed to, catching his eye once more.

She licked her lips before she looked back at his henchman.

"I'd love to," she said with a purr.

Leaving the other disappointed men behind, she followed the big guy on over and up into the private little area. As she got there, the bald, older man gave each of the women on his sides a gentle nudge and touched their asses, guiding them away.

"Go entertain my friends," he instructed them, and the two guards seemed to have lucked out on Angela's behalf as the ladies went into their laps.

The older man smiled up at her, wearing an expensive suit that fit his seemingly average body well. He had money, to be sure, and looked to be in his forties or fifties.

"Quite the show you put on," he said, no hint of any accent. He was likely local.

"I *love* the stage," she said as she joined him, sliding in next to him, though not sitting on his lap. If she was going to play the role of the classy whore, she couldn't give anything away for free.

Her hand, though, did grasp his bicep as she leaned into him, to better whisper in his ear. Her french vanilla perfume lightly scented the air between them.

"I'm Roxy."

He smiled at that contact, though one thing she noted was how hard his arm was. He looked like an average fella in an expensive suit, but beneath it he had some serious muscle. Which meant one of two things generally: ritzy CEO with money and time for a personal trainer. Or criminal.

With the two burly thugs, it was an easy guess.

"You know, I come here so often Roxy," he said to her, his eyes keen and studying her, soaking her in so intimately. "But you're the first woman who's really got a rise out of me without havin' to lay her hands on me," he said, the other two dancers still within ear shot.

She didn't have to fake how flattered she looked, that sparkle to her eyes, the way they dipped down for a second before returning to him seductively.

She leaned in, let him feel her breasts press against his arm from beneath her bra.

"Did you want to go somewhere more private?" she asked.

The older man stared at her a while then fished into his pocket. He plucked out a wad of bills, hundreds. He slid it across to her, leaving his fingers upon the edge of it.

"All the other ladies here have no issue getting nice and cozy with me right here," he said, such emphasis on 'nice and cozy' that led her to believe it was anything but nice. And judging by some of the lewd acts she'd seen about, she didn't need to think long on what such a powerful man might require of the women.

"All of the other ladies," she purred into his ear, "had to touch you to turn you on."

She pulled away, her fingers touching his across the bills.

"Besides," she added on coyly, "I'm not officially hired yet. I imagine Ernest will be coming to interrupt us any moment now."

That was a sly little way of getting the answer she needed. The older man, with his silvery goatee smirked at her just a little. He retracted his fingers from hers, but left that money in her grasp.

"Ernest works for me," he said, because just as she'd calculated, no man could resist such an opportunity to display his top dog status. "Which means, if you work here, you work for me too," he said, slowly licking his lower lip as he reached out, brushing the backs of his fingers along her arm, up to her shoulder along where the strap of her bra rested.

She fluttered her lashes, as if she wanted nothing more than for him to strip her then and there. Her gaze was seductive as she moved towards his ear once more, letting the bow of her lips tease against his flesh as she spoke.

"If I'm going to do a proper introduction, we should go somewhere we can really get to know one another," she said, a smile audible on her voice. "Nothing's worse than making a bad first impression on your new boss."

He gave her a scrutinizing look, studying her intently, and not just merely staring at her tits either. He looked like he was analyzing her.

"Where are you from, Roxy? You look too good to be a local girl," he said, lifting his hand up to brush his fingers against her cheek.

"I just got back," she said as she moved her face towards him. "Spent the last few years out west."

"You must be used to a lot of loose wallets, stuffed with oil money, no?" he said, licking at his lips again, thinking something over in his own head. "How would you like to accompany me to an exclusive party, Roxy? Then, maybe if you're a good girl, we can go have a little private party, just you and I."

He gave her such a devious little grin, looking sure that she'd accept.

She bit down on her lip as she squeezed his arm, moving just far enough away that she could meet his eyes, as if she had nothing to hide.

"Tonight?" she asked with a tilt of her head.

"You have plans already, Roxy?" he asked her

with a sly look. "I know you're a gorgeous lady, but you just got back in town," he said teasingly.

While off to the side she could hear the painfully faked giggles of the other two dancers as they sat on the guard's laps.

"For you, I can free up my night," she replied. Her eyes flashed deviously, and she stroked his arm. "I'm excited to see what types of parties you like."

"Mm," he responded, shutting his eyes and enjoying her contact for that moment. "I don't enjoy parties usually," he stated, looking back at her again. "Not without the proper company." He leaned in, speaking to her softly. "I was going to just have a bit of fun with these ladies, then head on over, feeling a little more relaxed. But you? I think you can actually make it a little enjoyable even."

"I've always enjoyed," she paused to lick her lips, "anticipation. Flirtation. The tease," her lips quirked. "Probably why I like dancing on the stage so much." Her hand left his bicep, one going to his chest as the other went to his waist, discreetly checking if he had a gun on him.

"It's so much better that way."

He was rather taken with her, it was easy enough to see. Though brushing her fingers against that large piece of his strapped beneath his blazer stole her attention.

"Get dressed," he said to her firmly. "And I'll take you to the finest party in the city," he stubbed out his cigar in the tray and looked sharply to the two thugs and dancers. "Get back to your work," he said in such a markedly callous tone of voice that so contrasted how he'd been speaking to Angela.

She stood in her platform heels, smiling at him excitedly even as her heart raced. She moved over to the side, finding some small privacy as she pulled on her dress, making it as sexy as possible. She knew his eyes would still be on her, and in that black minidress, with good reason.

Even covered, she was smokin' hot.

She reached for her phone, hitting dismiss on the alert once more.

As the other two women filtered on down to the club floor again, the two guards passed her by then up came her target, his arm extended to her in offering.

"The name is Lance, by the way," he said to her so smoothly, heading on down the stairs as her fingers coiled about his bicep once more.

"Lance," she said with a smile, squeezing his arm appreciatively.

Things were moving fast, and she only prayed the private party would be as private as Vitaly needed. Her mind raced, going through one scenario after another as she followed after her guide.

If there were any doubt as to who was in charge, when they passed off Ernest the sleazeball stepped up and tried to get Lance's attention, but was brushed off and ignored immediately, the older man instead focussing all his attention upon his new catch, Angela.

One of the guards vanished, but the reason became clear once they exited the club out onto the streets. There a sleek black car pulled up, and the door was opened for her.

"After you," Lance said, helping her to the door as he relayed some instruction to his other guard.

She slid into the expensive leather seats, and that was when fear really started to grip her. Away from the safety and security of the club, she knew she was taking a risk, but it was one she'd planned for.

She slid her hands under her bum, fixing her skirt, as she tucked some wayward strands of hair behind her ear.

Lance got in beside her and barely a moment after the guard shut the door for him, they were off. In back there was a glass barrier between them and the two in front, and the bald gentleman beside her had no qualms about cozying up tightly against her, his arm winding about her back and shoulders.

"A lovely lady like you shouldn't be working such clubs anyhow," he said to her in a deep voice. "You deserve to be well kept."

Inwardly she recognized the fact that it was a line, something she'd heard many times before by men who hadn't enough money, power, or ability to keep her.

He was different, though, and she couldn't help but be mildly flattered by the comment, though the expression on her face was quiet acceptance.

"Is that so?" she purred as her hand went to his knee, squeezing it. "You're too kind."

He was stronger than he looked, and so there was a moment of panic as he leaned over, his powerful grasp squeezing her shoulder and then the other hand rising up to slide over her breast. He squeezed tightly, and before she had much of an opportunity to respond he was grinning.

"Real?" He said, less a question and more surprise. "I would never have guessed with how perfect they look," he remarked with a shark-like grin.

She sucked in a breath. She hadn't been expecting that, and it set her off a little. Not just because it'd been a week since she last had sex and she was already getting those cravings.

No, it was because of how brazen he was. How entitled.

And she knew better than most that entitled men could easily be her downfall.

But she managed a devious smile to hide her shock, and she nodded her head.

"Completely real."

He was grabby sort, and that only added to the danger of the rest. She could only hope the car ride was a short one.

"I was going to play it all cool," he said to her. "But you have a way of making a man lose his patience, you know that?" He continued to feel her body, groping her breast through her dress and bra as he leaned in to press his lips to her neck.

She had practiced dealing with those types of guys in the past. The ones who wanted too much, touched where they weren't supposed to. It'd been years since she had to deal with one, though, and she wasn't sure they'd ever had a gun on them.

It added another element of fear and agitation to her that she hoped she wasn't showing.

She licked her lips as she squirmed in the seat, tilting her head towards him with the hope that it'd be enough to make him back off her sensitive throat. Her breathing was quickened, and she hoped that he'd mistake it for arousal.

"Maybe go right to the private party," she suggested.

That produced the proper reaction, as she saw his eyes glint with excitement at the prospect and his grin widen. He pressed in against her and kissed at her lips.

Though before things could progress much further, the car pulled to a halt and one of the guards were getting out of the front seat and coming around to the back.

Lance pulled back, and she could see the moment of indecision in his eyes.

"Soon," he promised her, opening the door then climbing out.

It was an expensive hotel, perhaps the finest in the city if she knew enough to say. A door man anxiously trying to help, but kept at bay by the presence of Lance's own private guards.

She let one long leg out of the car, followed by the other as she stood gracefully. As if she were a supermodel on the way to a show, rather than the high class escort she certainly looked to be.

Angela's eyes went up on the hotel, grabbing the name of it before looking towards the streets, trying to get a better idea of where she was. It had been hard to keep track of the turns they made in the car when she had more immediate problems in fending off Lance.

Her hand darted into her purse and she found her phone, dismissing the alert once more. She had to get him alone before letting Vitaly show up, and she hoped to have Lance disarmed and naked by that point.

Lance extended his arm to her, smiling so smugly as his guard escorted him on in as the other parked the car.

"You're going to be the most beautiful woman here tonight," he assured her as they headed through the lobby toward the elevators. Some of the staff again seemed to come close, eager to help, but were kept at bay by the buff guard.

Once inside the elevator, Angela watched as they headed for the top floor. Though once they got there, Lance took her around a corner to another, private elevator, where the guard had to use a key to access it.

That was going to be a problem.

She smiled up at Lance, as if she were impressed.

"King of the Castle," she murmured.

He gave a smug smile to her, seeming to appreciate the ego stroking as they rode their way up. Though once they came to the top, she was struck by music as the elevator doors open. Though another corridor stood between them and the party, the sound filtered on down.

Angela, however, felt a cold chill run down her spine. There before them was a metal detector, staffed by no less than five security guards. Lance's bodyguard even went ahead to put himself through, handing over a gun before stepping through.

Her heart skipped a beat and her blood seemed to freeze in her veins. She only carried forward on momentum and Lance's insistence. She felt panic as she tried to come up with some excuse, how she couldn't go further... but then her phone sounded again. Another message, and it distracted her, made her pause.

Lance stopped and looked to her, brow raised.

"Come along," he said, tinged with just a hint of impatience.

Angela's finger hovered over the screen of her phone, and she didn't know what to press. Though Lance took her aside, guided her away from the metal detector and one of the security guards lifted a cord to let them through around it.

Like that, a wave of relief washed over her and she dismissed the message once more.

"Everything okay?" he asked her as they walked up into the party itself.

She nodded, her face flushed as she leaned in towards him to whisper into his ear.

"I just thought I might've forgotten my pill today, but I remember taking it now," she said smoothly.

The glitz and glam of the party, the obviously wealthy men, the sexily dressed women who mostly functioned as ornamentation for the undoubtedly criminal businessmen surrounded her. She glanced around as if trying to take it all in, appreciate his connections and riches, but truly she was trying to find paths in and out, and how many people were there.

It was intimidating. There was no way around that. It had to be the most opulent of parties she'd been too, and in her younger days she'd been to some amazingly decadent blasts on the arm of rich and powerful men.

All about her were the signs of an old style of power, hyper masculine, with women as pretty objects for the criminals. She even thought she recognized a politician or two. Though amid the sea of testosterone she glimpsed at least a few women of power who stood out.

"Come along," Lance said, guiding her through the crowd, giving his nods to the other shady power brokers.

She followed after him with a sinking feeling of dread in the pit of her stomach. She'd done what Vitaly had asked, and all that she needed was a private area for them to go.

But she had no idea how the Russian biker could possibly infiltrate a place such as this.

Lance guided her through, and one of the servers brought them both champagne. The real deal no less, and the sound of the live music filtered on through the room.

"Lance!" came the soft-spoken voice of a pudgy little man that looked like he had to have been in politics, coming up to Angela's target. "I am so glad you made it, I was really hoping to get a chance to talk to you about your contributions for the upcoming race," he said toothily.

"Don't worry, I'll have you covered," Lance responded, seeming to have little patience for the man.

"Ah but, you see—" the short man interjected again.

"I said, I will have you covered," Lance insisted, tugging Angela along as he brushed past the man.

"Thinks just because he's in federal office now he can bust my balls for more contributions," he muttered to her in irritation.

She laughed, her hand squeezing his bicep in appreciation, in gratitude for him selecting her over the conversation with the man. Once more stroking his ego without using words.

She sipped her champagne, feeling it massage her throat and warm her cheeks.

"You know a lot of well-dressed people."

Lance laughed at that, though there was a slight edge of condescension for her words. Perhaps the politician had soured his mood somewhat.

The endless array of pumped up egos in suits continued, however, and Angela had to put the art of smiling attractively at unpleasant rich men to use again and again. Lance showed her off, and she caught a great deal of attention.

As they made their way through the crowds and Lance spoke to a woman, Angela's eyes landed upon another tall woman who radiated some authority. She looked familiar, but Angela couldn't place her immediately.

"So where did you find this one?" asked the pale woman speaking to Lance, who pumped up her own height with some high heels. She looked over Angela with a mix of predatory intent, as if she was both competition and prey. It wouldn't be the first time she'd come across a woman into her, however.

"Roxy here?" Lance said, stroking Angela's hand upon his bicep. "She is from out of town. Isn't she a dish though?" he said to the woman, who Angela hadn't gotten the name of. She was too busy mulling over who the darker woman was that commanded such attention elsewhere…

Her heart froze however when realization sank in. She missed the next thing the pale woman speaking to Lance said as she sought to reconcile the fact that woman was Evelyn Hevia, the same one she'd dined with that time, when Romy took her out to a fancy dinner.

Lance and the other lady looked at her expectantly.

"Ms. Eriks asked you where you are from, Roxy," Lance repeated.

Angela's eyes were drawn back to Ms. Eriks with a smile.

"I'm sorry, the music," she said, lightly tapping her fingers to her ear as she turned more towards Lance, her arm going to his chest as she tried to shield her face from Evelyn.

"Originally from Victoria," she continued. "Though I moved around a lot. Just got back from the oil sands."

Ms. Eriks recoiled at that.

"Dreadful place," she said with a curve to her upper lip. "I wouldn't set foot in such an awful wasteland if it cost me ten million," she said, and though that would've been hyperbole from any other, it came across instead as sincere from such a clearly rich and powerful woman.

Yet Angela's gaze was drawn back across the room as she watched Javier walk up beside Evelyn, the two standing side by side like some mob boss duo before a flock of lower rung businessmen and politicians.

She had to get Lance and herself out of there, before they sighted her and blew her cover.

She smiled at Ms. Eriks.

"Which is why I came here, to where the true life of the country is," she said before leaning up on her toes and pressing herself into Lance's body. Her breasts against his bicep, her breath on his ear.

"When does the private party start?" she purred.

Lance found himself licking his lips as he stared back into her eyes.

"You'll have to excuse Roxy here, Vanessa," Lance said to Ms. Eriks, barely able to tear his gaze away from Angela. "She's a rather feisty minx of a woman, this evening, it seems," he remarked so smugly, stroking his hand along her lower back, down from her spine over the swell of her rear.

"Ones like her are so hard to find, no?" she remarked, Ms. Eriks eyes upon her as well. The other woman's interest in her only slowing down her seduction. "Far be it for me to distract you two, however," she said almost coyly.

Angela gave Vanessa a wicked grin.

"I hardly think I can be blamed," she said with another squeeze of Lance's firm arm and a flirtatious giggle.

Vanessa gave her a smile and a tilt of her head that said she understood all too well what was going on. But it betrayed a hint of jealousy too.

"Well then," Vanessa said, tonguing her ruby lower lip, "I don't suppose I'll be able to tear this one away from you at all, Lance." The other woman displayed some hint of skill with seduction herself, batting her long, curved lashes and looking to the man.

"I had been kind of hoping to keep her for myself," Lance said, squeezing Angela's ass so lewdly amid the sea of upper crust clientele. "But if you care to join us, three's not a crowd in my book," he said with such a lascivious grin.

That would definitely put a monkey wrench in her plans.

Angela giggled again as Lance squeezed her sumptuous rear, her lips finding his throat as her hand played with his chest. Her face couldn't be seen, but her eyes darted to Vanessa, a look of warning hidden within the emerald gaze.

They exchanged knowing looks for a moment before Vanessa's lips crooked upwards into an almost sinister grin.

"That sounds just lovely, Lance," she remarked,

tipping back her drink and downing it. She handed it off to her own guard, a rather fetching man, who then himself passed it to a serving girl. "Your place or mine?" she asked as she walked on by Angela, brushing her long, manicured nails along the other woman's hip.

Angela knew things were in danger of going completely off the rails. It would be bad enough if she had to contend with both of them together at once, but if Vanessa talked Lance into going back to one of their places rather than, say… a hotel room, it could become very hard for Vitaly to come to her rescue at all.

Her heart was racing, her entire body feeling on edge as she continued to play with Lance's chest with her pink, manicured nails.

"Would any of us make it out of another car ride in one piece?" she asked with a thick purr to her voice, letting her breathlessness show through. She'd have to worry about getting rid of Vanessa another way. A whore turning down her client's third was never a good idea.

Lance chuckled at her words as they began to follow Vanessa, thankfully taking them away from Evelyn and Javier.

"You are such a frisky thing, aren't you?" he remarked with a toothy grin, leading her through the crowd, following in Vanessa's wake. "Can't even last the car ride back to my place, can you?" he teased as he molested her rear so shamelessly.

"We barely made it in here," she reminded him, sticking glued to his side.

Adrenaline was pumping through her, fear growing with his touches, though it was a double edged sword for a woman like her that was drawn to the edge. Her arousal, the way her body heated for him, couldn't be faked, and she had to work harder to keep her mind on the task.

She kept dismissing that little alert on her phone, but with each time, she grew closer to having to hit 'Shut Down'. Emergency.

"Hey Vanessa," he called out to the other woman as they walked through the hall, once more around the metal detector rather than through. "You have a room in the hotel here we can use?" he asked, brow cocked.

Ms. Eriks pivoted about on her high heels and looked at them both. It was clear she was mulling it over, strumming her red nails upon her hips as she thought. So much riding on what conclusion she came to.

"Hey you," she barked at one of the security staff. "Have the front desk arrange a penthouse room for us. Now," she said, that last word sounding more like a threat than a command. "Come on," she said, turning and leading both Lance and Angela again.

Once they were in the elevator and the doors

shut, Vanessa turned and reached out, running her pale fingers through Angela's hair.

"Does your girl here have a lot of experience eating cunt?" she asked so crassly, and it became clear to Angela that little warning look she'd given Ms. Eriks was a mistake. She'd taken it as some challenge, and seemed intent on pushing her now.

But perhaps she could make it work, in a makeshift way.

Angela let her arm drop from Lance's chest as she turned towards Vanessa, letting her nails trail across her scalp as she nodded and sucked in her lower lip.

"Yuhhuh," she murmured, and for the briefest moment, she was fully present and engaged in what she was doing. Ulterior motives and Romy forgotten for only a second as she felt herself lust for the threesome, some animal part of her craving the easier and more primal path.

Vanessa moved in at that, and shoved their mouths together for a kiss as Lance watched them. The elevator came to a stop and he motioned to his second guard, who still stood waiting outside the door to hold on. He didn't want to interrupt them.

Angela could feel Vanessa's tongue probe into her mouth, and the two of them made out. Ms. Eriks was an aggressive woman, and with how she grasped hold of Angela's breast and hip, it made Lance's powerful grip earlier seem mild by comparison.

When finally the kiss broke, Vanessa licked along her ruby lips and gave an approving smile.

"She's a good one, Lance. My congratulations. Usually your girls are such bores," she said as she strode out of the elevator, letting the men scurry out of her way as she led them to the penthouse rooms.

"Full of surprises, aren't you?" Lance murmured to her softly, giving her a half-appreciative, half-scrutinizing gaze before they followed in Vanessa's wake.

Part of her wondered if she was overselling it. If her very real desires and proclivities were so outlandish and foreign, that it would draw undue attention to her. Make him suspicious.

She flushed and looked to the floor, as if more embarrassed than titillated, her breathing quick and high in her large chest. She glanced to him from beneath her dark lashes, emerald eyes peering up.

"I love men, but variety is nice," she managed.

He stared at her a moment longer as they walked along, and she noted she hadn't succeeded in wiping away that scepticism from his look. Though it didn't matter, she just had to hold it together a little longer, right?

The moment was broken anyhow when one of the staff came literally running up in a huff, key card in hand.

"Sorry for the wait," he said, "if you'll follow me. Your room is just over here."

The middle-aged white man directed them over towards a particular room, and Ms. Eriks snatched the key card from the attendant's hand, swiping it open herself and leading them on inside.

"If you need anything else jus—" they strode on in, ignoring the man as the three guards all stood in his way.

Lance turned around, speaking to one of his men in particular.

"See to it we're brought some more champagne, and then go make sure my wife is taken care. I don't want her asking questions about my not getting home tonight, she's been anxious lately with that house guest of ours," he instructed before the door was shut and Angela was locked inside with the two crime lords.

Angela was struggling to pay attention to everything that was going on, her mind growing fuzzy as her fear really started to take hold. The room was huge, and she looked over it at the living room, towards the open bedroom. There was a large bar and a patio overlooking the city. Luckily she'd gotten the room number before they entered. She wasn't that careless.

Ms. Eriks spun around and eyed Angela up and down.

"How often have you taken this one for a ride anyhow, Lance?" she asked, plucking a cigarette from her own purse before tossing it aside. She lit it up and stalked about Angela like a feral cat.

"None," he responded, stepping away from Angela's side, leaving her there, standing alone before Vanessa's gaze. "Yet."

She had intended on excusing herself to go to the washroom when he'd brought her back to his room, sending a text to Vitaly with all the information, but now she didn't know if she could. The risk would be too high.

She gave a more timid smile to Vanessa, playing submissive to the other woman's clearly more dominant persona.

"I just got hired at his club," she said, flicking her eyes to Lance.

Vanessa reached her hand up, touching her smooth fingertips along Angela's arm and up to her shoulder. The scent of her cigarette filling the air as she circled around the presumed-dancer.

"From *your* club, Lance?" Vanessa said sceptically, just before taking hold of Angela's purse strap and pulling it away. "Hefty little purse she's got here," she remarked before giving it a toss onto a nearby table.

"She's the new gem of my club, what can I say?" Lance responded, loosening his tie as he eyed Angela up and down.

Angela begged herself not to flinch as the other woman took her purse, tossing it away, feeling her stomach roil.

How long before the alarm would be sent to Vitaly?

She swallowed and licked her lips with a smile.

"It's near to where I'm staying," she said as she watched Vanessa, her hand going to the woman's waist and thumb running along her hipbone. "How do you two know each other?" she asked curiously.

"So curious all of a sudden," Vanessa said back to her, giving such a sly look as she eyed her up and down.

"Vanessa and I go way back," Lance said as he shed his sports coat and received the bottle of champagne from his guard, dismissing him immediately as he went to fill their glasses.

"Oh yes, we rose up through the ranks long ago," she said to Angela before swatting the other woman's shapely ass. "Back when I started as a dancer with a hell of a lot of ambition."

Angela's hand rose up Vanessa's side, feeling her out, over her dress.

Manipulating a man was one thing, but manipulating a woman like Vanessa was quite another. No stripper worked their way up any ranks without being ruthless and cunning, and Angela couldn't help but feel a little admiration seeping into her actions, and a little jealousy sneaking into her mind.

Instead of climbing up any ranks, she'd been put in prison and did four years.

Angela's mouth went to Vanessa's once more,

silencing the woman's questions and, hopefully, her suspicions. She wasn't hard about it, just a soft, firm run of her tongue along the other woman's.

Vanessa responded to that at least, Angela had calculated well. If she'd come on too strong there, the older woman would have likely taken it as some sort of challenge. But the softer, affectionate kiss did the trick. It didn't challenge the other woman, it soothed her. And then Lance came up behind, his hand rested upon one of Angela's ass cheeks, while Vanessa groped the other.

"To think, you used to be in Roxy's position here once," Lance said with wry amusement, watching the two women make out.

Vanessa pulled back at last, giving Angela time to look her over up close, to see the subtle signs of age. Makeup and good keeping hid it, but it was clear she had to be about forty or more, at least ten years on Angela.

"Watch out for this one, Lance," Vanessa said, as he strolled away and plucked up her glass of champagne. "She's got more ambition than she lets on," she said as she peered over at Angela across her glass as she drank.

"Oh yeah?" he said, brow arched as he looked from Vanessa back to 'Roxy'.

Angela licked the taste of Vanessa from her mouth, her breathing heavy.

"We can't dance forever," she said gingerly.

"Nothing wrong with wanting to be taken care of." She lingered near to Vanessa, praying that the alert had been sent to Vitaly, but she was losing track of time. Her heart was pumping so hard, and she had no idea how much longer she could keep them controlled.

Worse still, doubts plagued her mind. There were two guards — maybe three, depending on how the second of Lance's guards intended to carry out his instructions — outside the door, and it was a swanky, high class hotel. Assuming he did make it to her in time, there were cameras everywhere as well. How'd he get through all that in a timely fashion without incriminating them both?

Vanessa, meanwhile was arching a brow, cigarette and champagne balance in one hand as she scrutinized Angela. Before she got to deliver anymore of her analysis on the other woman, Lance was grinding upon Roxy's ass and kissing at her neck.

"Nothing wrong at all, my dear," he said in a deep husk. "Especially not when one works so hard to make a man provide that care."

She had to buy more time.

Her stomach twisted, even if having him pressed against her felt so good. Her hand went to the hip his gun was at, pulling him in closer to see if it was still there. Her head turned so that she faced him, her mouth parting.

"This doesn't feel like work, even if it is... hard," she said as she racked her brain with what to do. The pressure was on, and adrenaline was racing through her along with more primal urges.

"And we have the night," she said as her gaze went to Vanessa with a saucier smile. "I'm... assuming you two..." she trailed off.

Vanessa gave an incredulous laugh before reaching down to tug off one of her heels, bending her leg at the knee before letting the obscenely expensive footwear fall to the carpet.

"No," Lance said with a chuckle. "Vanessa was a Grade-A cock tease from the moment I met her, but she somehow managed to get to the head of her own operation without ever putting out to another."

"Unless it pleased me immensely to," Vanessa amended with a devious smirk.

"And I'm not her type," Lance said as he ran his hands along Angela's thighs, rolling her dress up a little as he ground his dick against her.

That surprised her, genuinely, and she wasn't sure if she should be more afraid or less. It barely mattered, with how lovely their hands, their bodies, felt against her. Distracting, teasing touches that she so desperately craved, but wanted to stop all at once.

It was a difficult situation, to lose control and find her very body betraying her. She let out a low moan of pleasure, her hand reaching out to touch

Vanessa's shoulder, fingers teasing there as her breathing grew so heated.

She swallowed, and knew she had to get away. She needed to buy time and bit down on her lip.

"I'm so sorry, I really have to use the bathroom before we start," she said, wincing at the words. "I don't want to have to stop once we get going."

It of course didn't go over so well to interrupt the flow like that, but they of course allowed it. Lance pushed her away from his dick, nudging her towards the bathroom, and away from her purse as he began to unstrap his gun.

"Hurry up in there, we've got a party to start after all," he said as he dangled the holster over the dresser next to her things.

"Yes, do hurry love," Vanessa said, giving her a slow, pointed once-over.

She knew she couldn't go for her purse without being suspicious, though she weighed the chance that maybe they'd just assume she was on drugs. In the end, though, she knew the risks would outweigh the potential rewards and she reluctantly left it behind.

As she closed the bathroom door, she leaned her back against it and tried to calm her nerves.

She was terrified.

# CHAPTER 32

*V*italy had followed along with some of his crew. They'd ditched their usual motorcycles for a van. Heading the pack, Vitaly used the GPS in Angela's phone to track her the entire way. From the moment he'd seen what hotel she'd gone into, however, he knew things wouldn't be easy.

He was no longer the player he once was, but he was enough of one to recognize some of the faces that funneled up there with her. It was a gathering of some very important types, and there'd be security up the ass.

"You want we should go with you when the time comes, boss?" asked Sergei, one of Vitaly's henchmen.

"No," Vitaly responded after some thought. "I do

this myself still. You wait for my word and help carry the package when the time comes."

With that, Vitaly got out of the vehicle and made his way inside. Angela had not set off the alarm, but his curiosity was piqued. He had to know more about what was happening.

Dressed in a sleek black suit, he didn't look quite up to the stature of the other clients. But he got little notice as he followed behind some of the other, high class guests. He noted several things when they got to the top: the first being the locked, private elevator. The second was that the security cameras were all shut down on that floor.

Unlike the ones on lower floors, they showed no sign of being active. It struck him that the special guests had insisted upon it. There couldn't be video evidence of politicians and business owners meeting with criminal types, could there?

That meant all the more that he had to worry about the hired thugs, but at least he didn't have to fret about anything he did being caught on camera.

He monitored Angela's position for some time, but when he detected her approaching from above again, he took an elevator down several floors. Though once her position stabilized again, he knew she must've settled into another room and he traced his way back up.

There was no doubt about it once he saw the two

guards outside the room, and the GPS tracker pointing him right there towards Angela.

He had to casually appear to be another hotel guest wandering to his room as he checked them out, but then it simply became a game of waiting.

# CHAPTER 33

She splashed a bit of water on her face after flushing the toilet, looking into the mirror and trying to see what they'd see. An attractive dancer, ready for some fun?

Or someone with more ambition than brains?

She hoped it wasn't the latter, as she unlocked and opened the door. She went towards her purse, holding onto the table as she bent down, removing her own high platform heels.

"Sorry about that," she said with a grin to each of them. "All good now."

The timing couldn't have been worse, or better, it depended on perspective. As Lance and Vanessa turned their predatory gazes back upon her, Angela's ears perked to the sound of a light click in the door.

It was Vitaly who peeked through, and if he'd taken out the guards. Either the door was soundproof or he'd displayed some masterful levels of subtlety.

"We don't need any more champagne, dammit!" Lance said, turning his gaze to the door only to be greeted by the image of a towering Russian giant.

Shock set in. Vanessa was in a bad spot and was the last to be able to know what was going on.

Lance dove towards Angela, reaching for his gun beside her, but a mix of panic and Vitaly's training kicked in, and she extended her bare legs, tripping him up so that he tumbled into the dresser and upon the floor. Vanessa caught sight of Vitaly and him of her, she reached into her own jacket and pulled out a gun.

Vitaly was too fast for her, though. The towering man raining a blow down upon her wrists that knocked her over and sent the small gun bouncing across the carpet.

Everything was happening so fast, and as Angela reached for her own gun, Lance grasped hold of her legs and yanked her down. She stumbled, slipped, lost hold of her compact pistol for a second, but then Vitaly came to her rescue. He wrenched her from Lance's strong grasp, tossed her back a couple feet then pounded his leather-gloved fist into the man's face, bloodying his nose.

There was no time for Angela to relax though. She was clutching her purse with one hand as she watched Vanessa scurry towards her own gun. The woman was a fighter, Angela knew, and she had to get her gun out immediately and get her to surrender.

"Stop!" Angela cried, pulling out the sleek, black little gun and pointing it with shaking hands.

But Vanessa didn't stop.

She grasped her own gun and Angela was forced to pounce atop her, grabbing the woman's cherry-brown hair and slamming her face to the carpet.

"I said stop!" Angela reiterated, pulling back the hammer of her pistol as a warning sound to Vanessa, making her drop her gun back to the carpet.

While beside them, Vitaly finally finished beating Lance into submission, the older man's face bloodied as the Russian ex-military tied his arms up behind his back with a quick motion.

"We can't take both," Vitaly said to Angela, looking pointedly at the woman pinned beneath her.

Her stomach lurched.

It was bad. So bad.

Not only could the woman I.D. her, but there was no way Angela could deny her part in it all.

"The Hevia's are upstairs," she said, keeping Vanessa held in her shaking grasp, before bringing her emerald eyes to the other woman's. Vitaly's eyes went wide at that statement, obvious surprise marking his face even though he'd never lost his composure during the fight.

"You're a smart woman," Angela said with a

dangerous edge to her voice. "What will we do to you?"

Vanessa ground her teeth as she lay beneath Angela.

"You really thinking killing two of the most powerful people in this city— no, this country! — is going to go over well for you?" Vanessa hissed at Angela.

All the while Vitaly reached into his jacket and pulled out two things, a syringe and a black folded bag. He shot something into Lance without delay, the older man falling into unconsciousness through muttering curses as Vitaly began to unfurl the black bag and pull it over the man's entire body.

"I really don't," Angela said to Vanessa before bringing the butt of her pistol against the woman's temple with a solid 'crack'.

Vitaly watched Angela work, heard the dull crunch of metal on bone. He finished zipping up the bag then spoke up.

"That won't keep her unconscious," he said. "If we don't kill her, she will have you hunted down eventually." He picked up Lance's gun and stuffed it inside his jacket.

"A dozen people saw me leave the party with the two of them," she said with some disdain, looking to him with frantic eyes. She was way out of her league. They weren't just playing games anymore, and things had gotten far more real than she'd expected.

"You got more of that?" she asked, nodding to the syringe.

He looked to the syringe, and there was still a little left, but only a fraction of what he'd shot into Lance.

"Enough to keep her out for less than an hour maybe," he said, leaving the needle where it was on the floor. "I will finish her, you do not even need to be in the room," he offered once more, and she knew little was on him. After all, Vanessa had only gotten — at most — a brief glance at him.

It'd been so recently that she'd been worried about pulling off a robbery on a man with more money than he knew what to do with. Punishing the person who shot and possibly killed Romy was one thing, but Vanessa was just a player in the game who'd taken too much of an interest in Angela.

Her stomach lurched. She didn't have the luxury of fretting about her decision, thinking it through and questioning it and mulling things over. She had to trust her gut.

She grabbed for the syringe, injecting the woman with what remained of the drug before making her way to the kitchen, grabbing a cloth and some soap from the kitchen, quickly wiping down everything she'd touched.

"I wish ladies gloves were back in fashion." It was dark humour, given the situation, but she was terrified.

"Don't bother," he said to her, though it was too late. Luckily, she'd not laid her hands on much. "They won't be involving police in any of this," Vitaly assured her as he hefted the non-descript sack that contained Lance over his shoulders. It drew attention to just how big of a man Vitaly was, as Lance's body looked like little more than a sack of potatoes on his shoulder.

He went to the door, opened it and looked out carefully before peering back at her.

"You go right. Exit casually. Take a cab to the corner of Duckworth and Estrangue," he instructed her in that same calm, educational tone of his. "I will come get you there shortly," he said before slipping out the door.

She had so many things she wanted to say, but she knew there wasn't time. Instead she grabbed for her purse, putting her high heels back on. With another sad, lingering glance at Vanessa, she made her way out the door, letting the cloth drop to the floor as she exited.

She went to the elevator as if it were nothing, pressing the down button and waited for what seemed to be the slowest elevator in the world.

Stepping inside, she looked in the mirrored reflection as she selected the lobby, fixing her hair and lipstick. Just another whore after a job well done.

The quiet after a successful job was always so jarring. All that adrenaline, the anxiety, all of it lingering in her system, yet the world was calm and quiet. She'd walked out the front door of the building like nothing had happened, and nobody paid her any mind otherwise.

Nothing out of the ordinary happened, until late that summer night on the street corner, a dark van rolled up and the side door opened up leading into the back. Vitaly's hand reached out and he took hold of her and pulled her in.

In front were two of his men, while in back it was just the two of them… and Lance of course.

"Evelyn and Javier were at the meeting?" Vitaly asked her for confirmation, the first words out of his mouth as they began to roll down the street.

"Without a doubt," she said. The Cuban couple were unmistakable.

Javier owed Angela's lover, Jamal, a debt for doing time for him. He was the reason Jamal had the strip club she was supposed to be managing. Javier's mistress was their day manager.

And Abel... Abel had been more right than he knew.

The way Vitaly looked at Lance from the corner of his gaze suggested he had come to the same conclusion as her. The Hevia's and Lance were in business, and if they'd tried to take Vitaly out, they were both culpable.

Which also meant the man she'd turned to for help in finding Romy was an enemy of some very powerful people who had made her and Jamal's club a reality. She'd gotten herself tangled up in a huge mess.

"You should come stay under my protection for now," Vitaly said to her firmly. "Nothing is safe for you anymore."

Suddenly her decision to leave Vanessa alive seemed even more colossally dumb.

"No," she said sternly, immediately, shaking her head. "I'll disappear on my own." Already she was thinking it through. Go back to her place. She had enough money to find a new place, new haircut.

But in reality, she knew she was in deeper than

that. She'd not just edged her toe over the line, she'd obliterated it as she jumped over.

"What're you going to do with him?"

"I am going to question him just as we planned," Vitaly said. "Even though we know some of the answers already, he can offer us something of an advantage. I might even be able to use him to bargain with that woman you left behind for your safety. If you stay where I can look out for you," he said to her, reclining back in his seat, his large form sprawled upon the leather seat opposite her.

She leaned back, her arm folded beneath her chest, suddenly feeling so underdressed in her little black dress and perfect makeup. It had been such a long night, and now she was crashing hard.

"I'll be missed," she said, pointedly raising a brow.

"I will get word to whomever in due time," Vitaly said to her smoothly. "For now, we worry about finding out what this man knows, seeing if Romy is still alive. And getting appropriate revenge for us both, yes?" he queried, tilting his head as if challenging her to refute him.

She was too exhausted to fight any longer, and she knew the risks when she got into it.

Her gaze went to the side and she exhaled a long held breath.

"Do what you need to do," she conceded.

The smile Vitaly gave her said he'd intended to do that all along anyhow.

# CHAPTER 35

The van pulled into some sort of warehouse in a part of town she didn't recognize. She'd had no idea of where they were or how they got there when Vitaly pushed open the back doors and the Russian goons all assembled to heft out Lance's form.

Vitaly stayed back, extending his hand in offering to her as she looked out at a large, open warehouse filled with boxes and half-assembled equipment. Whatever he had going on, it looked like it wasn't quite underway yet.

"You will be my special guest, the accommodations are not the finest," he said to her, "but quality of service shall make up for it. And in the meantime, there is no reason not to cease our training, hm?"

Her mood was quickly souring as adrenaline

abandoned her and left in its wake frustration and worry.

She gave him a nod, though as she moved in closer, she whispered up at him.

"Javier gave a friend a club. I'm supposed to be the manager. He's going to be worried, but now I'm worried about him, understand?"

"I know of these things," he said to her so casually, helping her out of the back of the van, then leading her off down to some cargo elevator. He didn't take her up however, he took her down. "Your friend was the Hevia's hitman back in the day. Never failed to take out his target. Except once," he said casually as the elevator opened up, showing her a dark, shadowed hall beneath the warehouse, likely just another storage place.

It felt like her heart stopped in her chest, her throat constricting and she wasn't sure she heard him right.

It had to be wrong. There was no way.

Jamal wasn't a killer.

Her lips dropped open as the memories of him overwhelmed her. The times he'd held her as she cried, coming down from a bad trip. The way he took control over her, keep her safe and protected.

How he looked at her when he'd finally gotten out of prison.

She'd assumed it had just been drugs, taking the fall for his boss. Wasn't that what he'd implied? Said?

It was all a haze and she looked at Vitaly in horror, paying her creepy location so little mind.

But it made so much more sense that he'd kept it from her, if he was going away for his involvement in a murder. He'd never want her to know he'd done something so heinous.

Vitaly led her on down a corridor to a hall lined with metal doors, and then finally stopped at one, pushing it open and showing her the simple, Spartan room inside.

"I was not expecting company of such a caliber," he said to her as he stood aside, making room for her. "But this was my room, and now yours. If you're here longer than the night, I'll have nicer things brought in for you before the next," he said.

It was a bleak little room with a bed in one corner, thankfully not too small. A trunk at the foot of it, a mirror on one wall, and a coat rack that held an assortment of Vitaly's jackets and blazers.

Though despite the cold, it was hardly worse than her own apartment, in the gang riddled side of town. She stepped inside, and more than anything, she simply wanted to be alone.

"It's fine," she said, as though in a trance, and in a sense, she was.

Jamal...

"Hey," Vitaly said, reaching out and resting his large hand upon her shoulder. "Did you want to be informed when he wakes up for questioning? It likely won't be pretty," he cautioned her in his gravelly voice.

"No," she said with certainty in her voice. There was nothing that man would tell her that she wanted to hear first-hand.

"You know what to ask," Angela continued, catching Vitaly's gaze.

Their eyes locked, he gave her a firm nod.

"In the meantime, food? Drink? Company?" he asked.

She looked at him, her green eyes glittering with unspent tears and she forced her gaze away.

"Time," she finally managed through the cotton ball in her throat.

It all made sense. Too much sense.

The way Jamal'd always pushed aside her worries, her concerns. The odd hours, the desire to protect her from his job.

Her stomach turned once more, and she thought she might be side, but swallowed it back.

"Water, maybe."

Vitaly was already at the door when she said that, but he gave her a nod.

"I will be right back with it," he said, swinging the door shut behind him.

# CHAPTER 36

The room was dark, absolutely pitch black when Lance awoke. His nose was broken, he knew that for certain, and his jaw ached. He felt like utter hell with what was pumped into him too, groggy and unresponsive.

When he tried to get up and feel his way around, the world seemed to spin like he was drunk or high. He fell from the table he laid upon, striking the concrete floor with a pained cry. Though it wasn't long before that noise brought the sound of approaching feet.

Once the door swung open, Lance's world went from a black void to blinding white light. The white walls reflecting it all about so that his eyes could not adjust quickly.

"You are awake, at last," came a familiar, gravelly

voice. Strong hands took hold of Lance, lifted him up and placed him upon a chair.

He struggled to see, but whoever it was appeared as just a looming black silhouette before him.

"Do you know who you've fucked with?" Lance said in defiance, but a slap struck him across the face, causing him to sting and hurt.

"I know who you are, jackass," came that curiously accented voice once more, followed by another slap. Lance's eyes slowly came into focus, and the man before him slowly transformed from unknowable black ghost to a terrifying monster.

"V-Vi-Vitaly," Lance stammered out, panic setting in, replacing his tough guy front.

"Yez, you remember me now, hmm?" said the towering man, lighting a cigarette and taking a slow drag. "You tried to have me killed. That was not very nice of you," he remarked with such casual humour, smiling just a tad at the cowering man.

Lance was shaking. He'd, of course, been aware his life was in jeopardy by whoever had taken him captive. But knowing it was a man who had ample reason to want to make him suffer along the way to whatever their ends were…

"I-it wasn't my idea, Vitaly, I swear!"

Vitaly flicked some ash from his cigarette and it flew into the man's face, causing Lance to cry out from the stinging upon his wounds.

"I know you are too cowardly to make a

move on me just like that," Vitaly said, talking so casually as he pulled up another heavy, metal chair to sit in front of the mob boss. "That is why we are speaking, instead of other, more painful things."

"W-what do y-you want?" Lance asked in a soft whisper of a voice.

"Excuse me?" Vitaly said, craning his head and pushing back his thick hair to uncover his ear. "Speak up."

"What do you want?!" Lance repeated, his voice panicked as he struggled to please the man.

"Oh. Yes." Vitaly took a slow drag from his cigarette, then leaned over, stubbing it out on Lance's face, causing him to scream and squirm as Vitaly kept him pinned in that chair.

"I know you are not the one who gave the order," Vitaly continued casually as the screams subsided to sobs. "Another boss came to you for this favour, no? Who?" he asked firmly.

"The Hevia's!" he blurt out immediately, no hesitation in ratting out the other mob bosses.

Though that didn't win him much sympathy it seemed, as Vitaly stomped upon his foot, causing the sound of breaking bones to crunch in the air.

"I know that already," he said to Lance impatiently. "Which one of them was it?"

"Javier! Javier!" Lance cried.

Vitaly let that soak in as he thought it over.

"Good," he stated at last, pleased with the news. "Why?"

"They have their own system going, and they don't want you flooding the market with your meth again! And… and they are worried now that you're back. They know you're tough, and dangerous. They didn't want you to be a threat to them once you got established." He said quickly, apparently satisfying Vitaly, since no follow up blow came.

"So you agreed to help them even after all that happened? The two of you owing me this debt we all agreed upon?" Vitaly said, his perpetually calm and steady voice quaking slightly with rising anger.

"You know how it is, Vitaly! If I turn down their request, they know —" his words were cut off as Vitaly took his tortures up more than just a notch. Lance's cries chillingly filling the room for several minutes until Vitaly was sat back down across from him, waiting for the screams to subside.

"No excuses. Only honest answers," Vitaly said in that trademark calm again, despite the blood that stained them both. "Just one more thing for now…"

# CHAPTER 37

Her entire night had been filled with fitful, restless slumber. She couldn't rest without replaying the scenes and sensations over in her mind. Worrying about Vanessa and what would come of her.

More than that, though, Jamal was on her mind. She'd been so tempted to send him a text, to call him, but she resisted the urge. Half of her was scared of finding out the truth, but the other half was afraid of how she'd react to it.

It wasn't as though Vitaly was a good guy, but she'd walked into the arrangement knowing that about him. Jamal had let her believe for their entire relationship that he was just a drug dealer. Even after he paid his debt to society and to the mob, he came back and never once came clean to her about why he was really serving time.

What he'd really done to earn that club of theirs.

She woke early from another nightmare and grabbed for her phone, looking at it with such anguish. She'd gotten in so deep, all to try to find out who shot Romy. To try to make it right, to pay a debt she didn't owe to the young man.

Curling up in the bed, she let her head fall back to the pillow, swollen with anguish and sleeplessness.

It was too late to take anything back. She had to deal with the path she'd chosen.

A knock came to the door and with her say-so, it opened and Vitaly came in. The towering man holding two brown paper bags filled with warm food judging by the smell, and a tray containing two hot drinks.

"Good mornink," he said smoothly, placing one bag in her lap as he pulled over a chair next to the bed and opened his own, placing the coffee cups next to the bed. "There is cream and sugar there if you wish it," he said, pulling out his own breakfast and helping himself, treating the whole thing so naturally. Despite what she knew he must have done overnight.

She accepted her coffee, dumping all the sugar she could into it. She needed energy to get through the day, and that'd do well enough.

She was still in her skanky black dress and it always felt so much more shameful the morning after, even if she hadn't done anything. She exhaled as she crossed her legs, holding her coffee in her hands and letting it warm her.

She didn't want to ask, but she knew ignorance wasn't the answer. She'd just come up with the worst case scenarios.

"What happened?" she managed in her gritty, exhausted voice.

Vitaly was already halfway through his breakfast sandwich by the time she got around to asking, but patient as always with her he spoke calmly.

"It was Javier who ordered the hit on me. He had agreed to a peace upon my return, an agreement to work together. But he feared I would compete too hard with him. He couldn't take me out himself without breaking his word and letting it be known, so he contracted out to Lance to have the job done. But this means that the Hevia's can't retaliate against me for anything I've done so far, not without exposing their own treachery."

There was a lump in her throat.

"So far?" she said, her tired, green eyes going to his.

Vitaly finished his sandwich before plucking out a second, the large man clearly not satisfied with a single one. He gave her a casual shrug of his broad shoulders.

"The rest depends upon you and your decision," he said matter-of-factly. "I have to let Javier know that I know he tried this, otherwise he will try again. But how I do that," he shrugged once more. "I asked about your boy, Romy," he tacked on, though it was clear he was trying to tackle the subject as gently as he could.

Her heart fell at his tone.

"Tell me," she insisted, not looking away from him.

"He wasn't supposed to be there and they shot him by accident. One of Lance's men recognized him as a Cuban, and while Romy was bleeding out, brought him back just in case. It turned out wise, because Lance knew he was one of Javier's men. They held onto him long enough to try and save his life, or hold him hostage in case Javier got upset. But without proper treatment... he passed away."

Angela was surprised by how much anger she felt boiling into her veins, and shocked that tears sprung to her eyes.

Her breath quickened and her hand balled into a fist, her entire body trembling in rage. She didn't want to believe it, but the moment she saw the Hevia's at the party, deep down, she knew it was too late.

"Fucking careless pieces of shit," she hissed before drinking down some of her coffee. It felt good to be angry, that righteous sensation filling her.

"There is no justice, except that which we exercise through power," Vitaly said, his voice tempered just a little bit with sympathy. "We have our revenge on that prick Lance, though after the events of last night, it will be much harder to get at Javier."

He took a moment to look her over, sipping his own coffee.

"But the question is, where do you go from here, hmm?" he asked her delicately.

Her shoulders tensed. She didn't know what to make of that, initially. Where did she want to go?

Her body felt sore and exhausted, the events of the last twenty-four hours taking a toll on her not just physically, but mentally. Finding out that Romy was really dead and that Jamal was a hired hitman? There was nothing in the world that could've readied her for either of those things on their own, let alone together.

"I don't know," she admitted.

"I would not expect you to yet," Vitaly said gently. "As I see it you have a few options. You can go back to living a legit life, find a job somewhere. Go back to Jamal and hope Javier did not see you at the party even for a moment. Either way, if those are to have a shot at working I must go and kill this Vanessa Eriks, otherwise you have no shot at surviving beyond a week."

Vitaly took his time, blowing onto his coffee before taking a sip.

Her blood went cold as ice as she thought back to Vanessa, the woman so similar to herself, yet far more ruthless. She didn't doubt his words for a moment.

"Or…"

She couldn't meet his eyes.

"Or?"

"Work with me," he said it without hesitation. "I will protect you. What I did last night was retaliation. The other bosses will have to respect that, even Ms. Eriks. If you are my partner, she cannot retaliate against you, not like if you were just some random civilian or mook. You will be a boss, just like her. A boss who took her revenge, and she will have to respect that, or risk not just my retaliation by the angry hammer of the other bosses. And as a bonus?" he said, arching a brow and looking aside at her. "In time we will have our revenge on Javier too. Not fast or petty revenge. But the long lasting kind. The kind you savour."

He had a way of making it sound so enticing to her, like revenge were a delicious dish that made her mouth water.

"We will tear down all he has created," Vitaly said slowly. "Dismantle his empire, push him into poverty. Not through violence, but through business. He will find himself the king of an empire of dirt when we are done. And then our revenge can be complete."

She finished her coffee, but found neither warmth nor comfort in the overly sugared drink.

Her body still felt as though it were encased in ice.

What choice did she have? She couldn't have a woman's death on her head. A woman little different than her. Not just to save her own skin. She hadn't fallen that far.

Her face fell to her hands and she held herself there for a long while before speaking into her lap.

"No matter what Jamal's done, he's not to be harmed. Financially or otherwise."

Vitaly took a moment to think over her words before he nodded.

"One thing you must do for me — for us — if that is to be so," he countered. And that gave Angela hope, at least, that he was serious. He'd not bargain if it were a ploy. "The club is partially yours, is it not?" he asked, brow raised at her in question.

Angela nodded. Jamal had offered her an even split, to make up for leaving her without explanation. Letting her believe he'd dumped her and disappeared, setting her down the spiralled path towards prison.

"Keep your stake in the club," he said to her casually. "We need a chemist for our new operation here. Someone to produce our product so that we can compete with the Hevia's on price and quality. This will fall upon you."

The two points didn't seem connected to Angela.

She was certainly not a chemist by a long shot, and her brow arched at him in silent questioning.

"You have a woman who works for you there, yes? Svetlana," he asked Angela, receiving a nod. "I need you to go get her. Coax her into following you. Being your chemist." The emphasis on 'your' rather than 'our' didn't escape Angela.

Her arms folded beneath her breasts.

"Offering her the position of day manager was a condition that Javier gave Jamal for ownership of the club. She's Javier's girl on the side," she said easily. She'd caught her coming out of Javier's office, and that was enough to know they were fucking, but getting her a job? That was clearly mistress territory.

Vitaly took a deep breath but then nodded his head to Angela.

"Yes. Javier keeps her on a tight leash. Keeps her under control. Because he knows if she goes anywhere else, he will have stiff competition that his own chemist cannot beat. But she is a sweet girl, whose head was easily filled with lies while I lay in recovery. You can talk her into coming here with you. Trust me."

She listened to him carefully, reading between the lines before giving a gentle nod of her head. She was so exhausted, so tired. Ever since Romy's disappearance — death — she'd been running on adrenaline and now it was all depleted.

Even the coffee could barely perk her up.

"Then that's what I have to do," she said.

Vitaly watched her in quiet, but then he let spill more details. Angela could not claim he never seemed forthright with her.

"Svetlana and I came here as business partners only. I ran the business side, she made the stuff. I looked after her until Javier had me shot. And while I was hiding away, recovering, he took her. Filled her head with worries about being arrested or killed. Seduced her. Because he knows she is a sweet girl, with a vulnerable heart. A game I would never play with her."

He drained his cup of coffee, crumpled it up then dropped it in the brown paper bag.

"You are her boss at the club, no? She will listen to you," he said with certainty. "She is a good girl. Who has fallen in with a manipulative man that will not even give her the honour of publicly acknowledging it."

Angela looked at him as her arms tightened beneath her chest, giving him a single nod.

"You can trust me," she said, too tired and worn to have much more to say, her eyelids heavy as she looked at him, a frown on her lips.

She'd sacrificed all her hopes and dreams, her perfect life with Jamal, to see the killer of Romy punished, and knowing he was dead, she wanted to see it through. She wanted to do the right thing.

Even if that meant getting in deeper with the criminal gangs.

What other choice did she have? Backing away would mean others would suffer, and she'd be powerless.

$\mathcal{V}$italy had escorted her back to her place, helped her pack up her things, including her ill-gotten money. It wasn't safe for her there anymore, after all. But she got the opportunity to change out of her dress before heading over to the club.

It was, admittedly, not entirely her. The baggy blue sweater and the dark jeans were paired with sneakers rather than her usual heels. She wasn't feeling sexy, and she didn't want to draw any more attention to herself than she had to.

Though she knew she'd draw the attention of Jamal, but that was unavoidable after she'd skipped out on what was supposed to be her first week of work with not a word. She hadn't wanted to drag him into it, but more than that, she didn't want him to know what she'd gotten herself into.

Vitaly dropped her off outside her club, the large man accompanied in his car — as he'd eschewed the noisier, more conspicuous bikes since their mission the prior night — by two of his men.

"One of my men will be waiting down on the corner with a car, to escort you and Svetlana back to the hideaway," he told Angela. "Be careful. Your phone app is still active in the meantime. Use it if trouble arises, and I will come to the rescue."

"I'll be fine," she said sternly, her voice colder and harder than her usual sultry tone. She had to be strong if she was going to do it right.

She stepped away from the car, looking up over the signs outside. They'd already been replaced, and Angela felt a pang of... what? Gratitude? Excitement? Loss?

It was hard to tell, the way they all swirled within her, rearing their heads before being lost in the tide of emotions.

She made her way in, ignoring the bouncer and the woman at the coat check as she went towards the offices.

Svetlana was at the bar, doing cash. The chipper young woman brightening up at the sight of her.

"Oh! Jamal will be so glad to see you again!" she declared in an excited voice.

Angela slowed her step, looking at Svetlana in a new light, with a broader sense of respect.

"I need to talk to you once I'm done with him," she said. "So stick around a bit."

Svetlana didn't hesitate, but gave a bright smile and a nod.

"Of course!" she said. She'd never dreamt of leaving any sooner.

Off Angela went, back into the officers, where she found Jamal. The large man in shirt and pants, sorting through papers, looking for some receipt or another, she figured.

"Lana," he said, assuming Angela's approach was the day manager. "You know where that work order for the new sign went?" he asked before glancing back and doing a double take. "Angel!" he declared in relief and came to her, arms wide to embrace her.

She backed away, instead closing and locking the door behind her.

The sight of him, though, made her weak. She couldn't help it. He'd been her high school sweetheart, the man she'd grown into a woman with. The man who dominated her and helped her through some of the hardest parts of her life before dumping her and disappearing for years.

And then he waltzed back into her life, and her feelings were still there, beneath the rubble of hurt and broken trusts.

Somehow, even the knowledge that he was a hitman didn't extinguish that fire all the way.

"What'd you go to prison for, Jamal?" she asked, struggling to keep her voice hard.

Jamal's relief at seeing her return slowly melted from his broad, chiselled face, and he stared at her in confusion. It took him a while to muster up words.

"Why do you ask that now?" he said.

"Because I want to hear it from you," she said, though her tone crackled with emotion that she was trying to suppress.

Jamal's expression fell even further, but he didn't bullshit her then. He pushed back his shoulders, let his arms drop and said it plainly.

"Attempted murder."

Hearing him say it was beyond anything she could have prepared for, and she couldn't stop the tear that escaped her eye though she quickly swiped it away.

For a moment she thought she was going to throw up, her stomach roiling as her hand trembled. She just wanted to disappear, to run away and never come back. To hide from the mess she'd gotten into.

To hide from the man who'd broken her heart only to give her enough hope before smashing it again.

She had no words, not as her lip trembled, her throat choked off.

"That was the old me," he said, and shame sunk into Jamal's words. For the first time in all she'd known him, he sounded ashamed of himself. "I'm done with that life... done with being a monster, Angie. I... I didn't want you to know..."

"How long did you think you could keep something like that from me?" she asked, anger creeping into her tone as she threw her hands in the air. "Well, apparently you did for all of our relationship, so might as well keep up with the lies!" Fury masked her hurt, and it felt good to be mad.

"You come in, talking about starting fresh and clean, a new life together, but it was based on more of your lies."

Jamal looked defeated, like she'd never seen him before. The man who'd been her rock for so long, looking like a kicked puppy. He couldn't even meet her eyes anymore.

"That was why I ended things years ago... I didn't want you to know what I'd done. Didn't want the last thing I saw of you to be the look of horror and disgust on your face," he shook his head sadly, his shoulders sinking. "I wasn't strong enough to take that, Angie."

She couldn't hold back or hide her tears anymore. It felt like all the air had been pushed from her lungs, and all she wanted was for him to gather her in his arms and tell her it would be okay. That it was all a cruel game, that she'd be safe and protected from life. From him. From Vanessa. From everyone.

Things had just gotten so out of control, and her

entire life had been thrown upside down in so short of time.

She looked at him as tears streamed down her cheeks.

"Romy's dead," she said, and the words felt strange on her tongue, like a lie. He was so young, so filled with life, and now he was nothing more than a corpse, robbed of a future by the man he had so looked up to and admired. The man that was like a brother to him.

"I know," Jamal said and he stepped closer to her, and though hesitant with the revelation of what he'd done, he extended his arms to embrace her once more. "I'm sorry you're surrounded by this awful life, Angie."

She cringed away.

"You know who did it?" she asked, accusingly.

"No," he said immediately. "I don't have anything to do with that stuff. Svetlana told me." He sounded so wounded.

At least there was that. At least he wasn't the cause behind her last lover getting shot.

At least there was hope that he was telling the truth, and her gaze fell to the ground.

"I can't go clean," she finally said, arms tugged around her middle, hugging herself, trying to protect herself from her own broken heart and the fear that tainted her veins.

"But you can!" he said to her insistently, looking

so wounded by her words. "We've got our own place now, Angel! Fully legit, and I'm out! You've suffered enough," he said, afraid to try to touch her again for fear of seeing that reaction of hers.

It wounded him.

"This place is 100% ours! And I've got Javier's insistence I'm out. What could possibly keep you in it?"

Of course, Angela knew the value of Javier's word intimately.

"You're not out," she said, emotion drained of her voice. "He's a snake. You're only out, you're only clean, as long as he wants it that way." She was afraid to say more, afraid to bring him further into the choices she had made, and another couple tears managed to escape.

"And I'm not out. Your options are handing me the club in full and walking away," she said with a pause, a lick of her lips and a shrug of her shoulders.

Jamal's brows furrowed, he was troubled by what she was saying, and furthermore didn't quite seem to get the full meaning.

"I am committed to you, to making up for what I put you through. I'm not gonna walk away." He stepped in closer, "I'll help you with whatever comes, Angie. I'm in your corner. Always."

The conviction in his voice was undeniable. What she knew of him had changed, but not his commitment to her.

"I made some choices, and I'm going to be living with the consequences. This club is instrumental in that, as is Svetlana," she said, shoving her emotions down. She was hurt and afraid, and she couldn't help but wonder the things he'd done and seen behind her back as she was oblivious, drugged and fucked out of her mind.

But she didn't have the luxury of mourning the man she thought she knew so soon after he walked back into her life.

She licked her lips. She knew, once Javier got word of what happened, that Jamal would be as much in harm's way as she was, and there was a big part of her that wanted to protect him.

"I'll send you your share of the profits. Down on your beach, like you talked about."

Jamal's brows furrowed, the man's smooth, dark skin blemished by his confusion. His inner hurt as he studied her, trying to discern why she was saying what she was.

"I'm in this with you. It's all I ever wanted," he said in a low, firm voice. Unshakeable. "If you're wrapped up in some criminal shit… we can cut and run. But I ain't going without you, Angie," his voice filled with such certainty.

"There's no cutting, no running. Not this time, Jamal. I'm in this 'til it's done."

The desire to take down Javier had only grown.

He'd not just killed Romy, but had taken away

Jamal from her when she needed him most. When she was so broken, so vulnerable. If Jamal hadn't broken her heart, she never would've become so careless and had to do her own time.

She placed the blame on Javier.

She could see the conflict in him, the hurt, the confusion, the devotion to her.

"I'm not going. Whatever happens — if you never love me again — I'll be here. Waiting to help," Jamal said unflinchingly. Willing to put himself back on the line, even after those lost years to prison.

She stared at him for what felt like a long time before she gave a subtle nod of her head.

"There are things I need to do to protect myself," she said with a slight waiver of her voice. "We'll go from there."

Just a few moments later and Angela was strolling out of that back office alone. She passed by the bar, speaking clearly to Svetlana.

"Come with me, I've got something for you across town," direct, to the point.

Svetlana never argued.

# CHAPTER 39

It was broad daylight as Javier sat at his usual restaurant, waiting for Svetlana to show. But when someone slipped into the seat across from him, it was not the dainty little Russian girl, but the towering visage of a man Javier had long come to know and fear.

"Good day, old friend," Vitaly said, smiling unevenly across the table.

Immediately Javier twitched, his eyes darting to the nearby table where his guard waited inconspicuously like any other patron. Except, there he sat, another large Russian man, hand upon his shoulders, holding him hostage under the pretense of a friendly conversation.

"I'm not going with you anywhere," Javier said with a firm edge, trying to act unruffled by it all.

"That is fine, this is a nice place anyhow, no?"

Vitaly said, peering around the place. A waitress came by with Javier's wine and Vitaly took it for himself instead. "We need some time to get reacquainted," he told the waitress, slipping her a hundred and sending her on her way.

"What do you want?" Javier bit back at last, tension showing upon his brow. He wouldn't dare mention the truce, the arrangement they had. If Vitaly was there, it hinted at something dark.

"I want to be friends," Vitaly said. "I want to do business. To re-establish myself as a man of power without bloodshed. But... hey, we do not always get what we want, no?" He said it all so casually, his eyes zeroing in upon Javier's, hard and unforgiving.

"You tried to have me killed, that was not very nice."

Javier tried to speak up, but Vitaly held up a hand, silencing him.

"I have Lance still. Alive. Ready to talk if it keeps him that way," Vitaly said, and Javier's eyes went wide. "Of course, if our old pal Lance talks, then that brings down some very serious heat upon you, no? The Big Boss won't be happy to know it was you who violated a peace he brokered. That it was you who caused such a fuss in the streets that will bring the heat down upon his operations across the whole country."

Vitaly took his time drinking Javier's expensive wine as he made the man sweat, quite literally. The tension was ripe between them. Javier was not a man easily knocked off balance, but Vitaly had him anxious. Worried.

"You're here to rub it in my face then?" Javier said, wringing his hands.

"I am here to find terms between you and I. Even after what a lowdown, treacherous shit you have shown yourself to be, Javvy," he said condescendingly, that tinge of Russian accent colouring his words.

"What? What do you want?" Javier spat out, expecting it was all just some taunt from Vitaly. Some way to rub it in his face before the Russian brought down hell upon him.

"Our friend Lance can go away, all blame upon him, if…" He dragged out the silence, forcing Javier to prod him on.

"Yes?" Javier said anxiously.

"You back my claim on his turf. Back me up on all I've done as a necessary part of my revenge. There are some close allies of our old friend who won't be happy to see his territory fold, after all. Vanessa especially," Vitaly said, downing the last of that wine. "You back me, my new operation, with all due support. If Vanessa swears revenge on me or any of mine, you threaten her with consequences."

Javier was in a tough spot. If he said no, Lance would tell all, Javier would face the wrath of the national cartel head. The Big Boss would have to make a show of placating Vitaly, because he'd brokered the peace to begin with. To do anything less would mean his power was undermined for all the other bosses to see.

It'd mean the end of Javier's growing family empire at best.

"Fine." There was no point to bargain back. "But once the arrangements are made… Lance disappears for good, understood?" Javier gave as hard and serious a look as he could manage across at Vitaly.

"Of course. He will be of no use to anyone then. I will arrange the meet with the local bosses' tomorrow night." Vitaly said with a smile, rising up from his seat. Though before he walked off entirely he rested a hand upon Javier's shoulder and leaned in.

"Oh, and Svetlana is mine again. You will never see her again. Understood?" That last word was spoken so harshly, and Vitaly squeezed the man's shoulder so tight as he wrung that nod from the man.

All around, the restaurant was business as usual.

# CHAPTER 40

Vitaly had warned Angela to stay quiet until the meeting with the other bosses, and to throw away her phone. Though she'd hesitated on that last part. Just long enough to receive a call from Detective Luke Crusher.

She wasn't sure what perverse fascination caused her to answer it. Some news about Romy? Something that might sway her mind on the plethora of other matters she now had to weigh?"

"Officer Crusher?"

"Good to hear your voice, ma'am. I hope all's been well for you?"

"It hasn't. Is there news?" she asked, but already her stomach was turning. Cops were trained to ferret things out, things others didn't want them to know, and her heartbeat picked up as she held her phone in trembling hands.

"I was hoping you would meet with me about your man, Romy Agramonte. I've heard a few things and thought you might be able to enlighten me," he said, betraying that hope in his voice.

"Oh," she said, and her shoulders fell.

She knew the cops couldn't do anything. She'd had that gut feeling at first, the instinct that told her that it'd be covered up and forgotten about before long.

Maybe the fact that the detective was still looking into it brought her some small piece of mind. No matter how things had ended with Romy, he deserved so much better than being shot by his own adopted family.

"When?" she said tentatively.

"How about… right now? I can come get you, pick you up or meet you somewhere?" He wanted to do it immediately, and that gave her some sliver of hope at least.

"Sure. You know the Gelato place near me?" she asked, even though she'd abandoned her apartment. Another rank little home that was forgotten about almost as soon as she'd crossed the threshold.

"I'll be right there!" he said.

Coming and going required informing one of Vitaly's men and arranging an elaborate, secretive process. But the men obeyed her just as he'd told them to.

Angela was nervous, her heart nearly choking her. But the way she looked at it, she was getting needed information that could protect them. Protect her.

At least that's what she told herself.

He was already waiting when she got there, and he flashed her a smile as he waited in line.

"What'll you have? On me," he said, the handsome officer looking too good for his line of work.

And far too charming. She glanced at the menu, then at him before nodding to the case. "The almond-coconut in a cup," she said, forcing a small smile. It was a childish delight, something that could soothe her frayed nerves.

She was afraid she'd let something slip, that she'd be heading back to prison. But she knew, this time, prison wasn't going to be her highest concern. She was in deep.

All for revenge on Romy's killer. Guilt or righteousness? She didn't know.

The Detective returned to sit across from her,

placing down the cup of ice cream in front of her before sitting down.

"You'll be interested to know, we've come across some leads that suggest Romy was not only snatched up off the streets alive that day, but that we had some hints he's being held by a rival gang as insurance," he said without hesitation, spilling so much information at her, probably in the hopes of stirring a reaction.

She looked at him as she took the gelato into her hands, holding it for its cold comfort.

"Held?" she asked, confused. "What... what makes you think he's alive?"

"Well," he said in between licking his lips free of the ice cream. "I picked up a lead a few days ago after deducing your man Romy wasn't the intended target. He was just a bystander, at most a low rung member of a third, uninvolved gang. And that the shooters realized this, and decided to hold him and leverage him to make sure everything is cool between them, to not risk gaining a new enemy. I know, it's a bit murky and doesn't make entire sense, but that's what I heard."

Her own gelato was melting, but she felt that little, tiny flame that she'd thought had been extinguished flare up again. She'd given up hope for Romy, grieved him.

Her heart pound faster in her chest as she shook her head. It might've been true. It was true, for a time, and her stomach turned. A few days ago the detective had accurate information.

"Who told you that?"

"Well, I can't say exactly, but it was someone on the street, involved in one of the gangs. Not the one responsible for the shooting, or the intended target, mind you. A third party, more reliable. He didn't know all the details, but he said the bosses weren't worried about him because they knew he was alive."

He cracked a bit of a smile at her.

"I wouldn't get your hopes up if I wasn't sure, I took some time to corroborate other areas of the story even."

She looked down at her gelato, and she knew she should be appearing happier, more hopeful, but conflict was swirling within her and her smile was forced. Quickly, she brought the spoon to her lips and thoughtfully looked at him.

"What's your next move? How are you going to get him out alive? I mean, with all that blood, he'd need medical attention right away, right?"

"Well, that's why I'm speaking with you here," he said, sounding hopeful once more. "We don't know what gang has him, or where. I was hoping that... maybe, you might have some idea of who Romy had trafficked with. Anyone at all. Some tip to put us in the right direction, or any direction! So we can work towards finding Romy and saving him."

He sounded so impassioned, so dedicated to not only the work, but the premise of saving lives.

Her lower lip trembled and her gaze went to the table. Little flecks of black imbedded in the white, though her vision began to blur with tears as she drew in a ragged breath.

Briefly she wondered if the detective had looked her up, found her record, and that was why he was so hopeful. That she'd be back into it, and have more information for him.

She swallowed as she lifted her eyes to him, swiping away a wayward tear.

"I don't know who'd hold Romy like that," she lied, and hated to do it. But what other options did she have? Lance had probably already had everything cleaned up, and with him missing...

"It doesn't have to be that big. But... anyone he did business with? I'm not after piddling drug offenses here," he said in a whisper, sounding confidential. "I am trying to track down would-be killers, who shot up our streets, ma'am. And that is what I will be focussed on whoever's name you give me."

"Would you protect them?" she asked, curiosity edging her on. "If I knew of anyone, I mean," she clarified, though she was really thinking of Abel. Of what the bosses might do if they found out that he wasn't going to stop caring about his lost friend, or what he'd do if he ever discovered the truth.

"As best I could, ma'am. I won't risk exposing

them needlessly. I just need names, people I can talk to for hints. Find out what gang it is I need to go beating down the doors of for starters," he said, sounding more hopeful.

But she knew, even if she wanted to, that she couldn't give him Abel's name. The tentative truce that Vitaly was depending on to save her life required things to go to his plan, not hers.

She was just another pawn, and she took another spoonful of cold gelato into her mouth, nodding thoughtfully.

"Detective," she said gently, her head tilting to the side and her brow furrowing in frustration. "I wish I had more to tell you, but Romy and I had only gotten together. I didn't know what he was into. I guess he was trying to protect me from... this," she sighed, her shoulders slumping.

The Detective's face fell at that, he'd felt so close to some progress. Instead he sat back in his chair, looking a bit dumbfounded.

"Ma'am, like I said... we've got good intel that he's still out there. Alive. But for how long? I don't know. This could be your last chance to save him. And," he leaned back in, speaking quietly, "if you're into this yourself... your last chance to save yourself."

He took a look around cautiously.

"I can see about getting you taken to safety. Set up with a new identity, other side of the country maybe," he said. Though such a matter was certainly beyond the control of a lone Detective. It'd be an involved process.

And with a prior conviction? Be a lot harder sell.

She was stuck, and her eyes could no longer meet his.

"If I could help save him, I would, Detective Crusher. In a heartbeat."

Silence loomed over them for a while.

"You know something more, Angela," he said, using her name so familiarly. She had to ask about that protection for Abel, pointlessly, and now it'd made him suspicious. "I'm not looking to put away petty drug traffickers here. I'm looking into men that murder for a living. I want those guys locked away, to keep people like you, like me, like Romy, safe. To bring Romy home."

Men that murder for a living.

Men like the one she'd first loved, like the man who first broke her heart.

She pushed away her empty cup, liquid sugar staining the bottom, the sweet taste still lingering on her tongue.

"I want the same thing, Detective. But I'm completely in the dark."

Detective Crusher hesitated just a moment before he got up, looking disgusted.

"If you change your mind, you have my number," he said before simply leaving.

But his revulsion with her couldn't come close to matching her own, even though she knew the police would never get the major players. They'd get the shooter, maybe. The fall guys.

Only she and Vitaly could get the ones with actual power.

She had to remind herself of that as she stared into the empty carcass of her ice cream.

# CHAPTER 42

There they were, meeting upon a roof top, overlooking the city of Toronto. The skyline was beautiful, even if the purpose for Angela's being there felt anything but. Vitaly stood at her side, the towering man radiating such power and control. And under the circumstances it made sense. He'd orchestrated a lot for the sake of her safety. For their future business.

Dressed in a suit, he looked a far stretch from the gnarled, broken man she'd first seen wheel up on a motorcycle by her old place.

She'd splurged on the sleek outfit, the silk blouse and the high class, tailored suit. There were no itchy stockings, no uncomfortable pieces of fabric digging into her. It was pure luxury, and it made her stand taller, and more authoritatively. Even waiting didn't bother her as much as she felt it would, or should.

Then there came the other crime bosses. The lights were dark, and Angela didn't recognize most of them. Though among their ilk, Javier and Vanessa were impossible to miss.

"You've got a lot of balls calling a meeting of your betters after what you've done, Vitaly," Vanessa spat out, literally, upon the rooftop. The summer air was a little cooler up so high.

"What I did?" Vitaly retorted. "I was exacting vengeance upon a man who wronged me. A man who broke his word, not only to me, but to all of us, and the Big Boss."

Angela held no remorse or shame on her face. She was as stone cold as she could manage to be, her emotions tucked away.

They couldn't see her weakness, or else the house of cards might come fluttering down.

"You take that shit up the ladder, you pissant!" Vanessa snarled. "And you had damn well better hand over Lance if you hope to make it out of this alive!"

Vitaly took his time, smoking, blowing a puff of grey smoke out into the night air.

Strangely, it was Javier who spoke up first.

"We all know who it was that tried to take out Vitaly by now. What he did was simple reaction."

Vanessa could be heard to gasp, only that shock keeping her words in.

"As we all know, this shooting has brought some

heat on us. We'll have to be keeping quiet for a while. The Big Boss won't be happy about that. Lance is dead, I'm sure, and he dug his own grave. If we want to minimize issues, I say we report to the Big Boss we handled this all internally. Quietly. And there's nothing more to be done."

"You can't just—" Vanessa bit out, but was cut off by Vitaly's loud, booming voice.

"I will fold Lance's operations into my own. Take some of his people too, perhaps. But, since Ms. Eriks here has taken this all so personally, and I value peace… I will offer up Lance's manpower to her, if she so chooses. And his turf on the west end." He turned his gaze upon Vanessa hard, "Presuming she keeps any thoughts of further action to herself. And leaves me, and my people alone."

Vitaly pointedly reached over, wrapping his long, thick arm behind Angela's back to rest upon her shoulder.

Angela remained stoic, as tall and as firm as she could muster. As if no one could even imagine fucking with her.

"That little bitch?!" Vanessa hissed with such anger, and it was one Angela could perfectly understand. The woman was not only robbed of an ally, a friend. She was enticed and duped, then denied revenge. "She has to be handed over at lea—"

"No," Javier said firmly. "This is a fair price for peace. And what choice do we have? If we squabble now, it will draw more police attention upon us, and that will be but a small irritant in the face of the Big Boss, who'll likely come after you as Lance's ally," he said, pointing to Vanessa.

It struck the woman wordless, and the gathering of crime lords all looked about, coming to silent agreement with Javier's assessment.

"Then we have an agreement, good. I am pleased we could come to such accommodations, my friends," Vitaly responded, the words rolling off his tongue so easily. But the message was clear: he may have been but a low level lieutenant a few days ago, but now he was one of them.

A boss.

So when he put his hand to the small of Angela's back and guided her on out to the stairwell, she was walking away as not the girlfriend of some criminal thug. Not a girlfriend at all, in fact. No, she was partner to a crime lord that now owned a chunk of the richest part of the country in his iron grasp.

And beneath all the layers of righteousness and guilt, with so much sorrow and anger bottled up within her, she couldn't help but recognize there was something more beneath the surface. Excitement. Desire.

She wanted it.

She still wanted the world in her hands.

Vanessa had been right about her. Angela had

ambition. More than even she'd recognized until just then, after she'd already grasped that power.

It had come at a great price, but it was never one she had agreed to, only one she had to live with. She'd cried for Romy, and she'd cry for him again, she was sure. But at least now she might be in a position to prevent such tragedies from reoccurring in the future.

With power and money, she could have security. The security she'd longed for when she was filling out job applications.

When she'd first agreed to the deal with Romy.

# CHAPTER 43

*V*italy made his way across the grass in the dim moonlight. The overcast clouds kept him near invisible as he approached Lance's home. It was practically a little fortress on the edge of town, but Vitaly wasn't going for the guarded main home. He went instead for the hidden entrance. It was hard to find in the dark, but Lance's directions proved true.

Once inside he took a moment to take Lance's gun from his jacket and attach a silencer.

The corridors of the manor were tight below ground, and it seemed intended solely as a wine storage area at one point. But Vitaly made his way through, taking precise turns to come to the room in question.

After finishing his interrogation of Lance and checking on Angela to find her asleep, Vitaly went to complete the next part of his plan. The key card swept along the lock and it opened up perfectly. There the man found himself looking out over the interior of a lovely guest home. It was recessed into the earth beneath his manor, but around back the doors opened up to look over the waterfront beyond.

The living room was empty, but looked lived in, with several cushions astray.

Quietly, the large man headed on down the hall. His steps were careful this time, so light as he listened. The sound of a TV playing could be heard from the room at the end of the hall, and he knew that was the place he wanted.

After a quick check of the bathroom he moved on in with a sudden burst of speed.

There, sat atop the bed, was Romy; the man looking so startled he nearly fell off despite the bandaged wound over him.

"Vitaly!" he cried aloud, before Vitaly put a finger over his lips to quiet him.

"What are you doing here, man?" Romy said, eyes wide with shock still.

"Tying up loose ends," Vitaly said, looking about the very comfortable, lived-in room. "I see Lance had you taken well care of all this time, hm?"

"I didn't have much of a choice, Vitaly…" Romy said, his words a bit stammered.

"You don't even call to let your lady know you

are alive? So cruel," Vitaly said with a disappointed shake of his head.

"She'll know just as soon as —"

"Lance and Javier finish me off, hm? Yes, I imagine that was the plan." Vitaly studied the look on Romy's face, gauging his reaction before he sat down on the opposing edge of the bed. "So were you hiding out here until the smoke cleared, or was Lance holding you hostage to ensure Javier didn't hold him out to dry?" he asked with a quirked brow.

"I didn't know anything Vitaly, I swear," Romy pleaded, wearing just the sweat pants and bandages.

"Don't be silly boy," Vitaly said with a shake of his head. "Of course you didn't. You were lucky they didn't kill you in that fight. It was all rather bad timing, hm? But I guess I already know the answer to my question, no? Javier commissioned Lance to do the hit, it didn't work, but Lance didn't wish to take all the heat for the fuckup alone, so he was going to use you as a bargaining chip with Javier. Clever man, that Lance."

Romy eyed the large Russian up and down.

"What are you planning, Vitaly?" he asked softly.

"What any man plans really," he said with a shrug of his shoulders. "To settle down, have a place of my own. Someone to share it with. Ah, but the only problem with that is there is still someone in my way on the last point."

Romy's eyes slowly widened.

"What could I possibly hold over you man? I got nothin'! I'm just some lil' two-bit thug, a go-between!"

"Ah, you have one thing," Vitaly said.

"What, man?!"

"That woman of yours," Vitaly said it so casually.

"Angel?! She left me man! You don't need to worry about me!" Romy said with rising panic in his voice.

"Ah, but she is rather torn up about you and all. Especially with all the confusion that you ended upon. You thinking she was cheating and all. She is rather loyal that woman, even though you two were never really officially an item," Vitaly said all so calmly.

"You are cold man," Romy stated, his own voice beginning to edge with acceptance. "Why do you even want her? She is not your type."

"Ah, but she is," Vitaly said with a light chuckle. "And with a woman like that at my side, I will go very far. Very far indeed. So I am very sorry to say this, but you must be out of the picture. You are just another obstacle between me and what I want."

"No man, wait, please! I can t—"

Vitaly raised the gun and fired at Romy. Nobody heard the shot, nor saw the culprit slip out into the darkness.

# CHAPTER 44

ONE MONTH LATER...

Angela looked over her tanned, bared back. Golden chains hung from her neckline to tease down her spine, and she smiled. The black gown had been expensive, more than a year's rent in her last apartment, but it was worth it.

Custom tailored to her body, she wore it like a second skin and she smiled at herself in the mirror. Her dark hair was clipped up, curls cascading down along her high cheekbones and her vibrant eyes.

She'd wanted to live low for a little while, but she couldn't command her people from a dingy warehouse.

She certainly couldn't host a party in one.

So she turned and her high heels clicked on the hardwood floor of her bedroom.

Looking over her king sized bed with the one set of pillows, she couldn't help but feel a little mark of pride. She needed time, and space, to settle into her new role without the added complexities and drama of a relationship.

She took her long, black gloves and threaded each finger through.

The party was already full steam in her living room, but she enjoyed making them wait, especially in her own home.

Another small reminder that she was the one they had come to see. That she was the one with the upper hand.

Her new penthouse suite was large, and with more security than she'd ever dreamed of, and it was with a broad smile that she joined the other party-goers.

Politicians and businessmen courted her as the pleasant face of a criminal entity that was fast swelling. The same pudgy short man that had solicited Lance for political contributions fawned over her, and did his best to sway her to his way of thinking.

Most all of them buzzed with cocaine, all part of the celebrations.

Then out of the crowds came her well-dressed business partner, Vitaly.

"You have done so well," he said to her softly, the man able to drop his accent entirely for the sake of her formal affairs. "Even Lance took many years to put together such an invitation list," Vitaly added before offering her a bracelet that perfectly matched her dress. "I asked my men to keep an eye on what dresses you bought for the evening so I could help you accessorize."

She offered him her wrist, her green eyes going to his aqua blue.

But with him, there wasn't the expectation of gifts, or of doting upon her. They both understood that they were partners, and she didn't seek to treat him like anything else.

"Spies everywhere," she said with a small bit of teasing to her tone.

"Always good to remember," he said with a glint in his eyes as he slipped on that bracelet, the gold matching the chains upon her back so perfectly. "Lovely," he said approvingly. "You look like a far more luscious Audrey Hepburn," he complimented so sincerely.

She smiled genuinely at him, her lashes fluttering down over her eyes to hide them from him for a moment.

"Too kind," she said, but she was drinking up every compliment, the buzz in the air making her feel more alive than ever before.

She'd never dreamed of having so much in her life, and as her gaze went from Vitaly to the crowd of politicians and business people, to the biggest people in the city, she knew she had found what she was missing in her life.

"Come with me," he said, gesturing over towards a group of business people. "I think you will like to talk with them. They are looking to set up operations on some land we own, and they've already started to talk about producing a new perfume in your honour."

She dabbed her lower lip with her tongue as she laced her arm into his.

"My own perfume?" she practically purred.

She really had arrived.

THANK you so much for reading! I hope you enjoyed <3 If you have a moment, please leave a review. Other readers are dying to know what you thought.

I have plenty more bad boy romance for you, so make sure you check out my other books on the next couple of pages, and sign up for my newsletter to be notified when I have a new release on the way!

~Alexis Abbott

Killing For Her

Abducted

Stepbrothers:

Ruthless

Criminal

Standalones:

Betting on Love

Hunter's Baby

I Hired A Hitman

Vegas Boss

Rock Hard Bodyguard

Innocence For Sale: Jane

Redeeming Viktor

**<u>Romance:</u>**

Falling for her Boss (Novella)

Most Wanted: Lilly (Novella)

Bound as the World Burns (SFF)

**<u>Erotic Thriller:</u>**

The Dangerous Men Series:

The Narrow Path

Strayed from the Path

Path to Ruin

Alexis Abbott is a Wall Street Journal & USA Today bestselling author who writes about bad boys protecting their girls! Pick up her books today if you can't resist a bad boy who is a good man, and find yourself transported with super steamy sex, gritty suspense, and lots of romance.

She lives in beautiful St. John's, NL, Canada with her amazing husband.

facebook.com/abbottauthor

twitter.com/abbottauthor

instagram.com/alexisabbottauthor

bookbub.com/authors/alexis-abbott

pinterest.com/badboyromance

youtube.com/AlexisAbbott

## ACKNOWLEDGMENTS

Thank you to my amazing Patrons. I'm constantly humbled and grateful for your support.

*Ramona Cabrera*
*Melissa Hedrick*
*Virginia Swanson*
*Dawn Daughenbaugh*
*Don Doss*
*Stacie Currie*

If you'd like to join them — and get my ebooks or paperbacks — you can find me here on Patreon.
https://www.patreon.com/alexisabbott

www.ingramcontent.com/pod-product-compliance
Lightning Source LLC
Chambersburg PA
CBHW061341190726
48288CB00005B/1557